MISS WORLD

RANDI BLACK

FIRESPIRIT

FIRE SPIRIT

CHICAGO, ILLINOIS

Cover photo by Colby Underhill.
Cover design by Molly Rabbitt.
Fire Spirit logo and author photo by Karissa Lang.
Polished by Kaycee and Greta @ PWL Editing Services
4th ed.
ISBN: 0615475094
ISBN-13: 978-0615475097

THANK YOU.

Abra Adduci, Anndell Quintero, Beth Nugent, Bin Ramke, Carrie Bailey, Cina Pelayo, Colby Underhill, Dad, haters, James McManus, James Robert Baker, Jamie Kazay, Janet Desaulniers, Jennifer Steele, Joe Lindemann, Joe Pestilence, the John M. Flaxman Library, Karissa Lang, Katherine Southerland, Kenneth Crisler, LeAnne Ray, Mary Cross, Megan Lang, Michael Meyers, Miriam Pinchuk, Mom, Nicholl Montgomery, Ruth Margraff, Satan, Thomas Comerford.

This book is dedicated to me.

I've made my bed, I'll lie in it.

-Hole

1

Eight months of flirting and talking dirty over the phone since the tail end of sophomore year. Hoping she'd meet someone cooler than the idiots from high school, Kim had called a party line advertised in the back of a *Rolling Stone*. Rodney was one of two courteous guys who hadn't coaxed her into going to a private chat room just so they could get off and hang up.

She smiles, the width of an LP between them. "Holy shit. You *do* look like Greg Brady!"

Rodney reveals straight, white teeth. "I told you." He opens his arms. "Got a hug for me?"

"I guess." Kim makes sure her belly doesn't meet his crotch. He's twice her age plus three years. Sort of attractive. She's not sure if she wants to do anything.

He nods at the white Toyota pick-up truck in the driveway. "Ready?"

Kim sweeps a strand of hair towards her face. "Wait." She punches the four-digit alarm code. Hits the *AWAY* button. Once she's outside, she closes the door and double-checks that it's locked. "Ready."

"Don't worry. I'll get you home before your parents are back."

"Could you? They'd lock me up until I'm thirty."

He holds the passenger door, and she inhales lemon air freshener. The tan vinyl upholstery is spotless. Not a trace of trash. He pulls a cassette from the glove compartment. "I taped the Damned and the Buzzcocks for you."

She slips the tape into her purse. "Thank you!"

"Anything for my favorite niece."

His beer belly bulges beneath his charcoal sweater, and his jeans, the color of a smoggy L.A. afternoon, don't look right. She averts her eyes. In less than twenty minutes, they're going to be at Tower Records, where she can look at anything she wants without her parents breathing down her neck.

"How did you get to be a high school custodian, anyway?"

Rodney looks both ways. "I'm easygoing and hard-working."

"So have you fucked any of the girls from school?"

"Sweetheart. They're tempting, but not worth ruining my life over." He actually winks. At the corner, he looks both ways again. They pass the unnaturally green terrain of the fenced-in golf course and the row of two-story homes that snake up the long, winding hill. "Are you still chatting with that musician from L.A.?"

"I read him my lyrics, and he's teaching me how to play guitar over the phone. Once I turn eighteen, we're moving to Hollywood. We're going to be in a band together."

He pats her thigh. "Oh, Kim. Once you're legal, you should just date me."

"So you think he'll like me? You think I'm pretty enough? Not too fat?"

"You're fucking hot."

She wishes he'd make her a recording of himself saying that. She'd play it back until the tape wore out.

They pass Forest Lawn Cemetery where her mom's parents are buried. Every Sunday morning, she and her parents take turns standing in front of Grandpa Hsing's headstone, then Grandma Wai's. Three standing bows, three kneeling bows, and three standing bows again. Then Kim's mom looks to the sky and asks the ancestors to encourage Kim to study harder.

"What's up with those women you told me about?

Are you still seeing them?"

"Well, Kate stopped taking my calls. Cynthia and I don't have much in common outside of sex..."

"They were your age, though, right?"

"Yeah, but a lot of women my age are married or want to get married. When I tell them what I do, I get a moment of silence and then they're like, 'Oh. That's nice.'"

At Tower Records, they stand in front of the music magazines. In a few years, she's gonna be on the cover of *Spin* and *Alternative Press.* She just knows it.

"Whenever we come here, my parents follow me around and bitch about how everything and everyone's a bad influence. They're so lame! My dad loves lecturing me on how the First Amendment is a dangerous thing, then my mom grabs me by the elbow and makes me leave."

"This is gonna suck, but your parents come from a very different background and have never raised a teenage daughter before."

"They think we're still living in China!"

"But they love you." Rodney picks up a copy of *Spin* with Courtney Love and Kurt Cobain on the cover, so fragile and beautiful as he cradles baby Frances Bean.

Kim fights back tears. "All I want is to be in a band with someone like Kurt and never have to deal with my parents. Courtney's got the most glamorous life."

"Kim, heroin isn't glamorous."

"Yeah, but she's a famous rock star married to a famous rock star."

"You know, other guys have crushes on you." He puts *Spin* back onto the rack. "And you're missing out."

"I doubt it." She points at her fleshy belly hidden by a flowery blue baby doll dress. "I'm fat and ugly."

"If they're worth your time, they'll like you just the way you are."

She shudders. "Hey, Uncle Rod."

He leans closer. "Yes, dear?"

"Will you keep a secret?"

"I love secrets."

"Someone does have a crush on me."

"How come you've never told me?"

Kim motions Rodney closer. "Because he's retarded."

"What? You mean, really?"

She puts her hand on his shoulder and looks around the store again. "He eats lunch with the special-ed kids and rides the short bus."

"Aw, you have a special boyfriend!"

"Uncle Rod! Stop it!"

"I bet you two make the cutest couple!"

"Shut up, asshole!"

A group of high school boys eyes them from the other side of the newsstand. Good thing they don't look familiar.

He gives her a quick hug. "You love it."

She calms down, and they migrate to the next aisle. "Read *120 Days Of Sodom* to your favorite niece."

"How did a nice girl like you get tangled up with de Sade?"

"When I was fourteen, I came across the word 'sadism' in the dictionary."

"Here, I know. You'll dig *Story of the Eye*. " He pulls a

copy of it from the shelf. "Crush on de Sade, but I'm going to read you Bataille."

"I don't have a crush. I'm just morbidly fascinated with him."

In an isolated spot at the far corner of the store, he reads to her in a low, husky voice. The same one he uses when she calls him in the middle of the night and asks him to tell her stories, and she doesn't care if they're true or not. In the ether between them, they are. Like when he was this woman's "sissy panty slut" and she spanked him so hard that he couldn't sit down. Or when two women tied him up and made out with each other until he jizzed all over himself.

The one time Kim heard Rodney come, she had been mildly shocked. Then aroused. Breathy and guttural, he sounded almost like a woman. She can't decide how far she wants to go with him. Even after he buys her *Story Of The Eye*. Even when he takes her to Cinnabon, where they sit at the counter and have hot cinnamon rolls oozing with white icing. Iced cappuccinos with mountains of whipped cream that Rodney licks off his pink straw.

"You could come here with your special boyfriend."

"Eww! Stop it!" Kim punches his arm. Then she spots a chubby blonde and a thin brunette at the entrance. They look her way and she huddles closer.

"Shit! It's Traci's little sister and her friend!"

"Is she the cute blonde in the red dress?"

"They better not be coming in!"

"They're walking away. You can stop hiding."

Kim sits back up and sighs. "That was close!"

Rodney kisses her on the cheek. The smell of sugar and cinnamon lingers. "Once you have me, you won't be able to keep it a secret."

2

Onstage, Kim hovers above a grand piano. Temporarily beautiful in the spotlight. Weightless in her black lace gown as she plays Beethoven's *Moonlight Sonata*. Her long fingers glide back and forth. The soles of her Doc Martins maneuver the foot pedals with precise control. Every note and chord is magnified.

She's rolling around on a big bed with her Kurt. Rose petals strewn on ivory silk sheets. Candlelight. His chiseled bones beneath pale skin. Golden hair. Blue liquor eyes. In perfect rhythm, they move together, their shadows making love on the wall, voices composing a song in the air. Music spreads from her fingers, across the concert hall, onto the wooden floors and towards the high ceiling, and bounces off brick walls.

Silence hurtles her back, and she rests her hands in her lap for three seconds before she gets up and takes a bow. The applause follows as she walks offstage and climbs the carpeted steps to sit next to Melinda, a pretty cocoa-skinned girl a year younger than her.

"I sucked so bad! My parents are gonna give me so much shit later!"

"So are mine! I'm telling you, they're as bad as yours. If not worse!"

After every performance, tight shoulders, her head slightly bowed, she prepares for the worst by pretending she's onstage at Lollapalooza. Ethereal from the heat and sweat. Playing guitar and screaming into a microphone, everyone in the audience entranced by her beauty and the power of her voice. Her Kurt's gonna rescue her soon.

"Keep walking," Kim whispers. She and Melinda scurry towards the exit, smiling and nodding at men in suits and ties, women in evening dresses. Trying not to sneeze from someone's crime of too much *Giorgio*. In the lobby, they make a beeline for the folding table covered with a red tablecloth. For the platter of holiday cookies next to a large crystal bowl filled with red punch. Illicit sweetness.

"I'm so hungry!" Melinda grabs two white paper plates, two Santa napkins, and hands her one of each.

Kim feels a hard jab on her left side. One she recognizes.

"You must be considerate and save some for others."

She wants to run or turn and take a swing at her dad, but her body doesn't work. She opens her mouth. Nothing.

"Since you are not losing weight fast enough, I must remind you." Kim's dad pats her shoulder hard. Too hard to be a standard pat, too soft to be an actual slap. Her shoulders and upper back stiffen. She exhales twice before she can breathe normally.

"Fine." Sugary red liquid swirls as Melinda hands her punch in a red plastic cup.

After they get their cookies, there's still plenty left.

Kim rolls her eyes. "I'm so sick of him!"

"I wish I could have a body like yours." Melinda's lanky in a long, burgundy velvet dress with short puffy sleeves and a white satin collar.

If Kim wore it, she'd shred the hem to her knees and accessorize with torn fishnets and Doc Martins. "Are you shitting me?"

"No. My parents give me shit for being too skinny. It's like we can't win, either way."

Other performers, their friends and family, crowd the lobby, echoing with revolving conversations. Their piano teacher, Diana, chatting with Kim's dad, waves them over, puts her arms around their shoulders. "Both of you played beautifully tonight!"

Her dad shakes his head. "Kim's performance would have been even better if she respected our heritage and played *Yellow River.*"

"I only take suggestions from a professional," Kim says.

Diana shrugs. "Mr. Ho, regardless of what Kim performs, we can videotape her recitals and send them to the UC Admissions Committee."

"Yes. We want to insure that Kim will be accepted to UC Irvine next spring."

"Her recitals count as a contribution to the community. I am confident that they will be impressed."

Kim's has no intention of going to her arranged college. Her parents have already decided that she's going to major in Information and Computer Science, because she isn't smart enough to be a doctor.

Diana and her dad resume talking as Traci and Michelle, Kim's only friends from high school, hug her and give her a bouquet of pink carnations and a Nirvana shirt inside a pink gift bag. They barely acknowledge Melinda. Kim stands closer to her. Wishes Melinda's Baptist parents would let them hang out more often.

Kim's dad looks towards the auditorium. "Please excuse me." He shakes Diana's hand and nods at Kim before disappearing into the chilly night.

"Kimmy-ah!"

Her mom makes pounding strides towards her, Evil Aunt Tai and Cousin Jessie in tow. Her aunt's fingers make a flesh handcuff around her cousin's wrist. Kim's own wrist throbs.

"Kimmy-ah! Aunt Tai and Jessie drive two hour to see your recital! Do you know how to thank them?"

As Traci and Michelle slip away to the refreshments, Kim and Cousin Jessie exchange dirty looks.

"Thank you for coming, Aunt Tai and Cousin Jessie."

"When I little, I want to play piano, but we can't afford class!" Evil Aunt Tai says.

Right when Kim opens her mouth, Diana puts an arm around her. "Yan, your daughter performed beautifully tonight, as always. She is one of my best students."

Kim's mom grins. "That's because I push her! If I don't do that, then she no practice!"

Kim excuses herself and Melinda follows. Her dad's still nowhere to be seen, but her friends are eating cookies on the concrete steps outside. She and Melinda swipe some more refreshments before rushing up the staircase at the back of the lobby to lean against the wall. Putting off the inevitable.

💣

"You still coming on New Year's Eve, right?" Traci asks Kim while her dad drives them home. Evil Aunt Tai and Cousin Jessie are heading in the opposite direction, towards their spotless house with grandfather clocks that don't know the art of ticking subtly, and porcelain figurines fucked by the devil.

"Hell yeah!"

"Those hockey boys from San Dimas are coming, too," Michelle says.

"Are they hot?"

"No, Kim. None of them look like Kurt Cobain."

From the right, Traci leans closer to her. "So how is your Kurt, anyway?"

From the left, Michelle leans closer to her. "Are you gonna see him soon?"

"Hey, I need to have fun." She leans closer to Traci. "So is there gonna be pot?"

"Maybe. There's definitely gonna be champagne at

midnight."

After her friends are dropped off, it's uncomfortably silent except for the chamber music from the car stereo. Her mom turns around. Under her black marble glare, Kim fights to breathe.

"Kimmy-ah! Cousin Jessie say she try to talk to you and your friend, but you ignore her!"

"That's not true!"

"Why Jessie lie? She premed at UC Berkeley and have perfect GPA!"

"Yan!" Kim's dad snaps, "Jessie does not like Kim and her friends, so why would she want to talk to them?"

"Kimmy-ah! You must call and apologize!"

Her dad sighs, the back of his head solid and shiny. Kim's mom shakes his shoulder. He swats her hand away, then ignores her. Kim catches his stoic reflection in the rearview mirror as her mom starts bitching about keeping Cousin Jessie happy because Uncle Liang died before she was born. Her poor cousin doesn't have an easy life like she does. Kim flips the bird and reaches for her Discman, when her mom turns around again. "You play wrong note! And your crescendo no good!"

Kim throws on her headphones. Presses play and turns the volume all the way up. The jarring guitars and Courtney Love's spine-scraping howl save her. Her mom turns around and snaps her fingers. She pretends not to notice. The music drowns out her mom's shrill voice. Colored lights bleed into darkness as Kim dives into Courtney's body. Takes on her tall, strong form. Messy platinum hair. Smudged lipstick and eyeliner. A tattered ivory dress. One foot propped up on the monitor, she assaults her guitar, vocal chords on the verge of tearing.

She's going to be onstage one day. Because her Kurt is going to pay her visit three days after Christmas.

Kim knows he'll change her life.

3

Kevin's baby face leers at Kim from the front porch. "Aren't you gonna let me in?" His hair's a black Brillo Pad. An albatross of a Minolta SLR dangles from his neck.

"Yeah," she looks away, "but take off your shoes."

"Is that an Oriental custom?"

"I guess."

After he lays his battered navy blue Vans in a haphazard pile on the doormat, he takes her hand. Kisses it. "I'm so glad to finally meet you."

Kevin had described himself as good-looking over the phone. More like pale and scruffy, with small brown eyes. His smile makes her uncomfortable, but she can't figure out why. So she ignores the goose bumps, the chaos in her belly, and lets him in, anyway.

"Can I see your bedroom?"

"Sure." In the hallway, she points to the room on the right.

Kevin nods at her white Fender Squire and practice amp. "So that's the famous guitar I've been teaching you songs over the phone on, huh?"

His teeth are yellow. His breath milky, slightly foul.

"Want me to play for you?"

"Later."

In the guest room, he unzips his battered black backpack. Hands her a stuffed white lamb, and a paper box with Christmas trees on it. "Merry Christmas, Cutie."

"Oh, cool!"

"I taped you Blondie and Patti Smith. There's some New York Dolls, too, because you know how much I love them. I used that guitar strap onstage when I toured with my last band a few years ago, and we opened for Hole."

"Wow! Thank you so much!" Kim's mom refused to buy her a guitar strap. The excuse? She wasn't ever going to play in public, anyway. And she couldn't buy one with her allowance, because it was still her parents' money.

"There are other ways I prefer to be thanked." He chuckles, sits on the bed. "I brought some pictures, too." He holds up a black and red paisley photo album. Pats the mattress. "Come see."

Kim switches on the lights and sits next to him. Do other guys have this many white hairs at twenty-six? Kevin's got as many as Rodney, who's nine years older. "Um, Kevin, what's with your hair?"

He smiles. The light emphasizes the crinkled skin beneath his eyes. "What do you mean?"

"Why do you have so many white hairs?"

"Oh," he looks at the ceiling, then at her again, "it happened when I was twenty-one. Runs in the family."

"I started getting a few in seventh grade." Kim admits.

"That's because you're smarter than most people your age. And prettier than I imagined."

"Wow!" Kim smiles. "Thank you!"

"It's true." His denim thigh brushes hers. His thick, musty scent reminds her of the girls locker room, where she changes as fast as she can. Every day is humiliating when she has to wear the white cotton briefs and sports bras her mom buys in bulk from Costco.

Kevin shows her picture after picture of his two *Les Pauls*. A mahogany one, and her sleek black sister. They rest on their stands, recline across couches.

There are no pictures of him onstage. None of him actually playing. But he wears a guitar strapped low across his body, or holds one in each hand by their necks. Or sits with one in his lap. Kim acts interested, even though she starts to wonder what she'll buy at Tower Records next time.

Kevin puts the photo album away and takes off his leather jacket. His frame is narrow, but his stained white T-shirt stretches over his gut, sleeves pinching the insides of his wobbly arms. But Kim doesn't have any right to complain, not when she's fat and isn't allowed to pick. She can only be picked.

She looks at the white closet door, her mom's suits and dresses hiding behind it. Something unzips. Fabric rustles. He's pasty and hirsute. Her upper lip twitches when she sees the black bush above his hardened member. He lies down on top of the beige bedspread, crushes the silkscreened bed of red and pink roses. "Time for my gift."

In the cafeteria, Slow Boy's at the special-ed table. The *Be Cool, Stay In School* poster above him on the wall. Spiky hair as black as his shirt. The scruffy guy sitting beside him nods Kim's way. Slow Boy lifts his head and stares at her. Again.

She imagines kissing Kevin under the starry sky in Hollywood. Imagines the boys who will want her when she weighs 120 and plays The Palladium.

Slow Boy's unfazed by animal noises and the balled-up napkins being thrown at the special-ed table. He leans forward. Alert. Kim walks taller, looks straight ahead, holds her Styrofoam lunch tray a little tighter. She feels him watching her until she's out of the cafeteria.

It's been like this since the first day of junior year.

Traci and Michelle giggle on the ledge between the B and C buildings, in identical brown corduroy pants and long-sleeved T-shirts. Red for Traci, baby blue for Michelle. They must've went to X-Girl without her.

"Hey." She sits on the ledge and rests her tray on her lap. Today it's a bean and cheese burrito, a small carton of skim milk. "What's going on?"

Michelle grins. "It was so fucking funny when you turned red on New Year's Eve!"

Traci leans against her, laughing. "I've never seen someone hurl so much! All you had was half a wine cooler and a glass of champagne!" They look at each other, faces contorting. Scrunched eyes on the verge of tears.

"Whatever." Her friends new clothes are way too small for them. Their hockey boys are nowhere as cool as Kevin, whose former band appeared on a New York Dolls tribute CD. Kim smirks before she takes a bite. She and Kevin will be playing out as soon as she's eighteen.

💣

Kim clutches her backpack straps as she walks into Chemistry. The bitches are already in their seats. Inmates appraising the newest guy on their cellblock. Monica Thomas is the head bitch, and her followers are Brandi Simmons and Robyn Humphrey. Brandi and Robyn are skinny blondes, but Monica's built like a linebacker. Pancake make-up is caked over her round, freckly face. Shoulder-length hair dyed red. People have mistaken her for Sydney from *Melrose Place.* Or so she says.

"I wanna be a wannabe!" Monica sings.

"Yeah, Kim Ho is so cool!" Brandi adds, "I wannabe just like her!"

Robyn giggles. "Yo, Ho! I wanna be in your band!"

Kim sits at the back of the classroom, glowering. In ten years, they'll be dowdy, alcoholic housewives. Popping out baby after baby. Their husbands will cheat on them. And she and Kevin will be cutting their fourth record for DGC and touring Europe.

The classroom door opens. In stalks Ms. Manning, red stilettos clicking, rhythmic spankings on a bare ass. Long red hair flames around her pale face, white lab coat snug on her tall, thick frame. She slaps her yardstick onto Monica's desk. "Quit making fun of people more interesting than you."

"Ms. *Man*-ning! We're not making fun of Kim, we're complimenting her!"

"Bullshit."

After school, Kim takes her time, strutting onstage in a black Anna Sui dress. Holding her black Les Paul. Her mom's beige Camry is parked next to the curb, in front of the short yellow bus. She cuts across the grass so she won't have to walk right next to it.

Slow Boy stares from his window seat.

Kim looks straight ahead. Why does he have to be the only boy at school who notices her? And why does her mom always park in front of the short bus, blasting Mandarin talk radio with the windows open? A group of kids tuck their lower lips beneath their upper teeth. Put their palms together and bow. *Ah-so* and *ching-chong*, followed by laughter. There's no way they'll see her fighting back tears. She gets into the back seat, sits behind her mom, and wipes at her eyes.

"How was school?"

She puts on her seatbelt. "Fine."

"What you do in school today?"

"I went to class and had lunch."

"What class you go to?"

"The classes I go to every day."

"Do you go to Trigonometry and Chemistry? Those two most important!"

"Geez, mom! Why do you have to ask me this every day?"

"Kimmy-ah! I listen to Chinese talk radio show. If I not ask you, then is very possible you do drug or get pregnant!"

"Whatever." She can't trust a radio station with a special hour for parents to call in and boast about what colleges their kids got into.

💣

Kim finishes her Trig homework in half an hour, then picks up her guitar. Kevin's strap hugs her as she tunes it. Her amp turned down to one step above unplugged. She hits her favorite chord. E minor. Then she hits the power chords on the low E and A strings Kevin taught her last week. The beginning of Hole's *Garbage Man*. Kim's voice, nowhere as abrasive as Courtney's, is out of sync with her fingers. At the chorus, her fingers slide back and forth between two chords. She sings as loud as she can.

Without without a doubt, come on and let me out. Hey where the fuck where you when my and people sing along.

She falls backwards into the audience. They hold her up as she keeps playing. Anonymous palms brush her face and guitar. They call her name as...

"Kimmy-ah! Shut up!"

A hot sting on her right cheek. Her fingers stop moving. Her arms fall to her sides. Her guitar hangs like an impotent cock.

"Who you think you are?" Her mom's face is scarlet, with narrowed eyes. The corners of her tight lips curve upwards. "No one want to see fat, ugly Chinese girl on stage!"

Kim wants to yell, *shut the fuck up!* but her throat's wired shut. She blinks. Forces her shaking hands to grip the body of her guitar. Holding it across her chest, she takes one step backwards, then another. And another. Until her back hits the wooden chest of drawers.

"Do you steal guitar strap? Huh?" She's sprayed with her mom's saliva.

"D-D-Don't spit on me!"

Pfffffft! A stream of spit hits Kim's right cheek. "Take off guitar and do homework!"

"I did my homework already!" Her chest pulls into a dead knot, old air trapped in her throat. Her mom raises her right arm, open palm ready to strike again. Kim flinches. An uncomfortable tingle in her sacrum.

"Then you do math homework again on kitchen table!"

She and her mom sit together, sides touching. She scoots away. Her mom scoots closer. She scoots away again and hits the empty chair next to her. The empty chair blocked by the wall. Her mom smirks. Under the microscope, Kim is a specimen stuck to a glass slide. Dissected. Judged. She wonders if she's writing down the right numbers. If she's sitting in her chair and holding her pencil the right way. And only her mom can decide what's right. Whenever she begins to write down the wrong answer, her mom pounds the tabletop. *Nonononono! You stupid!*

After Kim finishes, she's ordered to do her homework a third time. But she makes it through, doesn't break down. Tries not to look too excited when she has to be excused.

"Daddy come home in one hour! If I don't have dinner ready, is all your fault!" Her mom sighs. Kim's limbs retract when she feels her mom's arms around her. Her mom's chest is too hot and soft. "Kimmy-ah, Aunt Tai and Jessie think I have fat, stupid daughter! You earn their respect, and they stop making fun of me!"

She wants to push her mom away. She wants to scream, *Let go of me, you cunt!* But she's a statue. When her mom lets go, she's unsure of herself when she tries to move.

*

"I miss you so much, Kimmy," Kevin says on the other line.

She giggles, bats her lashes at the ceiling. "I miss you, too."

"I'm so glad we met. You're everything I ever wanted in a girl."

"Really?"

"You're fun to be with, you like great music, and you're the most beautiful girl I've ever seen. We're soul mates, Kimmy."

"We so are."

She smells his foul breath. His stubble scrapes her face. Her eyes close as he pounds away. A grunting pile of sweat when he comes. For Kim, there's no orgasm. She's grateful someone even wants to fuck her. It'll be better next time. She knows it'll be.

"We'll play music and fuck all the time at our apartment. I'll get a job so I can move out of my mom's house when you're eighteen."

"Can we live near all the cool clubs?"

"Of course! I'm gonna rescue you from your parents. Trust me. They don't know how great you are."

"But I still have to live with them for two more years!" And she hopes they're not listening in, or she'll be dead.

"Don't worry, Baby. I'm gonna make sure you'll never have to deal with them again." He pauses. "You're gonna spend Martin Luther King Day with me, right?"

"Hell yeah!"

"God, I want you so much right now, Kimmy. You know what I was thinking while I fucked you from behind?"

"What?"

"That you have such a tiny asshole and I want to be the first one to fuck it."

She grimaces. "Um, I don't know."

"But Kimmy, it'll feel so good!"

"I've read about it at Tower Records, but I'm not sure I'm ready yet."

"It'll be really special!"

"Don't you think we should wait?"

"Don't you trust me?"

"Yes! It's not that! It's...it's...I'm kind of scared, you know? But I'm sorry I..."

"Come on, Kimmy! We're soul mates!" Then his voice turns icy. "You caught me at a bad time. I'll talk to you when you change your mind."

An hour later, she calls him again. Cringing as she tells him she's changed her mind. But she has to let him do it. He's her only way out of this house, this life.

4

"Kimmy-ah!" Kim's mom rushes to the kitchen table in a red skirt suit, an ivory and gold scarf tied around her neck. "Why you no dress for school yet? You making me late!"

She rubs at her belly. "Mom, I don't feel good."

"School make you feel better!"

"But I told you! I don't feel good!" She shifts in her seat, winces when she's at an awkward angle. The uncomfortable sting hasn't gone away since Kevin left yesterday.

"You no talk back to me! Get dress now!"

There's no way she's going to school. Not after that painful shit she took this morning, blood on the toilet paper.

Kim's mom slaps a plate onto the counter, slams the cabinet door, hurls packaged bread. "I counting to three! One! Two!"

"Kim, why are you not dressed for school?" Her dad asks.

Her sigh of relief shifts into a distressed moan. "Daddy, I don't feel good!"

Her mom puts on her sad mask. "Chao, is hopeless!" She puts a hand on his shoulder, lowers her head. "I doing everything I can, but she still disobey me!"

He touches Kim's forehead. "You do feel warmer. Where are you not feeling good?"

"Everywhere, but especially my stomach." She groans and rubs at her belly again. Resists the urge to sneer at her mom. "Please, Daddy, may I stay home?"

"Do you know what tonight's homework is?"

"Yes, it's on the syllabus."

Kim's mom stomps her foot. "Is trauncy if you no go to school!"

You mean "truancy," right, Mom? "I'll do my homework. I promise."

"Okay, Kim," her dad says, "but only today." He nods at his wife. "You call the school secretary, Yan."

Her mom looks ready to strangle her when she has to repeat herself three times to the school secretary.

After her parents leave, she throws on a faded black cardigan over her Nirvana shirt and plaid pajama pants. Gets a cushion from the family room couch, trudges into the backyard. The sky is dusty blue, sunless. A black iron gate separates her from the steep hill that drops down to the golf course. She tosses the cushion onto the concrete platform and sits, inhaling cool, crisp air. She shifts in her seat, makes a face. The sting is still there.

The Northridge Earthquake was a sign from the universe. It damaged the freeway Kevin had to take to get to her. She pretended to be sad, but she was relieved to spend Martin Luther King Day alone. She never should've taken his calls after that.

She has a mini-pizza for lunch, imagines Slow Boy on the lookout for her. Does her homework while watching Jenny Jones. She's relatively good, compared to those out-of-control teenage girls who antagonize the audience. By the time school's out, she's finished all her homework. Slow Boy's looking for her from his window on the short bus. He'll keep looking until it drives away.

When Kim checks the mail, there's two yellow padded envelopes for her. Rodney's package includes a small box from Godiva. A half-ounce bottle of perfume oil that smells of roses and salty ocean air. *Once Upon A Time, The Scream, Join Hands,* and *Kaleidoscope* from Siouxsie and the Banshees, all dubbed onto two cassettes. A silver card with an embossed heart. Rodney's small, neat handwriting in black.

To my favorite precocious niece. From your dirty Uncle Rod. P.S. Sorry this is late.

From Kevin, there's a dubbed cassette with The Heartbreakers and The Dead Boys. A small Valentine with Tweety Bird holding a heart-shaped balloon. She turns it over.

To the most beautiful face I've ever come across. I'm Kurt, you're Courtney, and we share the microphone of life. And beneath it, *My cock, your face* scrawled inside a heart.

She stuffs Kevin's package into her bottom dresser drawer, beneath the oversized tops her mom bought. Picks up the phone.

"Hey, Rodney, thank you so much for that Valentine's Day package! I already had a chocolate, and can't wait to listen to Siouxsie!"

"I'm glad you're happy! How was VD, anyway?"

Kim frowns. Yesterday was both Lincoln's Birthday and Valentine's Day. "Shitty."

"But didn't your Special Valentine get you a lifetime's supply of orgasms?"

"Uncle Rod!"

"I bet he's fantasizing about making love to you as we speak."

"Eww, no!"

"Honey, you won't be saying that when his face is between your legs."

She can't stop laughing. The most she's laughed in days. Her entire body shakes. "Oh my god! If you were here, I'd smack you!" She takes a deep breath. "So how was your Valentine's Day?"

"Boring. That's why we should stay on the phone and make up for it."

💣

Kim's mom answers the phone during dinner. "Hello?" She raises an eyebrow. "Hello?" She hangs up, shaking her head. "Someone hang up on me!"

"Probably a wrong number," Kim says.

Kim's dad nods. "It also could have been a telemarketer. When they hear your accent, they would rather not go through the trouble."

"What you mean, Chao? I no have accent!" She glares. "We in America almost twenty-five year!"

* * *

On President's Day, her parents take her to the West Covina Mall, and let her go to Tower Records for an hour. The longest they've ever let her be alone there. She wishes she were one of Bunny Yeager's honeys, carefree at the beach in a leopard swimsuit. Or a pulp vixen in a black dress and heels. To cheer herself up, she buys the latest issue of *Ben Is Dead,* and *Junkyard* by The Birthday Party. Four answering machine messages wait for them at home, each one the sound of a phone slamming into a receiver.

She wakes to a fishy odor coming from her vagina. She's also itching and burning, discharging gray. It hurts to piss. She can barely sit still in class or at the piano bench. Showers with lots of soap and hot water don't wash it away. Nor does wishing it'll disappear.

After a week, it's still there. Kim has to tell her mom, because she can't drive herself to a clinic. Her parents let her get her license, but she's not allowed to drive until she turns 18 or gets at least a 1300 on the SATs. Traci and Michelle can't be trusted anymore. Diana and Melinda are out of the question. And her dad? Fuck, no. So on the drive home from school, Kim takes a deep breath before she tells her mom she has a yeast infection.

Her mom's narrowed eyes meet hers in the rearview mirror. "Kimmy-ah! Are you having sex?"

She forces herself not to look away, even when her heart skips a beat. Her shoulders tremble. "No, Mom, I've never had sex before!"

"What I tell you when you get your period at eleven, huh?"

That afternoon, her mom ordered her not to have sex before marriage, or she'd end up like that Chinese girl who got pregnant and shamed her entire family. Or that Chinese girl found naked and dead in a ditch. Or the one cut in half at the waist, her throat slashed from ear to ear. It wouldn't matter if she lied about having sex to her parents. The ancestors would be watching, no matter what. If they saw her having sex, they'd make sure she was punished. But thank goodness she had nothing to worry about. Not when she was so fat and ugly, anyway.

Kim swats the upholstery. "I told you! I'm still a virgin!"

"You no wiping yourself after you use bathroom?"

"No, Mom, I always wipe myself!"

"Ai-ya! You need wipe from front to back! You must cover public toilet seat and wash yourself right!"

"Mom! Stop it!"

"I just trying to help!" She shakes her head. "Fine! We go to Target and buy you medicine!"

"I going in with you!" Kim's mom says in the waiting room of the OB/GYN at Kaiser Permanente.

Kim sinks into the purple-cushioned chair. "No."

Her mom's eyes narrow. "How come yeast infection medicine no work, huh? Do you not use it right?"

"Mom!" She massages her temples. "I used it every night for a week!"

A short, chubby Hispanic nurse calls Kim's name. Smoky eyes give her the once-over. Her mom walks too closely behind her. "Kim, since you are sixteen, you can go in without your mom."

"She not adult yet! I going in with her!"

"I'm sorry, Mrs. Ho, but it is our policy."

"I'll go in by myself." Kim turns at the door and waves. "See you later."

The defeat on her mom's face is priceless.

"One hundred and sixty-five is overweight for a teenage girl who's five foot four," the nurse says gently as she weighs Kim.

She stares at the digital numbers. "Oh, my god! I was only one fifty one when I was here in September!"

The nurse pats her shoulder. "You're young. It'll be easy to lose."

Her medical history is gone through. Her blood pressure and temperature taken. In her assigned room, she changes into a white gown. Lies down on the examination table. Smiles at the galaxy of black dots on the beige ceiling. Right when she's getting comfortable, there's a knock at the door.

Alison Yang, RN, a diminutive Chinese woman with soft features and a dulcet voice. "Hello, Kim, what brings you here today?"

She's the opposite of those tight-lipped Asian doctors her mom made her see in the past. "This is gonna sound really dumb, but I had sex with my boyfriend and we didn't use a condom. I think I have a yeast infection now."

"Well, let's take a look."

💣

A week later, the phone rings.

"Hello, Kim. This is Alison from Kaiser Baldwin Park. Sorry to tell you, but you've got Chlamydia."

5

"Hey, Ho! Let's go!" Kevin says when Kim finally answers the door.

She winces. Still dripping, still itchy. The antibiotics no match for whatever she has. "Don't call me that!"

"Come on, Kimmy. Aren't you gonna to let me in?"

"Um, my parents are coming home early.

"That's cool. We can get a room."

"But they're gonna be home around one!"

"No big deal. I can get you home before that."

She follows him to his gray Tercel. Shakes her head at his charcoal sweatpants, a hole beneath his right buttock. Bags from McDonald's and Taco Bell litter the floor and the backseat. The stink of old grease lingers. When she's about to put on her seatbelt, he chokes her with his bad breath, paws at her breasts. Her fingernails dig into her palms. Her lips go dead.

Kevin pulls away. "What's wrong with you?"

Kim wipes his saliva off her face. Presses herself into the car seat. "Nothing. Just take me to Tower Records, then to a motel, and we'll fuck."

He squeezes her thigh. "Can you pay for half the room? I just got canned."

"Can we go to Tower Records first?

"I thought your parents were coming home early."

"I need to pick something up real quick, okay?"

"As long as you get me off afterwards." He starts the engine. "So did you like your Valentine's Day gift?"

It hurts to smile. "Yeah."

On the drive to Tower Records, Kim looks out at the foothills and strip malls in the distance. Kevin and Bean, KROQ's weekday morning deejays, are quiet and forlorn. Kurt Cobain's been missing from rehab for the past few days. His body was found at the greenhouse in his Seattle home earlier this morning.

Kevin strokes Kim's thigh. Snakes slithers through her jeans. Then he squeezes her crotch. "It's okay, Baby. You're my little pink muff."

She wants to slap his hand away, but looks out the window. The sun has yet to come out.

💣

Sadness looms inside Tower Records. The acoustic version of *Something In the Way* is a dirge. Everywhere Kim goes, she hears sobs, sniffles. Wishes she could join the clusters of kids hugging each other.

"Are you ready?" Kevin asks.

She rolls her eyes. The latest issue of *Spin* in her hand. Courtney Love on the cover, wearing a black dress with a white collar and cuffs. A tiara on her messy platinum hair. "Let me pay for my magazine."

The lanky clerk with horn-rimmed glasses shakes his head, eyes red and wet. He hands back Kim's magazine in a yellow bag with red letters. "Telling you to have a nice day seems so fake. So I hope you feel better. You know, hang in there and all that."

Kim looks at him as a tear slides down her cheek. "You too."

At the news stand, Kevin taps his foot while flipping through a magazine. She stares at the exit door, limbs tingling. Begging to go in that direction. She looks back at him, then at the door. Realizes how badly she wants to run out of Tower and into the mall so she won't have to go to a motel with him. If he followed her, she'd deny knowing him. *He's harassing me. Make him stop.* But how would she get home?

Her eyes dart around the store for shiny golden hair. Blue eyes. Light, delicate limbs. Walking like he floats. Like his feet are an inch above the ground.

Where the fuck is he? Prince of the air. Hiding in the ozone. Doppelganger dead man.

Someone taps her shoulder. "Let's go."

"What?"

"Come on, Kimmy. Let's go."

She keeps looking back, feet dragging to his car. They take side streets, and at every red light, she wants to shove open the passenger door. And run. Her head throbs. A voice screams, *Get out of the car! You don't even wanna be with him! Fucking run, dammit!* The door's unlocked. All she needs to do is take off her seatbelt. Push open the door. Jump out. Run as fast as she can.

But her ass and thighs are stuck to the seat. Her feet nailed to the floor. She tries, but can't get her arms to move.

Kevin parks at the Motel 6 in downtown San Dimas, cuts the engine. "Got the money?"

Kim hands him a twenty she should've used for something else. "Here."

He disappears into the main lobby. She should get out of the car and run as fast as she can. Go find a pay phone. Call her mom collect and lie. Her hands shake. She blinks again. That scream comes back. *Open the fucking door and run! Do it! Fucking do it!*

Kevin opens the door. "Let's go, Ho."

Kim stares.

"What are you waiting for?"

She recoils into the passenger seat.

"I got us a room. Only twenty bucks."

She looks down at the asphalt. "G-Give me my ten dollars back."

He throws a ten at her lap. "What's wrong?"
"Kurt's dead."

"So what? You don't need to cry just because KROQ says you should." He holds his hand out to her. "Come on, it'll take your mind off him."

Room 216. Forest green carpet. A floral quilt on the king-sized bed. Wooden chest of drawers with a TV on top. Large mirror at the center of the blue and white striped wall. The room is dim, even with the lights on. The air reeks of stale cigarette smoke. A nameless, faceless history.

"I'd eat your pussy if it didn't stink so much," Kevin says before ramming it into her.

Kim fights tears. It burns so much. She can't even pretend she's having fun, but she goes through the motions. She's relieved when Kevin comes. Her alone time precious while he's in the bathroom. She rolls onto her side. Looks through the sheer white drapes, at the outlines of the gloomy world outside. Rain beats against the window and rooftop. Even the sky mourns for Kurt.

When Kevin lies back down, she shudders. "You need to go on the Pill."

"My parents won't let me."

"You're not in China anymore. Go to the clinic."

"Shut the fuck up."

She rolls onto her back. Covers her eyes with her forearm. She shouldn't have answered the door. Should've ditched him while she could. And why did she let him talk her into seeing him again after he gave her Chlamydia? After he made her have anal sex, even when it hurt? Why couldn't she have just trusted the Northridge Earthquake?

Kim turns to face Kevin. Wishes they'd never met. "I wanna go home. Please? I don't feel good."

He pinches her left nipple. "I wanna get off again."

She lies, eyes shut, ignoring the sound of his fist moving up and down. His heavy breathing. It's too late to run away. Way too late when he slaps his erection against her thigh. "Come on, Kimmy, you're so fucking hot."

"I really don't feel good. Could you please take me home?"

"I drove all the way from L.A. We paid for this room. You're totally teasing me, and I wanna get off."

"No," she says, but it barely comes out of her mouth.

"Come on. Suck it." He straddles her chest. Crushing her. The fur on his ass and thighs prickles her skin. No matter what she does, she can't move. He smacks himself against her chin. "I'll drive you home after I come."

She shakes her head. "No." Barely audible. A wisp of air.

"Just suck it a little. Then you can go home."

He pushes himself into her mouth. Hits the back of her throat. His balls collide with her chin. She fights for air, gets the stench of his genitals and sweat. The knot in her chest tightens.

"Open your mouth wider, or I'll fuck you with it." He drives himself deeper into her. She hears herself gag. Even deeper. She gags again. Her lower back tightens. Even deeper. She gags again. Water oozes from her eyes, nostrils and mouth. Her jaws shake, then clamp together, teeth biting down hard. Sinking into flesh and membrane. Her entire body stiffening from the shock.

"Fuck!" Kevin yanks himself from her mouth.

She covers her face, waits for a slap. A punch. A violent tug of her hair.

"Look what you did! Look!"

Kim opens her eyes. Raises her head. The king's been dethroned. Grimacing. Rubbing at his still-erect member. He shoves a wide, stubby finger in front of her face. A faint splotch of red at its tip. "Now I'm gonna fuck you with it!"

She wipes water from her face, shivers at his thick hand. His eyes cold obsidian. She's scared. So scared that her mouth widens into a scream, but nothing comes out. Before she can even push him away, he pulls her legs apart. Shoves himself into her. She closes. Hears him grunting. Slamming in and out of her. But she can't feel a thing. Next to the bed, fully clothed, she watches Kevin pound away at the dead girl, his belly flopping against it, hands gripping its thighs, holding them up and apart.

Kevin pulls out of the dead girl, comes all over its chest, then laughs, and Kim wants to beat that naked dead thing on the bed for lying there, for letting him do those things and not fighting back. She fucking hates that stupid fucking thing. Stupid stupid stupid piece of shit.

The dead girl's eyes flicker. Feeling and movement return. It gets up, follows Kim into the bathroom, the harsh light makes them look older. She leans against the wall, crying. It scrubs Kevin's mess off its chest with hot, soapy water, and Kim moves closer as the dead girl stares at itself in the mirror. Defeated. Betrayed. The dead girl lowers its eyes. Teardrops slide onto ashen cheeks. They cry together. It follows her out of the bathroom towards the bed, where Kevin waits with his camera.

"Lemme get some pictures of you."

"I wanna go home."

"Just a few pictures. I'll take you home after that."

"You fucking asshole!" she hollers, but he doesn't hear. No one does.

The shutter goes off while she puts on her white sports bra, bends over for her white briefs. "Ooh, I love your cute widdle girl undies!" Kevin coos. *Click. Click. Click.* "I wanna tear them off and make you my cute widdle cum slut!"

The dead girl and Kim stare at each other. Mirror images. Long, tangled black hair. Short, thick bodies. One is enraged, the other resigned. They walk towards each other, eyes not breaking contact until they're together again.

Kim glares. "Take me home right now!"

"Hey, Ho, no need to get all bitchy with me!"

She's home four minutes before one. Sobbing from the disembodied voices that have been calling KROQ about Kurt's suicide. She wishes she could join Kurt, wherever he is.

Kevin tries to kiss her. She pushes him away. Hard.

"What the-"

"Asshole!" She gets out, slams the door behind her. He speeds off as she runs up the driveway. The alarm screeches as soon as she opens the front door. After she turns it off, she dials Traci's number. No one's there. She tries calling Michelle. No answer. They're probably crying and drinking with the hockey boys. Why does she even bother?

She's so relieved when Rodney answers. "Uncle Rod! Help me!"

"Kim! I've been trying to call you ever since I heard the news! Are you gonna be okay?"

She collapses onto the couch. "I don't know!"

6

In the cafeteria, Kim looks right at Slow Boy. His spork slips through his fingers. She turns away. Forces her iron feet to propel her forward. Away from his gaze. She listens to Traci and Michelle commiserate about Kurt. Not saying much as she eats her chicken fried steak and peas. Only agreeing when she needs to. The conversation shifts to a party they'll be going to this weekend.

Kim gets up, throws her backpack over her left shoulder. "Fuck this."

"Your mommy won't let you stay out past nine!"

"The parties we go to aren't cool enough for you, anyway!"

She finishes lunch behind the C building, surrounded by gray stucco walls and cement. Watches cars zoom by. She used to wish for one of them to come take her away, as long as the driver was a cute guy who looked like Kurt. Today, she'd rather get run over. The bell reminds her that things can get even worse. When she walks into Chemistry, the bitches are waiting.

"Oh, Kimmy, you must be so angst-ridden!"

"Oh, woe is Kimmy! Kurt Cobain's dead!"

"You're so poetic and tragic! Are you gonna write a song about him for the band you think you're in?"

Kim wishes she had a gun. She'd blow their brains out.

A combustion of blood. Chunks of white and gray. She presses herself into the chair. Hopes no one sees. The classroom door opens again. It's the boys from Varsity Football, who have their own Pearl Jam cover band. Their hair shaggy, yet shampooed. Pressed flannels, clean shirts, artfully ripped jeans. The bitches tell them they should start covering Nirvana songs.

Ms. Manning spanks the chalkboard with her yardstick. "Ladies and gentleman, of course I'm making you do presentations the day you come back from spring break. Now who's going first?"

No one volunteers. She calls on Kim.

She rests her homemade poster against the chalkboard. The chemical structure for Vitamin K at the top center. Inside the grid are symptoms of what happens when someone doesn't get enough. Or gets too much.

Twenty-nine pairs of eyes dissect her hair, her face, her dress. None of them look away. Sweat drips down her forehead, but she's covered with goose bumps. She wants to start talking. Her throat stays closed.

"Hurry up!" Monica says. "The rest of us need to go, too!"

"Did you forget how to speak English?" Robyn asks.

Ms. Manning slaps her yardstick against the wall. "Shut the fuck up!"

"You're not going home until I come. Come on, Kimmy, open your mouth wider and suck it. Suck it."

She gags. Gags.

She rushes out the door. Braces herself against the gray stucco wall. Her legs give out, and her ass hits concrete.

The door squeals open. "Kim!" Ms. Manning looks down at her. "If you don't do your presentation, you'll get a zero!"

She shrugs at the Amazonian form of her Chemistry teacher. "Fine."

"If you want a B in my class, then you will need to get perfect scores from now on."

"Okay."

"Is that all you have to say?"

"Yeah."

She can't bring herself to go back in, so she basks in the warm breeze and listens to birds sing. Chemistry can go on without her. When the coast is clear, she presses her fingers to her crotch. Rubs them back and forth for a few seconds. She still itches. Still burns. She imagines the discharge eating away at her underwear. Her hand goes back to her lap. The last thing she wants is for someone to accuse her of masturbating.

Footsteps approach. It's Slow Boy. Slumped shoulders. Awkward stride. Holding something to his right cheek. His left arm dangling at his side. His black t-shirt clings to his skinny frame. The legs of his black pants straight and narrow.

"Um..." He stares at the concrete. An ice pack over his right eye. "C-C-Can I sit with you?"

"I guess."

He sits down in jerky increments, stretches his legs in front of him. Apart from his stutter, he talks like a normal teenage boy. His voice is deep for such a skinny guy. Up close, he looks like a normal teenage boy. As normal as he can get with his large nose and sharp-boned face. Thick eyebrows and long lashes. Full, wide lips. He's got the kind of face that inspires jeers and nicknames.

Kim raises an eyebrow at the pointy toes of his black boots. "So who kicked your ass?"

"I-I got hit w-with a volleyball."

"Right."

During their lapse of silence, an airplane flies past.

"A-Are you sad?"

"Yeah. Why?"

"M-Me too. I hate this place."

"Wanna burn it down?"

"I kind of do. But why is someone like you sad?"

"What do you mean, someone like me?"

"Y-You're so pretty. Y-You destavate...no, y-you deva- devastate me. You devastate me."

"Are you fucking blind?"

"B-B-Bullshit. I can see you just fine. W-Will you go

out with me?"

A prominent erection bulges beneath his pants. She scoots away from him.

"Wh-Wh-What's wrong?"

"Look down."

He peers at the cement walkway. "I don't see anything."

"Look. Down."

He turns even redder when he sees what she's referring to. "Shit! I'm sorry!"

"I'm going now."

The bell rings as soon as she's back in Chemistry. She rushes to her desk, gathers her belongings, and the bitches give her dirty looks. Right when she's at the door, Ms. Manning tells her to stay. But she doesn't. Disabling the ringers and answering machine tonight sounds like a good idea.

Slow Boy is nowhere to be seen. Instead of US History, Kim goes into the library, where it's cool and quiet. She admires the librarian, who sits behind the front desk in glasses and a yellow cardigan. The student workers wheel carts of books to shelve. She never considered it before, but working at a library sounds like a great idea.

Towards the back, she finds a wooden desk. Opens the May 1994 issue of *Sassy*. She'd usually devour a new issue as soon as it arrived. Finding outfits she wanted. Deciding which bands and books to check out. Today, she's indifferent. The chatty tone annoys her. The dresses are too colorful. Too happy. She's sick of smiling models. Sick of their outdoorsy glows and natural make-up.

She imagines clothes that don't bloom or dance. Only in black. Heavy velvet or ghostly chiffon and lace. The models would look like the walking dead. Pale faces, shadowy eyes. Bleeding lips. She wishes she could be that beautiful, funereal. Rising from the grave. Haunting everyone who did her wrong.

She'd go after Kevin first. Tie him up, then gag him with her white cotton briefs. Make sure he never calls her a cute widdle girl again.

7

"Kim, you know you are only allowed to eat at the kitchen table," her dad says.

Her parents stand in front of her, wearing matching gray sweat pants and white polo shirts. Her dad stern. Her mom smirking. Waiting for her to fuck up.

"Good morning." She puts her half eaten-banana onto the counter, presses her back into it. Forces herself to exhale. Forces herself to smile.

Neither replies as they look her up and down. Two slices of bread pop out of the toaster.

Kim's dad tilts his head. "You have been getting a lot of pimples."

She runs a finger down her cheek, skin bumpy and moist. "Thanks a lot, Dad."

Kim's mom runs to the master bedroom, reappears with a red plastic comb. Attacks her forehead with its long, thin handle. "You must comb your hair better!"

The sharp tip of the comb scrapes her scalp, makes a straight line backwards. Her mom's wrist bumps into her forehead. The comb yanks through tangles, tugs at roots.

Kim slaps her hand away. "Stop it!"

Her mom stares. Rough fingers poke at her right cheek. "Why you have rash?"

Blood rushes to Kim's cheeks, boiling at the summit of every pimple on her face.

"You look awful lately," Kim's dad says.

Kim's mom grabs the inner crook of her right arm. The place she hates being grabbed. "Sit down! I make you pretty!"

There's less than half a foot of space for her to breathe. Her pores enlarge and shrink. Enlarge and shrink. The tip of a knife traces its downfall on her back. Kim shoves past them, rushes into the bathroom. Locks the door. She stares at her reflection. Her mom was right. No one would ever want to see her onstage.

"Kevin, it hurts!" Kim yells into the mattress.

"Come on, Kimmy. It won't hurt if you relax."

Her jaw shakes. Her teeth clatter. The discharge so corrosive it could eat its way through her underwear. A knot forms in her chest. Ants crawl up her legs and sleeves. Every time she scratches, another one bites. She's covered with them, covered with

"Kimmy·ah!" Her mom bangs on the door. "What you doing in there?"

She whirls around. A scream charges through her body. It unties the knots. Fumigates the ants. Her right leg pulls back, and she thrusts it at Kevin's head. Breaking his cheekbones and nose. Shattering his jaw. The insides of her cheeks tingle. Blood rolls down her tongue. She doesn't even feel her bare foot go through the wall, but now it's a mass of throbbing tissue and bone.

"Kim! Do not destroy your parent's property!"

"Ugh!" She plops her butt onto the bathroom floor, drives her knuckles into her heart. Trapped air breaks out. She lifts up her right foot. Swollen red, but its bones are intact.

"I don't know what her problem is, Chao! She so sour now, wear black every day!"

"If you worked harder at raising her, she would not behave this way!"

"But I can't control her at school! Maybe she taking drug there! Normal people no act like her!"

"How is she able to afford drugs?"

"What if she sell her body?" Her mom pummels the door. "Kimmy-ah! You come out right now! I counting to three! One! Two! Three!"
"Yan! You are ineffective!"

Kim snickers as she rubs at her toes.

Gentler knocking. "Kim? Are you having a temper tantrum because we will not let you to see *The Crow?* You cannot see R-Rated movies until you are eighteen. That is final."

She shakes her head, laughs the way someone would after intentionally running down a pedestrian.

"Tell Daddy what you think is so funny."

She leans her head back and closes her eyes. Holds her knees to her chest. The doorknob rattles again. She's safer in the bathroom.

"Chao, something wrong with Kimmy! I know it! She spending more time in bathroom lately!"

Before she stops wearing her cute widdle girl briefs, she'll have to tell mom she's still got an infection. The thick crust on them motivates her to do the laundry more often, much to her parents' delight. But she only does it because she's afraid her mom will get to it first.

"Yan! Do not get so excited!" Another knock. "Kim?"

"What, Daddy?"

"Today we will go to the West Covina Mall and have lunch. You may have pizza. We will let you go to Tower for an hour. I will give you money to buy something, but it must not offend us. Kim?"

"What, Daddy?"

"You must apologize for your behavior when you come out."

They walk away. Sun shines through the window above the white tiles. Kim tilts her head. Rests it on a thin, warm shoulder. An arm wraps around her. Hair, lighter and finer than hers, tickles her cheek. She's in a field of flowers. Pretty. Untouched. Wearing a white silk gown. Birds of every color fly above her. They know the melody to every Nirvana song, but they never chirp *Rape Me*. Kurt takes her hand, a crown of light above his golden hair.

"Mom, Dad, I'm sorry for behaving like that," Kim says as they watch the Chinese news on Channel 18.

Her dad nods. "We accept your apology."

"We go as soon as you get ready!" Her mom says.

"Actually, mom, could you please cut my hair before we leave?"

When was the last time her mom looked this happy? "Okay! We go to backyard!"

They stand on the concrete rectangle patio next to the lawn. Away from where the sun hits. Kim keeps reminding her mom to cut it no shorter than shoulder length. She better listen, and not give her that awful haircut she and Cousin Jessie used to have. The kind that looks like someone put a bowl over her head and started snipping. One time her mom even nicked her ear. Blood dripped down her neck.

Her eyes squeeze shut when her mom takes the first cut. The blade grazes her right below her shoulder. She opens her eyes. Chunks of hair fall to the concrete. Her mom continues to cut. Right to left. A neighbor is mowing the lawn. The warm breeze on her face. The way it'd feel with Kurt.

Her mom hands her a mirror. "Is so much better!"

She looks lighter. Feels lighter. The ends of her hair just below her collarbone. More than two years of growth scattered at her feet. Ever since *Nevermind* came out.

That dream is over.

"Did you have a good time today?" Kim's dad asks at the dinner table.

"Yes, Daddy. Thank you." Chopsticks pick at salmon, rice, and boiled cabbage.

"I'm glad. You look better, too." He takes a bite of salmon. "But only diet and exercise will make you truly attractive." He nods at Kim's mom. "You too, Yan."

She's glad she bought *Destroy Me, Lover* by the Pain Teens with his money. The cover and song titles offensive. The music is sludgy, and abrasive. Neither of her parents asked to see what she purchased. Nor did she volunteer. Now that he mentions it, she'll be collecting an asshole tax from him later. The plunder always sweeter, and justified, when they talk shit about her body.

Kim's mom pats her shoulder. "We must look good for Daddy, Kimmy. Is our duty."

Her mom's purse sits next to the living room couch. She'll be sniffing through there, too.

"When people see us as a family, I do not want to be judged wrongly. Nor do I want people to think you lack self-control."

"Okay, Chao," Kim's mom says in earnest, "I working harder. You too, Kimmy."

She shrugs. "Fine."

Her dad looks at her. "Kim, we have forgiven you for your behavior, but I still want you to explain yourself."

"Be an obedient Chinese girl and concentrate on your dad. He's easier to fool!" Someone behind her says.

The back of her neck tingles. She turns around. There's no one.

"Trust me. Just do it." The voice belongs to someone her age. She can't tell if it's a boy or a girl.

"I'm sorry, Daddy," Kim lowers her head, "you're right. I've been depressed lately, but that's no excuse." She sighs. "I am just lazy and need more self-control."

Both her parents nod furiously, and look way too proud. "That is true, Kim. You have a very easy life. You have no right to be depressed."

"Tell them you're ready to change!" The voice hisses.

"I am ready to change." She smiles at her mom. "Thanks for cutting my hair, Mom. It really makes a difference."

She beams. "Now you can be good Kimmy!"

"After dinner, we will take away your guitar and amplifier," Kim's dad says.

She hasn't been able to bring herself to play or sing since Lincoln's Birthday. Since Valentine's Day. She bought and devoured *Live Through This* the day it came out, but it just wasn't the same anymore. "I agree." The skin of her face crackles. "It's been disruptive to my schoolwork."

"You also may not go out with Traci and Michelle until school's over, nor can you talk to them on the phone."

"They're lame, anyway!" the voice says.

"I can still go to Lollapalooza with them, right?" But she's not looking forward to it.

"As long as your GPA is over 3.5. You will devote all your time to schoolwork."

"That's fair." Kim feigns innocent curiosity. "Is that all? Aren't you going to ground me?"

"There is no need."

She feels delicate hands on her shoulders. Smells strawberries, roses, baby powder. The voice giggles. "Told you so."

8

"So how's my favorite niece?" Rodney asks.

"Better," Kim stretches out on her bed, "I've been studying for the SATs."

"Really? You were trying your hardest not to get into UCI."

"I don't have any other choice."

"What about Kevin?"

She stares at the ceiling. "We're not seeing each other anymore."

"What happened?"

Kevin's hands on her inner thighs. Hot. Itching. Her skin red and bumpy from scratching so much. "He turned out to be an asshole."

"Sorry to hear that, Honey."

His saliva burns her face. "He wasn't who he said he was, you know?" Her face is dry when she wipes at it.
"I do. You deserve much better."

She's suffocated by his rotten milk breath. His soft, hairy belly flaps against hers. "You're right. I do."

"That son of a bitch didn't hurt you, did he?"

"No one will believe you." Kevin's clownish grin stretches from ear to ear. Black marble eyes. The way he looks when he visits her in dreams. Fucking her mouth, pussy, ass. No matter how much she tries, she can't move or speak. She'll wake up in a cold sweat, shaking. This is how it's been since Kurt died.

"N-No. He didn't." She covers her eyes with her palm. "It was all about his dick, so I dumped him."

"Good for you," Rodney says, "it needs to be all about your pussy, too."

The itch and discharge have yet to go away. "True."

"What about your special boyfriend? Has he talked to you again?"

"Not since that day." But he's resumed staring at her during lunch and after school.

"Why don't you approach him?"

"I don't know if I should."

"You know, Kim, I really mean it when I say that you deserve better."

Tears escape. "I know you do."

"Oh, honey, don't be sad. I'll mail you a care package this week, okay?"

💣

While her mom parks her car in the garage, Kim slips the large padded envelope into her backpack. It's been her duty to get the mail since she was little. Her mom never thinks to search her. If she's not being the homework Nazi, then she's watching Chinese soap operas.

There's a used copy of *Blue of Noon*. A box of Pinson hard candies. Two dubbed cassettes of Public Image Ltd. and Joy Division. Purple scented soap and another bottle of perfume oil from Andromeda's Potions. She sees Rodney in a dark shop lit with candles, sniffing everything until he finds just the right ones. Nesting them carefully in bubble wrap before putting them into the envelope.

Packages come every other Friday afternoon. Copies of *Laure: The Collected Writings. My Mother/Madame Edwarda/The Dead Man. Maldoror. La Bas.* All inscribed with suggestive messages from her dirty Uncle Rod. Colorful chunks of lye and tiny amber bottles temporarily take her mind off the smell, the itch, the discharge. She's the most exotic-smelling girl at school, who snacks on European candy. Getting a fast education of post-punk bands from the late seventies and early eighties.

Before New Order, there was Joy Division and Warsaw. Modern English cut a dark, aggressive record before they were known for that romantic pop song. The Fall's not just a book by Camus. There's more to Bauhaus than "Bela Lugosi's Dead." And who gives a fuck about the Sex Pistols when there's PiL? While the idiots at school rave about Green Day and The Offspring, she cavorts with Gang of Four and Wire. The angular bass and spastic drums just feel right. The scraping guitars in her blood. Atonal vocals with heavy accents voice her anger, her disillusion, better than any riot grrrls can.

"I call Kaiser," Kim's mom says on the drive home from school, "they don't have appointment with Alison until last day of school. I make one for you then."

She's riding in the passenger seat for once. "Thanks." She tilts her head back. "I can wait a few more weeks."

"I hope this time, they take care of it. Is not good you have infection so long."

Tell her about it. "Mom, you know I'm a virgin, right? I really don't know why I have it in the first place."

"I know." She pats her shoulder. "I so proud of you, study instead of go to prom. I hear many girl have sex that night."

"It's true." Traci and Michelle rented a limo and a room at the Long Beach Hilton, bought gowns from Windsor Fashions. The hockey boys were their dates. Kim hears about it every day at lunch. They accuse her of being jealous.

"Is good we put more pressure on you. If we don't, your grade not so good and you don't study so hard for SAT." Her mom smiles. "But you good girl now."

The voice bursts out laughing from the backseat. When Kim turns, she doesn't see anyone.

She stares into the dressing room mirror at Robinson's May. A girl wears a black mesh bra and matching panties over her navel-grazing briefs. Her dark eyes gleam. She's luminous, despite a few pimples. A raven's wing of black hair falls into her face. Her full lips curled into a slight smile. Standing tall with her shoulders back.

For the first time, Kim likes how she looks.

Three black bras. Nine pairs of panties. All Calvin Klein. Thanks to her mom, she remembers to use a twenty-percent off coupon torn from the *L.A. Times.* There's enough left over for a tube of blackberry lip gloss from the Clinique counter. In a bathroom stall, she unloads everything into her purse. Stuffs the shopping bags into the trash. She knows where she's going to hide it all. There will be covert washing. Stowaways inside towels. Clandestine air-drying. When she meets her parents at the Broadway in fifteen minutes, they'll have no idea.

She's a good girl now.

9

On the last day of school, Slow Boy loiters in front of the lunch room, hands stuffed into his pockets. "Kim?"

"How do you know my name?"

His foot shuffles back and forth on the blacktop. "Someone told me. W-Will you have lunch with me?"

"Did you just ask me to have sex with you?" She lowers her chin, looks up. Smiles.

Blood rushes to his face. His thick brown eyebrows pull together. "Shit! D-D-Did I?"

"What, you don't want to have sex with me? Don't you think I'm pretty?"

It's her black bra's fault.

"I do!" He groans in dismay. "B-But I didn't mean..."

A group of boys walk by, making animal noises. The tall one in a Blind Melon shirt slaps the side of his hand into his chest. "My name is Waltard! Will you be my special boyfriend?" His tongue lolls from his mouth. His friends high-five him.

Slow Boy grits his teeth, stares at the ground.

Kim stifles a laugh. "Hey, that wasn't cool."

He wraps his arms around his chest. His forearms

pale, with prominent veins. Dusted with fine brown hairs. "He should talk, with that Blind Melon shirt."

"Let's go somewhere quiet," she says after they pay for their food. His friends wave from the special-ed table. He waves back.

His grin is the sudden burst of electricity that ends a blackout. "Y-You mean, be alone with you?"

"Ye-ah."

Behind the gym. Towards the field. She walks fast, but he keeps up. Smiling and looking at her. The sea of grass stretches in front of them. She nods at a spot underneath the tree. Confirms they're isolated before she sits down. "So what's your name, anyway?"

He sits across from her. Puts his navy blue backpack over his lap. Rests his lunch tray onto it. "W-Walter. Walter Aaron Riordan."

She removes the top bun from her burger. Half the melted cheese's stuck to the charred meat. The other half's stuck to the spongy white underside. Her nails rip open ketchup, then mustard. Squirting them onto the patty. A circle of yellow lies in a blob of red. "Aren't I a little old for you?"

He squirts ketchup all over his fries. Leans closer. "I-I just turned sixteen." His face is smooth. Unblemished.

Her pimples swell in protest. "What are you, a

sophomore?"

"A freshman. I flunked third grade."

"Oh. What are you doing in special-ed?"

"I'm retarded."

"No, you're not!"

"Are you telling me I'm not special? I think *you're* special."

Kim bursts out laughing. Hurls a wadded napkin at him. "You're such a dork!"

"Y-You're so sexy when you laugh." His piercing gaze strokes her face, brushes her lips. The flecks of gold and green in his hazel eyes swim and swirl. No one's ever looked at her that way before.

"Shut up!"

"It's true!"

Buzzing heat spreads through her. She hovers a centimeter above the grass. Her face flushes. Despite the discharge, this unmistakable throb between her legs. She feels herself getting wet. So she deliberately sneers. Flips him the bird. "Seriously. Why are you in special-ed?"

"I'm dyslexic." His short, messy black hair is freshly dyed. Her fingers ache to mess it up even more.

"I'm sorry."

"I'm not."

The bell rings. They take slow, short steps back to the main part of campus. Kim can't picture herself squealing *I miss you!* and hugging anyone, the way so many other girls are. It would take at least a heavy dose of X for her to do that. She and Walter are the only ones wearing head-to-toe black. Everyone else in summery clothes as they sign each other's yearbooks.

He stops in front of the library. They face each other. She's still plagued by a monstrous arousal. Traci and Michelle are nowhere in sight, but other classmates walk by. Do double takes. Whisper. Almost everyone she knows sees them. Her only safe spot is Walter's face.

"M-My dad's getting me Lollapalooza tickets for my birthday. Do you wanna go? He'll take us."

The flittering in Kim's belly intensifies. "I'm going with some other friends."

His face falls, but then he nods. "M-Maybe I'll see you there. D-Do you want to have dinner? And go see *The Crow?*"

"My parents took me to see it a couple weeks ago."

At the movies, Walter will yawn. Raise his arms over his head. One of them will accidentally fall around her. "I-If you wanna see it again, that's cool. Or we can see anything else you want. As long as it's not *Forrest Gump.*"

What the hell? She's already gotten fucked in the ass and had an STD, but she's never gone on a date before. "I'd love to, but my parents are total control freaks."

"My dad can talk to them when we pick you up. O-Or

your parents can take us. I don't care."

Not when she's a human petri dish. "Look, I should really get to class."

The bitches give her knowing smiles as she walks into Chemistry. Who cares if she got an A on her final? She shifts in her seat. Wet and tingling and feverish. She sees Walter's face. Pushes it away. He keeps coming back. What would it be like to go out with him? She yanks on her hair as hard as she can. He has nice lips. What would it be like to kiss him? She jabs her fingernails into her forearm.

"Kim's got a boyfriend! Kim's got a boyfriend!" The disembodied voice sings. Hiding in plain sight.

💣

After school, she sidles up to Walter's window on the short bus. No one's ever looked that happy to see her. She kisses the insides of her fingertips, makes a flicking motion. He catches her kiss, slips it into his shirt pocket. She feels him blush through the spotty window. He puts his palm against the glass. So does she. Their palms are the same size. Their eyes lock. Her lips part. She lingers longer than she should. Her shoulders tighten. Someone's seen her. She takes her hand away.   At least it's not her mom, who's parked in front of them.

The bus obscures any incriminating reflections in the side and rearview mirrors. Nosy eyes can't witness anything from the driver's seat. They wave once more before Kim turns. Hoping her appointment with Alison will destroy what Kevin left inside her, once and for all.

10

Michelle starts the engine. "Where the hell were you yesterday?"

Alone in the backseat, Kim makes a face. If she tells the truth, it'll be one more thing to make fun of her about. They slowly back out of her parents' driveway. Michelle keeps glancing at her, curiosity in her tired eyes. Kim looks out the window. How long has her neighbor had that wood-paneled station wagon, anyway?

A cool hand on her shoulder. "Fuck with them!"

She takes a deep breath, puts on a straight face. The center that keeps her together tilts to the side. "Don't tell anyone, but I had an abortion." Kim says while giving into the voice.

Traci gawks from the passenger seat. Her bleached blonde pigtails swish back and forth. "Oh my god! You were pregnant?"

"Eww!" Michelle shrieks over those whiny Beastie Boys. "You didn't use rubbers?"

The voice giggles. "They are so stupid!"

"I wanted to feel his flesh so bad." Kim blinks. Swears she sees a pale, skinny leg. Golden hair.

Traci shakes her head. "But-but, your parents! Do they know?"

"Nah, I did it behind their backs. Guess who was the father?"

"Your guitar teacher?"

"Nah, I dumped him a couple months ago. He was a lousy fuck." Kim digs her nails into her palms.

"'Cause you should know." Michelle smirks in the rearview mirror.

She forces herself to smirk right back. "It was Uncle Rod's baby."

"You mean that janitor from Simi Valley?"

"Eww, Kim! He's twice your age!"

"What can I say? He's my Uncle Rod. We went to Planned Parenthood to get our baby scraped out of me."

"Good one!" Blue eyes. Long, golden lashes. She just saw them. Really.

Gasps and oh-my-gods fly from the front seat. Kim struggles not to laugh, but her cackle shoots out like machine gun bullets.

"Oh my god! You just psyched us out!"

"You fucking bitch! How dare you!"

"Haha! Hockey boy jizz makes you dumb!" The disembodied voice says.

Spasms charge through Kim's body. She hasn't laughed this hard in a long time.

"Where the fuck were you yesterday? Tell the truth."
Michelle's voice cuts through her laughter.

"Why's it so important to you?"

They don't acknowledge her the rest of the way. A line
has already formed around Tower Records. Kim sits
behind Traci and Michelle, her back to the wall. She looks
for Walter. He's nowhere in sight. She's surrounded by
guys, but doesn't want any of them. It's the first time she
hasn't bothered to gauge who might fuck her. Who's out of
her league. She looks down at the curb. The Flagyl Alison
prescribed for her chronic bacterial infection is doing its job.

The early morning sun burns her eyes, makes her
dizzy. She shields them with her hands. Every time she
takes them away, she sees spots of gold and blue. Licks of
white with pink at the edges.

That yellow hair. Those blue eyes. His pale skin.

"Wasn't last night's party awesome?" Traci asks.

Michelle laughs nervously. "Fuck yeah! I'm still so
hung over!"

"It was so funny when Trevor and Alex showed us their
hard-ons!"

"Alex's balls are totally gross!"

The doors opens. Everyone stands up. Kim braces
herself against the brick wall. Her forehead sweaty. Her
head swims. She wants to lie down, far away from everyone
else. Metal rubs against her tongue. Fur grows over her
taste buds. The contents of her stomach shift. Pangs of

nausea can't get past her throat. The light bouncing off
bumpers and mirrors are streaks and splotches of white.
So bright she can't look straight at them.

The whites of his eyes. The color of his bones.

Kim squeezes her right hand into a fist. Feels her hand
in another's. Warm. Frail. She smells roses, strawberries,
baby powder. What's the air and heat hiding from her?
Fragments of gold. Blue. White. The hand still in hers.

"Look harder. I'm right next to you."

That voice has returned, but Kim doesn't see him. Or
her. Or both.

The orange label on the side of the Flagyl bottle warned
her to avoid prolonged exposure to the sun. Some of the
known side effects are confusion, irritability, and
dizziness.

It's the fucking medication.

"No, it's not."

Whoever it is disappears when Kim enters Tower
Records behind Traci and Michelle. Later, when they're at
the mall, she's still a couple steps behind. They ignore her.
Everywhere she looks, she sees gold, yellow, white. Every
time she sees a skinny boy with shoulder-length blond hair,
her heart skips. It starts again when she sees stand-offish
faces. Not him. None of them is him. His young ghost. Her
real Kurt. Lights keep flickering. But she doesn't see him.
She doesn't hear or feel him.

"Hey, Kim! What the fuck's wrong with you?"

"Yeah, you've been acting so weird lately!"

She stops. Traci and Michelle stare at her like she just told them she's a born-again Christian. They're clustered in front of Bath & Body Works. The store's chemical sweetness and pounding techno make her nausea and dizziness worse. There's no way she can give another listen to those weird Throbbing Gristle tapes Rodney dubbed her. Not this afternoon, at least.

The hand is on her shoulder again. "Hide me."

"I'm kind of tired." She groans, rubs at her forehead. "Can you take me home soon?"

"We'll take you home right now!" Michelle says while Traci nods furiously.

He waits on her bed. Pale legs dangling over the edge. Lily hands in his lap. Light from the window leaves a halo above his long golden hair. Fine bones beneath alabaster skin. Blue eyes plucked from a dead feline. His pink dress with puffy sleeves hangs from his slight frame. Skinny legs end in white anklets with black Mary Janes.

Against the door, Kim braces herself. "Oh, my god."

"Hi." That voice she's been hearing comes from his full, rosy lips. Too high and sweet to be a guy's. Too low and tough to be a girl's. Its lilt creeps towards singsong, crackling with staccatos and inflections.

"How did you get in here?"

When he smiles, his pink lip gloss glitters. So pink it smells like strawberries. Up close, his skin will smell like roses and baby powder.

"Walls and doors mean shit to me." Sunlight bounces off the metal barrette in his hair. It shines, a freshly-sharpened knife. "I've just been waiting for the right time."

"What's your name, anyway?"

He smoothes his dress. "Joey."

11

At night, Joey cuddles with her on their canopy bed, the walls glowing in the moonlight. He recites naughty renditions of nursery rhymes and sings an off-key *All the Pretty Little Horses.* They eat flowers and twirl around, then lie together on the grass. Sleep always comes fast and deep. When she opens her eyes again, it's already daylight. Back in her bedroom, where she's been the entire night, she swears the walls are now pink. The furniture white.

When Kim's parents criticize her, Joey points out their flaws. Cuts loud, rambling farts that stink of angel food cake and butter cream frosting. Lifts up his dress, exposing skinny legs and white bloomers. "My piss tastes like lemonade, and my shit tastes like brownies."

It's always a struggle not to burst out laughing, but she's learned the art of being the obedient Chinese daughter. All she has to do is speak in an agreeable voice with her head slightly bowed. Constantly praise them and never talk back. They don't suspect a thing.

But when the phone rings one afternoon in August, even Joey can't keep her safe.

"Hey, Kimmy," Kevin's voice is cold slime against her ear, "I miss you, Baby."

She holds the phone away. "Shit!" She looks at Joey. "What should I do?"

He twirls his hair around his index finger. "Hang up, and we'll have a tea party!"

"I...I..." She can't bring herself to hang up. Kevin's

heavy breathing tightens the knots in her chest and shoulders. *His thick palm covers her mouth and nose. Her limbs go dead. He looks down at her, baby face smirk and weasel laugh.*

Joey tugs at her paralyzed arm. "Come on, hang up!"

"Kimmy? You there?"

She winces. "Yeah, I'm here."

"I started a new band last month. We've put some songs together but we still need a singer. I told those guys how hot and beautiful you are. Wanna come jam with us?"

Joey touches Kim's arm. "Hang up, so we can have rose tea and chocolate chip scones! And cake with lots of strawberries and whipped cream!"

"I'm busy." Her voice barely gets through the steel door in her throat.

"With what?" Kevin asks.

"Tell him you don't want to be in a band with him, even though we don't know who the hell he is!" Joey nods to himself, then at Kim.

"Well," the word drops from her tongue as she raises an eyebrow, "I don't want to be in a band with you anymore."

He gives her the thumbs-up.

"Kimmy, why are you doing this to us?"

"What?" She and Joey are the only people sitting at the

kitchen table, but she's suddenly crowded. Pushed into the wall.

"Why the hell are you doing this to us?"

With her free hand, Kim flips through the A's in her SAT vocabulary study guide. The letters flicker in front of her. Black splotches bleed into white.

Joey's eyes narrow. "Tell that deluded psycho to go find someone else."

"Go find someone else," she says, her voice an ice pick, "you deluded psycho."

"Well, geez," Kevin says, "there are singers out there who are way better, not to mention skinnier and prettier."

"Ugh!" Kim's hands shake. "There are better guitarists out there, without so many white hairs! And you're not so hot yourself, so just fuck off!"

Joey jumps up and down. "Yes! Let him have it!"

"Well, God, Kimmy! Don't get all hysterical! If you were a real musician, it would still matter! I wanna start playing out again, dammit! I'm thirty-three and not getting any younger! I-"

Joey gasps. "Eww! He's how old again?"

Kim sucks in air through her teeth. "How old are you again?" She closes her vocabulary guide, pushes it towards the other end of the kitchen table.

"I told you, I'm twenty-six! I was born in sixty-eight and I'm ten years older than you!"

Uni-brow and deep-set dark eyes with lines carved around them. Weathered skin covered with stubble. His belly slapping against hers.

Joey stares at her, his hands gripping her shoulders as he shakes his head and repeatedly tells her no, no, no, he's looking for another Kim and we're just messing with him!

"Oh, my god! That's so gross! You really are thirty-three, aren't you?"

"Why would I lie about my age, Kimmy?"

Joey snatches the phone from her. "You should be in jail, getting butt-fucked by big, scary guys!"

"Kimmy? I didn't mean to diss your looks. You know I didn't. You pissed me off, but I forgive you. I don't want you to feel unwanted because you are wanted, you know that, right, Baby?"

"You deserve to be shitting into a bag for the rest of your life!" Joey tosses the phone onto the floor, yanks the cord from the wall.

"Let's get out of here!" Kim manages to say as she propels herself upwards. They run into her bedroom. Gather the cassettes Kevin dubbed, those lying notes he wrote, the stuffed lamb, the guitar strap that still constricts her. They rush into the laundry room, then the dark, oppressive heat of the garage. Trying not to bump into cabinets and boxes until they reach the door that opens to daylight.

Everything falls out of her hands. Clatters onto the concrete walkway. She can barely breathe as she flips up a trashcan lid. She hurls cassettes into the trash, and is rewarded with the sound of breaking plastic. But when she tosses in the guitar strap, it's hushed voices. Sideway glances. Her dad's roses blow knowingly in the breeze, then nudge each other.

She bites down onto her lower lip and tastes blood. The knots grow tighter as she stares at the lamb, the fucking lamb she wants to rip apart limb by limb but when she pulls at one of its stubby legs, it doesn't give. Silently laughing at her for not being strong enough. There's nothing else to do but scream. Scream so loud she trembles from her sock-covered feet to her scalp. Dogs start barking. She tosses the lamb into the trashcan, slams its lid back on.

Back in the hallway, the guestroom door is open. Floral drapes and white curtains barely hide her secrets. The bed is sloppily made. The sheets haven't been laundered since February. There's a not-so-fresh smell Kim can't quite figure out.

Joey nods. She slams the door shut.

The guest room has been filled with concrete from carpet to ceiling. Its door disappears into the wall.

It's not there. It was never there.

12

"So, Kim," Michelle says over *Brass Monkey* by the Beastie Boys, "someone said they saw you with Walter Riordan on the last day of school!" She smirks in the rearview mirror.

"Yeah," Traci adds from her shotgun throne, "what were you guys doing behind the gym that day?"

In the backseat, Joey sits next to Kim with his legs crossed. The lacy white hem of his pink dress demurely grazes his knobby knees. He pouts as he asks, "How come we never get to hang out with your boyfriend?"

An annoyed growl slides from her throat. She looks out at the palm trees and rolling hills. "He's not my boyfriend! And you know my parents are making me take that SAT preparation class!"

"Oh my god!" Traci swats Michelle's arm. "No wonder! She's been seeing him all this time!"

"That's why she's been listening to all those British bands and looking like a wannabe vampire, too!" Michelle says. "She's doing it to impress the retard!"

"And just so she can be cooler than everyone else, because no one's allowed to like what she likes!"

"Well, they're definitely not welcome at our tea parties!" Joey says.

Kim leans into the car door, holding up her head with her palm. The sun is a spotlight on her forehead, warming her skin through the glass. "Fuck off." Right as she speaks, dirty air is trapped in her throat. She looks down at her black lace lap. Hopes neither of them see her eyes water. They don't hear her exhaling loudly over the Beastie Boys. Or they don't care.

Joey tugs at her arm. "Let's ditch them later!"

"Kim!" Michelle laughs. "When he asked you out, did he say, 'My name is Walter! Can I be your special boyfriend?'"

Traci slaps the sides of her thumb and forefinger into her chest. "Let's have retarded sex!"

A "hmmph" comes from Joey. Kim spots the green sign. *Cal State Dominguez Hills, next exit.* It's easier to breathe. She remembers Walter's eyes. The look in them. The way he made her feel. Traci and Michelle's hysterical laughter are cacophonous sour notes, metal banging against metal. Their faces belong to nightmarish circus clowns.

Joey twirls his hair, bats his long, golden lashes. "He's totally cute, isn't he?"

She scowls. "Nuh-uh!"

He grins and nods slowly. "Uh-huh!"

After they exit the freeway, Michelle makes a sharp stop at the intersection. Joey leans over, slaps her upside the head. She doesn't notice. "We've put up with a lot of your shit, Kim. Every show we go to, you make out with a different guy during every band. And once, we had to wait for you because you were too busy fucking someone in their backseat. But you're not ditching us for the retard."

"I mean, really, Kim, a retarded freshman? You're a pedophile!" Traci says.

"What are you? The Mother Theresa of sluts?"

"Are you gonna fuck blind guys and amputees next?"

Joey puts his hand on Kim's thigh. "She's not welcome at our tea parties, either!"

"So what's he like in bed?" Michelle asks after she pays for parking.

"I haven't fucked him, Stupid," Kim says.

Joey nods. "Good. Besides, sex is so...so...nasty. I'd rather go shopping."

"Yeah, right!" Traci says as they begin to circle for a spot in the crowded parking lot. "I bet he drools and makes weird sounds!"

Kim rolls her eyes. "Shut up."

After Michelle parks, she turns to glare at her. "It's us or the retard."

Traci turns, too. "We're just looking out for you."

"And so am I." Joey nods at the car door. "Let's run for it!"

Kim shoves the door open. Joey's already waiting on the blacktop. Their fingers clasp together as they run from Michelle's car. He glides in the early morning heat as she gasps for air, forces herself to keep going. Traci and Michelle are yelling. She doesn't look back.

With each second, she and Joey lift a little more off the ground. A little more until they can straighten their arms and legs and glide, but they fall back to earth when they're at the end of the line. It's already wrapped around the fence. Kim puts her hands on her thighs, panting and choking while Joey puts on pink lipstick. They're swallowed up by everyone else who gets in line behind them. By that smell of sweat and cigarettes and shampoo, with a sprinkle of marijuana.

💣

At high noon, the sun burns Kim's scalp. The rays don't penetrate Joey, who stays porcelain. He's also exempt from perspiration. The crowd in front of the stage stretches all the way across the field and towards the midway.

"Last year was much cooler," she says after they've secured a spot against the railing, front and center.

He snorts. "That's because Ethyl Meatplow played the second stage, and they had a dancing she-male with pierced nipples."

The four women of L7 saunter onstage. They nonchalantly assume their positions, and start playing *Death Wish.* Joey dances and sings along at the top of his lungs. Kim's a stiff mute. Her head bobs out of rhythm. She knows she looks like an idiot. After L7's first song, he grabs her hand. "I have a bad feeling about the gross guy standing behind us. Move closer to the barricade and don't turn around. Oh, shit! Oh, no-"

A pair of tan arms wrap around her waist. Wrinkled hands with dirty fingernails rest on her belly. She can't move. Her eyes widen. Her lips part, curl downwards. Maybe she's seeing things. Maybe they'll just go away. But they don't. "What's wrong with me, Joey? Why can't I move?"

He slips over the barricade, yanks at Gross Guy's wrists. They refuse to budge. "I don't know, stomp on his foot or elbow him!"

She grits her teeth, takes a deep breath. On the count of three, she snaps her head in Gross Guy's direction. Oh, he's definitely gross. Wrap-around Oakley sunglasses on his sunken face. His greasy chin-length hair crowned with a receding hairline. His shirt used to be white. Right when she opens her mouth, he kisses her. Both of Joey's hands are on Gross Guy's head, but his tongue forces open her lips. Mashes against hers. His breath stinks of beer and cigarettes. She pulls away, spits through the side of her mouth. Saliva lands onto the front of her new black dress.

"No!" Joey's fist hits the side of Gross Guy's head. "She's my girl!" He hits him again. Nothing.

Kim is so humiliated in front of the band she once worshipped. So ashamed they're witnessing this. They've got to be rolling their eyes behind their sunglasses. Do they think she's too stupid to stand up for herself, or worse yet, a slut?

She used to love almost every band with loud guitars and a raucous female vocalist. They understood her, made her stronger. Now they just make her feel like a wannabe. Everyone from L7 is skinny and gorgeous. All the girls in those bands are. She shakes her head. She could never be a true rebel grrrl rocker. Especially not after Kevin.

She's still a statue when Gross Guy kisses the side of her neck. He pinches her nipples through her dress, ignores Joey's attempts to stop him. Gross guy's hairy hand slides up her skirt, strokes her pantyhose-covered crotch. Tickles her like the legs of a fly.

Fat security guards stand in front of the stage with their arms crossed. Expressionless. Eyes dart in their direction, then look away. And she can't get away from Gross Guy dry-humping her ass. Kim feels an uneasy tightness at the base of her spine. Her skin crumples above fat and bones and tendon. The knots she's all too familiar with return.

After L7's set, Gross Guy is still pressed up against her. Joey hugs her from across the barricade, keeps apologizing for being such a lousy friend. Kim forces herself to scoot to the right, where there's a welcome gap of empty space behind her.

"Wait!" Joey perks up. "Ask him to hang out with you!"

"No! I don't wanna see Nick Cave with that fucker!"

"I'm serious! Please trust me!"

"Fine, Joey. I trust you." She turns to Gross Guy. "Wanna hang out?"

"Sure, Baby, let's go."

Joey prances besides her. "Ask him how old he is!"

Kim smiles at Gross Guy. "How old are you, anyway?"

His elbow bumps into hers. "Twenty-five. You?"

"I just turned seventeen on August seventeenth." Kim scans the crowd to make sure she doesn't see anyone she knows.

"*She's only seventeen/se-ven-teen/daddy says she's too young/but she's old enough for me.*" Gross Guy gives her two thumbs up after he's done singing Winger. "So what are you, a senior?"

Joey sticks out his tongue. "So what are you, a child molester?"

She tries not to laugh. "Yeah."

"My name's Bob. What's yours?"

"Jennifer." Jennifer Finch and the rest of L7 must hate her, but there's still a chance they don't.

"You're so pretty, Jennifer."

In his sunglass lenses, her doppelgangers are small and scared. "You think so?"

"I know so."

They sit cross-legged in the grassy area between the midway and main stage, with Joey holding her hand. Bob stretches his deeply tanned legs in front of him. His plaid shorts ride up his muscular, hairy thighs.

Joey wiggles his left pinky. "Hey little girl, wanna see my worm?"

Kim giggles. Bob scoots closer. She scoots away.

"Nice shoes!" Joey points at the battered brown

moccasins Bob wears without socks. "You'll attract lots of teenage girls with those!"

Bob smiles at Kim. "Do you do this often?"

"Do what often?"

He shifts in his seat, hands resting above his crotch. "Tease strangers at shows."

"No. Never."

Joey nudges her. "Ask him if he'll be your human toilet. Do it."

"Hey, Bob. Will you be my human toilet, and let me use your tongue as my toilet paper?" Kim smiles, tilts her head from side to side.

He leans closer. She turns away from her doppelgangers. "Come on, Baby, you know you wanna get your pussy pounded, so let's find a place to fuck."

"Pull off his sunglasses!" Joey says.

Kim takes a deep breath, yanks off his Oakleys, holds them behind her back. "Yeah, right, asshole!"

"Hey! That's not cool!" Bob's face is tan, with pale circles around his bloodshot blue eyes. She holds his gaze, even though she'd rather not. He reaches for his sunglasses. She scoots away. "Give 'em back!"

Kim and Joey look at each other and nod. They get up.

"Twenty-five my ass!" She dangles Bob's sunglasses in front of him before they rush away.

"Hey! Bitch! Give 'em back!"

They giggle as she tosses Bob's Oakleys into a trashcan.
On the main stage, the road crew is still doing sound check.
As they push their way past the sea of people, a hand
touches her shoulder. She gasps. Her entire body stiffens.
Then a familiar voice says her name.

13

Joey jumps up and down. "Your boyfriend is so ugly he's hot!"

"He's not my boyfriend, Joey!"

There's no denying Walter's angular face. His big lips and freshly dyed black hair. If her vision were in grayscale, he'd belong in a publicity photo for a British post-punk band, circa 1979. It would conceal his sun burnt skin. But even in black and white, he'd still look at her the way no one else has before.

That feeling she had on the last day of school returns with a vengeance.

He stares. "Y-You look hot."

She smiles shyly. "Thank you." Or maybe he was telling her she looked uncomfortable from the heat?

"Are you alone?"

Joey rolls his eyes. "No!"

"Well, I'm no longer friends with the girls who gave me a ride."

Walter lights up. "D-Do you need a ride home?"

"I'd love a ride," she smiles with her chin tilted down. Winks.

"Okay," he gulps, Adam's Apple quivering beneath his

skin, "I-I, um..."

"Walt," the middle-aged man standing next to him grins, "aren't you going to introduce me to your girlfriend?"

Walter shakes his head. "Dad!"

Kim turns even redder. Joey points and laughs while she and Walter's dad shake hands. "Just call me Neil." He looks at her knowingly. "It's nice to finally meet you. My son talks about you all the time."

"I bet his dad caught him touching himself while he was saying your name!" Joey says.

"Joey! Stop it!" She raises an eyebrow at Walter. "He does?"

"Dad!" Walter's jaw drops as he shakes his head.

Neil nods. "Oh, yes, he-"

Cheers cut their conversation short. They turn to the stage, where Nick Cave sarcastically greets his audience. Under the sun, he and The Bad Seeds are impenetrable in their dark suits. Their music too heavy for broad daylight. And there's no band she detests more as she stands next to Walter.

Half their set consists of love songs that obliterate the feeling in her legs, make her heart race. Every time he looks at her, she melts a little more. Joey's kissy faces make it worse. There's a make-believe gap between the soles of her Docs and the ground. He leans closer, points out the dark-haired guitarist as James Johnston from Gallon Drunk.

His warm breath on her ear. Their sweaty forearms touch. Their eyes meet again. The back of Walter's hand touches hers. She looks away, then looks back at him. His fingers graze her knuckles. She can't imagine how dumb she looks with her eyes wide. Her lips in an O. He takes her hand. His fingers intertwine with hers. His palm hot, moist. It's the first time she's held hands with someone other than Joey.

A chill runs down her spine as the band plays *I Let Love In* and *From Her To Eternity*. Fighting back tears as she looks at him. At first, she can't recognize the pretty girl with dark eyes and blackberry lips in Walter's dilated pupils, but realizes it's her when he squeezes her hand.

"Kim and Tard sitting in a tree, K-I-S-S-I-N-G. First comes love, then comes marriage. Then comes Little Tard in a baby carriage!" Joey sings into her ear.

"I hate you!"

She's never been so happy for a band to get offstage.

"That was the best Leonard Cohen tribute band I've ever heard!" Neil says.

"Th-they sound nothing like him!" Walter shakes his head, then looks at Kim. "Don't mind Dad."

"At least he learned how to sing. Remember when you were playing the Birthday Party and I thought he sounded like a rabid dog?"

Kim looks at Walter incredulously. "You like The Birthday Party?"

"I-I love them."

Neil laughs, gives his son three pats on his back. Walter wrinkles his nose, gives his dad a sidelong glance. "You should've seen my reaction when I found out that Walt started liking Nick Cave when he was twelve."

"Really? You got into him when you were that young?" Back when Kim was twelve, she loved hair metal, along with regular doses of The Outfield and Eddie Money.

Walter nods. "I like Social Distortion and Johnny Cash a lot, too. D-Do you like them?"

Joey snorts. "He'll say anything to impress you!"

Kim nods, tugs at a strand of her hair. "Yeah."

Neil clears his throat, wipes the sweat from his forehead. "But yeah. When I found out Walt liked that stuff, I was worried he was going to start wearing eyeliner and Aqua Net. If he did, the kids at school would be making fun of him even more." He slaps his thigh and laughs loudly.

Joey sticks his tongue at Kim. "Like it made a difference."

Walter makes a face. "L-Like I said, d-don't mind him."

Neil waves a dismissive hand, smiles. "Would you like to have lunch with us? You are Walt's girlfriend, so I ought to treat you right."

She raises an eyebrow as Walter looks at the ground. "Um, sure."

Joey nudges her. "Tard had an erection the entire time!"

And she and Walter are still holding hands.

Neil buys them vegetarian burritos and soda. They sit in the field, not too far from where she and Joey pulled a fast one on Bob. Walter places his paper plate over his lap. Kim pretends not to notice as she unwraps her burrito. Joey winks at her before taking long, slow licks from a large rainbow lollipop.

"So what are you doing after graduation, Kim?" Neil smiles at her, oblivious to the young and questionably fashionable, who raise their eyebrows at his golf shirt and khakis.

"My parents want me to major in computer science at UCI, but I really like books and want to be a librarian."

Walter's eyes widen. "Wow! You're smart!"

Neil laughs. "You're the reason my son got a library card."

"Ooh, Tard got smarter over the summer!" Joey makes slurping sounds as he licks his lollipop. Dark saliva drips down his chin.

Kim glances at Walter. "I guess that's good news. What kind of books do you like?"

Neil nudges him. "Hey, Walt, should I tell your girlfriend which books you checked out recently?"

"I-I checked out *A Clockwork Orange* a-and *The Catcher in the Rye.*"

"Right."

"He checked out sex manuals!" Joey wags his discolored tongue before attacking his lollipop again.

"How did you like them?" Kim asks.

"I loved *The Catcher in the Rye,* but *A Clockwork Orange* was kind of weird. I checked out some poetry books, too, because I thought they'd be easier to read than novels."

"I've been trying to get my dyslexic son to read more for years," Neil says, "then all of a sudden, he wants a library card."

"He's like, your pet retard." Joey licks the corner of his mouth.

Kim nods. "It's great that you're reading more."

Walter blushes. "Th-Thank you."

"Am I really your only friend around here?"

"No. Steve Perez, th-that greasy kid who sits with me in the cafeteria, is my friend, too. But w-we moved the summer before freshman year."

Neil nods. "My ex-wife and I divorced nine years ago, then I got promoted to a position in Southern California. It was time for a fresh start." Walter sits with hunched shoulders, looks down at his lap. Pulling up blades of grass and letting them slip through his fingers. "Walt's had a hard time adjusting, especially since his golden retriever died."

Kim puts down her burrito. "I'm sorry. What happened?"

"Well, I-I was walking Harry last summer. H-H-He started barking when he heard the ice cream truck. I tried to calm him down. I really tried. But-But he broke away and ran right in front of it. The driver stopped, but it was too late. Then the bastard drove away." Walter fingers the scratched metal tag hanging from a silver ball chain around his neck. "Th-This was his tag."

Joey frowns. "Poor doggy."

She eyes the circle of metal with Harry's name engraved on it. "Where are you guys from?"

"Hayward," Walter says. "It's not so bad anymore, but I still miss my mom a-and my friends."

Neil's lips tighten. But they switch to a smile just as quickly. "I'm curious, Kim. You seem to have goals and good study habits. So what is a smart, attractive girl like you doing with my son, anyway?" Neil asks, taking a big bite of his burrito.

"You wanna see the snake in his stovepipes!" Joey says.

Kim shifts in her seat. "I don't know." She laughs nervously as Walter watches her. "Because he's more interesting than the friends I came here with?"

Neil shrugs. "Well, he is kind of special."

💣

After the show, Neil takes them to Denny's for a late night breakfast. They do whiny impressions of Billy Corgan complaining about how much he hates L.A. She and

Walter sit next to each other at a respectable distance, but it doesn't stop her from kicking him under the table. Stepping onto his foot. He smiles shyly as the toe of his boot brushes hers.

"Oh! My! God!" A familiar voice says.

A server seats Traci and Michelle a few booths away. Kim makes eye contact with them, smiles sweetly. Traci mouths two monosyllabic words at her. Michelle slashes her index finger across her own throat.

Joey lets out an angel food cake and butter cream frosting fart. "The first day of school is gonna be fun."

14

Joey bounces up and down on their bed. A white leather
purse swings back and forth from his wrist. "Hey, look
what I've got!" He giggles, stops bouncing. His hair
disheveled, his cheeks rosy. He unclasps his purse, takes
out a silver revolver. A small yellow box of bullets. "It's the
first day of school. We should make it count!"

"Oh! Oh! You're my girl!"

They laugh and jump up and down together. Ruffled
white curtains ripple in the hot breeze. They waltz beneath
the white canopy staked by columns at the four corners of
the bed. The bubble gum walls swirl as they collapse into a
giggling heap. After they get up, they do their hair and
make-up at the vanity table. Then they have scones with
dried strawberries, rose-scented black tea with cream.
Joey's My Little Ponies fly off their shelves to soiree at
their Dream Castle beside their bed.

It's little girl heaven. Or little girl hell.

After her mom drops them off at school, they creep
behind Traci and her little sister.

"You ready?" Joey takes out his gun, aims at Traci's
back.

"Kill her."

He pulls the trigger. Traci screams, topples forward.
Her little sister keeps walking. Kim and Joey giggle as

they pass her. She's sprawled face down on the cement. The back of her sky blue dress stained red.

Kim blows a kiss at Traci's dead body. "Have a nice life."

In zero period English, everyone is already sweating in their first-day finery. The school district deems air conditioning an unnecessary extravagance. There's no relief in opening doors or being outside. The Santa Ana winds are a perpetual furnace blast.   Next it's first period Economics. Second period Spanish.

Classmates reunite in fits of hugs and laughter. No one speaks to Kim. She doesn't expect them to. In every class, Joey sits at the desk on her right. Her classmates look at the empty seat and go sit somewhere else. He's giddy in his Catholic schoolgirl uniform, stroking the barrel of the revolver. He keeps reminding her he'll shoot anyone she wants.

Before third period, the bitches head straight for them. Their smirks visible from a distance. They all wear some sort of baby tee under some sort of ankle-length slip dress, and Docs. She walks with her shoulders back, doesn't look away. Joey cocks the hammer as he sashays besides her.

"Yo, Ho!" Monica whistles. "Did you have fun with your special boyfriend at Lollapalooza?"

Kim and Joey look at each other, shaking their heads.

Robyn cackles. "So what's Waltard Riortard like in bed, huh?"

"Does he drool when he comes?" Brandi asks.

"Kill 'em all," Kim says.

Joey kisses her hand. "My pleasure."

He shoots Monica between the eyes. Blood splatters, she stumbles backwards. The rest of the bitches are too busy giggling to notice. Next comes Robyn, who gets shot in the chin. The back of her head hits the concrete ledge that separates the C and D buildings. Brandi keeps running her mouth until she's shot in the forehead. She tumbles into a twisted pile on top of her friends.

Their living schoolmates continue to walk in oblivion.

The Chinese kids give Kim sidelong glances as they walk into Intro to Calculus. She sits down at one of the empty seats up front. Hears the word *banana* in Mandarin, followed by snickers. Joey starts firing. One. Two. Empty chamber. He holds six fresh bullets in his right palm. Reload. *Click. Click. Click. Click. Click. Click.*

The Chinese kids are still twittering about Kim. *She fat. She Twinkie. She not even that smart. I hear she having sex with mentally retarded boy.* Three. Four. Five. Six. Seven. Eight. Nine kids are still slumped over their desks when class is over.

On the way to fourth period, this hairy Armenian kid with a uni-brow calls Kim a "retard-fucker." Joey shoots him in the crotch. He falls to his knees, clutching himself and groaning.

All jocks and cheerleaders are shot on principle. So is anyone who's ever made fun of her. Then they zero in on Michelle, who's walking alone in a clingy white baby tee and a red miniskirt. Kim's former friend is about to say something. She is shut up with a gunshot. They laugh as she flies backwards and hits the concrete. The blood that spreads through her shirt as red as her freshly dyed hair.

"I can't believe Ad-Rock married that bitch Ione Skye! I mean, I can barely fit into the largest size at X-Girl, but he picked her over me!" Joey says in a high voice, his puckered pink lips blowing glittery gunpowder from the barrel.

A halo shines around his head. His pale skin glimmers like melted candle wax. His eyes are even brighter. A small blue bird lands onto his left shoulder, chirps gleefully. Two mewling kittens rub up against his calves.

As they walk into computer class, people glance up and talk in hushed voices. They find a workstation at the far corner, next to the coat closet. Debate what spreads faster, a crabs outbreak in a whorehouse, or a rumor at a high school, when they're interrupted by laughter. Kim stops talking. Her body starts tingling.

Joey claps. "Your pet retard is here!"

Her eyes face the safety of her computer screen. "He doesn't see me."

"He's walking towards us! I dare you to kiss him in front of everyone!"

"Shut up, asshole! Why don't you shoot him, already?"

"If I did, then I'd have no one to laugh at."

Footsteps approach. A backpack hits the floor. Someone sits down next to her. Something unzips.

"H-Hi, Kim."

Joey clears his throat. "Look at him, silly."

When she does, she's warm all over. "Hey, Walter. I had fun at Lollapalooza."

"Yeah. S-So did I."

"I heard they were totally kissing and feeling each other up at Lolla!" A girl says.

"Really?" Her friend asks. "I heard Riortard's a fag!"

Walter rolls his eyes. "Wrong."

The instructor doesn't look up from reading the *L.A. Times* at his desk. Joey shoots both girls in the chest. They tumble backwards in their chairs. No one else notices. Then he shoots a fat girl who used to make fun of Kim for being fat. A rainbow forms above Joey's head. The blue bird on his shoulder laughs even harder. The kittens hop onto his lap, purring with approval.

"I heard Riortard was banging Ho-Bag since he was a freshman!" Some guy says. "And they did it behind the gym on the last day of school!"

Bang. Whoever said that falls out of his chair.

"I bet she gave him retarded head!" His friend says.

Joey shrugs, pulls the trigger. Shoots him in the face. He collapses over his keyboard. Daisies spurt from the classroom floor and tabletops. The bluebird and kittens rush away from Joey, towards the freshly bloomed blossoms.

The instructor's still hiding behind the *L.A. Times*

when the tardy bell rings.

"Kim," Walter begins, "why are people saying w-we've...you know?"

"That he likes it when you pee on him?" Joey asks. "I started that one."

"Because the girls who gave me a ride to Lollapalooza suck."

"Steve Perez and the rest of the guys from special-ed asked if w-we had done it. They were so sad wh-when I told them we hadn't."

"Well, we should make those rumors true."

Walter covers the side of his face with his palm. "W-We should get to know each other more before w-we...you know. Like, hang out a-and go on more dates."

"Hey, I was just kidding."

"Um, okay. Y-You got me."

Joey laughs so hard he falls off the table.

💣

Lunch is Salisbury steak, mashed potatoes, and peas. Kim's flanked by Walter and Joey as they walk out of the lunchroom. The kids from the special-ed table give Walter the thumbs-up. She shakes her head, rolls her eyes. They pass laughter silenced by gunshots, to their secluded spot behind the gym. When they sit down in the grass, Walter puts his backpack over his lap again.

"It's okay, Walter," Kim pokes at her mashed potatoes with a spork, "you don't have to do that."

"Ooh, I wanna see his dick, too!" Joey takes a pink lunch bag from his purse, turns it upside down. Halloween-sized servings of candy clatter to the grass. Boxes upon boxes of Red Hots. Kim's eyes widen at the pile of sugar. Joey rips open one of them. "Unlike other people, I never get fat or have bad skin."

Walter's forehead scrunches as he rips open his milk carton. "You sure?"

"Since people say we're fucking, why not?"

"Okay. Wh-Why not, right?" He takes his backpack from his lap.

Kim eyes the outline of his erection through his snug black jeans. Tugs on a strand of her hair. "It's flattering."

"Ooh! Get him to whip it out!" Joey tosses a fresh handful of candy into his mouth, munching with his mouth open. Red chunks fall from his lips and onto the grass. Kim wrinkles her nose. He sticks his red-stained tongue at her.

"Hey, Walter," she gives her best cutie-pie smile as Joey claps his hands together, "whip it out."

"Uh..." He stares at the grass. Scratches his head. "I don't think I..."

"I'll show you my tits."

"No. I-If I do, you should show me your pussy."

"This is so fucking awesome!" Joey rolls around in the grass. Candy spews as he convulses from his wailing laugh. His lips and teeth artificial red.

"You shouldn't be so shy. Could you show me? Please?" Kim asks.

"Well, as long as y-you show me yours." His right hand rests uncertainly on his stomach, right at his waistband.

"Tell you what." She rests her lunch tray on the grass. Spreads her legs. Joey hoots, kicks his own legs into the air. Kim's upper teeth scrape her lower lip. She pulls up her dress, exposing pale skin and black fishnet stockings. She presses her right hand into her crotch. Covers black mesh that barely hides her. She shudders as she feels wet heat. "Is that better?"

A moan escapes from the back of Walter's throat. "Yes." His voice is hoarse. His wide eyes on her thighs. "Y-You have nice legs."

Joey blows a raspberry. "I have better ones!"

Kim laughs. "Oh-kay."

Walter scoots closer, leans forward, cranes his neck to the right. Sweat shines on his forehead. "P-Please move your hand."

"Uh-uh."

"Pretty, pretty princess, please?"

"Please don't!" Joey says.

"Show me yours, and I will."

"Okay." Walter unbuckles his belt, unzips his fly. Reveals a white elastic waistband leading to his tighty-whities. "Should I stand up? O-Or should I..."

Joey sits back up, stares at him intently. "Just take it out, Tard."

Kim winks. "Just take it out, Walter."

"Ladies first."

"No, be a gentleman."

Walter's hand disappears beneath his waistband. Kim bursts out laughing. She finds a half-chewed Red Hot, sticky with spit, hurls it at Joey's head. He throws a fresh handful at her.

A tomato-red Walter zips and buttons up his jeans. Buckles his belt. "I'm gonna get you for this."

"Ooh, I'm so scared."

After lunch, they have Graphic Arts with Mr. Wu, a balding Chinese man with silver-rimmed glasses. A tight red cardigan over his white polo and grey bellbottoms. In his bored monotone, he mentions they're not allowed to use profanity, pot leaves, pentagrams or suspected gang symbols in their projects. Kim and Walter look at each other and groan. Mr. Wu shakes a finger, announces he'll be keeping an eye on them.

Some of their classmates giggle. She hears their names, coupled with "did it in a porta-potty at Lollapalooza." She rolls her eyes, shakes her head. Turns red when Walter looks at her.

"Are you taking the bus home?" She asks after class.

"You mean, the Tard bus?" Joey shoots a tall blonde she doesn't recognize.

She's not even sure how many people he's killed. After fifteen, she stopped paying attention to the body count. There's no longer a halo or even a rainbow shining around his head. His skin and eyes have grown dull. The blue bird and kittens are nowhere to be seen.

Walter sighs. "Yeah. Do you drive?"

"Not until I get a 1300 on the SATs, or turn eighteen. Are you trying to get me to drive you around?"

Joey snickers. "He wants to diddle you while you drive. And get a hand job."

"Why wouldn't I want a hot librarian to drive me around?"

"Can't you drive yourself?"

"H-Here's the thing. Dad won't let me drive until I'm eighteen. He's totally paranoid that I-I'll try to go back up north."

Joey snickers. "Sure, if you can even read the road signs properly."

Kim raises an eyebrow, stares at Walter. "But if you wanted to leave that badly, all you'd have to do is go to the Greyhound station."

"He thinks I'm too stupid to."

"He shouldn't underestimate you."

"Yes, but Greyhound doesn't have short buses," Joey clucks his tongue and twirls his hair, "it's such a pity."

Walter leans closer to Kim. "But I haven't really wanted to go back lately. C-Can I have your number?"

"Sure," she tattoos her phone number onto his palm with her pen.

"Here. You can have mine, too," he scrawls it onto a torn piece of notebook paper, "I'll call you tonight."

"You don't have to."

"I want to."

"Give me a hug before you go, then."

His eyes widen as she puts his hands on his shoulders. "Really?"

She tilts her head up, looks at him. "Yeah."

Walter slips his arms around Kim's waist. She wraps hers around his shoulders. The heat of his palms soothes her lower back. She smells dryer sheets and soap. The slight musky undercurrent of his skin. His breath is light and fast, racing with his heartbeat. His back stiffens when he realizes he's pressing his erection into her stomach. She presses the front of her body into his, hears a gasp from the back of his throat.

Their eyes meet. Their faces tilt towards each other.

His fingers on the nape of her neck. She pulls him closer to her, parts her lips. Not caring who actually slips the tongue first. Her body hot and tingling. About to float away. She thinks she hears the glorious feedback you get when you hold your guitar to your amp. Laughter and gunshots in the distance.

When Kim pulls away, he can't stop smiling. "I'll see you later."

"He definitely came in his pants," Joey says as they walk to six period Physics.

"How your first day of school?" Kim's mom asks over Chinese talk radio. After Kim and Walter briefly touched their palms against the glass of the short bus, and Joey flashed his frilly pink briefs to no one in particular.

Joey cringes, rubs at his ears. "She has no right to complain about your music when she turns this shit up so loud!"

"I know, right?" Kim puts on her seatbelt. "It was good, Mom."

"Good. Do you make new friend?"
She tries to keep a straight face as she thinks about kissing Walter. "Yes."

"You mean, you gave your pet retard blue balls!" Joey says.

"Who you make friend with?"

"Walter Riordan. He's a sophomore, and has a learning disability."

Her mom looks back at her as they pull out of the parking lot. "You know, Mommy very popular math teacher in Taiwan. Many of my male student visit me after class, tell me I'm their favorite. Some of them bring sweet and flower. Before I have you, I have eighteen-inch waist and Daddy can wrap one arm around it."

"I know, Mom. You've told me that before."

Joey pats her on the shoulder. "And then you came along and made her fat and bitter."

"When you done with SAT, your little friend can come to our house after school. I help him with math, and you help him with reading and writing. I take you and your little friend to West Covina Mall on weekend, too!"

Kim's jaw drops. "Huh?" She looks at Joey. "Isn't she worried about me getting pregnant?"

"I bet Walter's sperm is so strong that it can jump right through the air to impregnate you!"

Kim's mom turns around and smiles. "Yes! Today I talk to Daddy, we trust you can do math homework all by yourself now. But if you need help, I still help you. We also raising your allowance to fifty a week because you new Kimmy now, more responsible and studying harder!"

"Really, Mom?"

Joey scoffs. "So now you don't have to steal their loose change to buy lingerie!"

"When you good, your parents reward you!"

It's the best first day of school Kim has ever had.

15

"Where is application for UC school?" Kim's mom asks.

Joey rolls his eyes, brushes the purple mane of a white My Little Pony unicorn. "Up your butt."

"On the kitchen table." Kim doesn't look up from studying SAT analogies on the living room couch.

"I filling it out for you!"

She whirls around. Stares at her mom. "I want to fill it out myself!"

"You taking SAT in two day, need more time to study!" Her mom gives that sharp, triumphant nod before she walks into the den. She reappears with a typewriter in her arms. It lands onto the kitchen table with a tender thud. "We let you write your own admission essay. Is good enough."

Kim catapults from the couch. "It's my life! I have the right to type it myself!" She stomps towards her mom. Joey follows suit.

Her mom shoves at her. "Is not your life! You go study!"

"I'm going to college, not you!"

"We paying your tuition!"

Kim grabs Joey's hand. "Come on! Shoot her!"

He sighs. "She's a bitch, but she takes care of us."

For the first time, she doesn't feel light and explosive. Like anything in the world is possible. She grits her teeth. Tries to push past her mom to get to her college application. She's blocked by her wide figure. Suffocated by her heavy floral perfume."If you don't sit down, I hit you!"

Kim's a statue again. Her mom brims with victory as she sits at the kitchen table, switches on the typewriter. She and Joey retreat to the couch. She's a trembling mess of cold sweat. Joey exhales through pursed lips, tugs at his hair. Her mom types away.

Dogged fingers slam down onto the keys. Joey moves closer to her. She squeezes his hand so hard she's about to crush his bones. The little ringing bell precedes a mechanical ripping sound every time a new line starts.

"We applying for every UC school, and telling Aunt Tai and Jessie which one accept us!" Kim's mom says. "I will prove I good mommy and have smart daughter, too!"

She shakes her head. "You are a selfish bitch."

Her mom pretends not to hear. She has better things to do, like choosing her major for her. At UC Berkeley, she's undeclared. At UC Davis, she's engineering. And of course, at UCI, she's Information and Computer Science.

Kim wants to yank the application from the typewriter. Rip it to shreds. A scream slides its way towards her throat. It's lodged there, a chunk of rotten meat. Choking her. Every time she inhales, she can't take a complete breath. Every time she exhales, there's still more dirty air trapped inside her.

Kim tries to breathe long, relaxing breaths. All she gets are short, shallow ones that fray her nerves even more. Kevin pushes in further. "Ow! You're hurting me!"

"But I'm being gentle and using lube! Most guys would just go crazy when they're in an asshole as tight as yours!"

"Ow! Stop!"

"Come on, Kimmy! I drove all the way from L.A.! You can't change your mind now!"

"Tell her you're gonna change majors behind her back!" Joey says.

Her entire body trembles. Her teeth clatter. Another scream snowballs inside her stomach, pushes up her windpipe. She opens her mouth wide. Balls her fists at her sides. There's nothing. She squeezes her eyes shut and tries again. She's still mute.

"God, Kimmy. You're such a girl. You let me fuck you in the poopie, but now you're telling me you don't want it anymore?"

Joey swats her right knuckle. "Tell her!"

She turns around. Glares. "I'll just change majors behind your back!"

"You no allowed to! If you change, school call and tell us!"

Her nails dig deeper into her palms. "So what? I'll be eighteen!"

"But you no independent, no getting financial aid until

you twenty-four!"

"Tell her you'll just get pregnant, then!" Joey hisses, gripping Kim's hand.

"Fine! I'll just get pregnant so financial aid will consider me independent!"

"If you get pregnant, I kill you!"

"I don't care! I'm tired of having you as my mother!"

Joey cheers. "Damn right! Let that bitch have it!"

Kim's mom stops typing, shoots up from her seat. The wooden chair falls backwards onto the floor. "I killing you!"

"Go ahead bitch," Kim says calmly.

Her mom raises her hand, fingers spread for maximum impact. Kim and Joey get up. The couch is the only thing that separates them from her mom.

"Maybe you secretly want me to get pregnant," she smirks, puts her hands on her hips, "so you can kick me in the stomach and give me a miscarriage."

"I taught you well," Joey says.

Kim's mom's face boils red. "Nobody want to sleep with you! You want to run away and be prostitute, fine! At least prostitute have pretty face, good body!"

"Well, look in the mirror before you open your stupid fucking mouth!" Kim steps around the side of the couch so they're face to face. Joey stands behind her, his hands on her shoulders. "I bet Daddy's cheating on you! He wants someone younger and thinner, instead of a fat pig like you!"

Joey gasps, tightens his grip on her shoulders. "Um, I think you went too far."

Kim's mom's lower lip quivers. Her shoulders slump forward. "I tell Daddy you say that. I tell him we sacrifice so much, but you threaten to kill us."

"Go ahead! Maybe he'll fuck you out of pity!"

"Jesus Christ, Kim!" Joey yells. "Just shut up!"

Tears stream down her mom's cheeks. "Kimmy-ah, you say bad things to Mommy, but you only hurting yourself."

"Oh, really?" She cackles. "That's because the truth hurts!"

Her mom wipes at her face. "I trying my best! Aunt Tai single mom, need to take out loan so Jessie go to Berkeley. You have two parents paying for your college education! How many other children have parents that love so them much, when they so rotten?"

"Shut up with your stupid guilt trips, Mom! You don't give a shit about me! All you care about is what Aunt Tai and Cousin Jessie think!"

Joey steps between them. "Stop it!"

"No! She has it coming!"

"What the hell, Kim? UCI means we can get out of here! Remember when your dad mentioned you'd be living on campus because it's gonna be too much of a commute every day?"

She looks at him helplessly, ignores her mom's loud sobs. "I'm so sick of her manipulating me like this!"

He throws his hands into the air. "But don't you see? You'll be living an hour away from them!"

"Oh." She's a rapidly deflating balloon. Why didn't she realize that in the first place? She sighs, shakes her head. "I'm sorry, Mom." Puts on her most obedient face. "I'm a bad daughter. I do not deserve this opportunity you're giving me."

Kim's mom nods. "You very bad daughter, deserve to be flush down toilet. One day, you learn I right, and you appreciate me. Nobody love you as much as I do."

"One day." She holds her mask over her face. "Mom, I really appreciate you filling out my application while I study. I'll sign it when you're done."

Joey tugs at Kim's hand. "Now let's go have a fucking tea party."

16

"So what do you wanna do during that stupid rally?" Walter asks as the fifth period bell rings.

Joey giggles. "You know what he wants to do!"

Homecoming is tonight. The crowd at the rally is going to be extra-obnoxious, not to mention malodorous, since many of them are zombies. As they walk towards the library, she takes Walter's hand. "Let's hang out behind Graphic Arts."

"Walter," Joey bats his lashes, "wanna make out with me behind Graphic Arts?" He lifts up his pink pinafore, revealing bloomers.

"You go make out with him, then." Kim hisses at Joey.

Walter pauses. "I-It's kind of secluded, right?"

"Yeah." She smiles at him. The walking definition of the dorky boy next door, even with his dyed hair and black stovepipes and Social Distortion shirt.

"Ahh," Joey says slowly, "what have you got today?"

Kim pats her backpack. "Bataille."

He shrugs, straightens up the rounded collar of his crisp white blouse. "That'll do."

Kim and Joey wrinkle their noses at the stench of their dead schoolmates. Zombies trudge towards the school gym.

Muddled voices chatter about tonight's game and dance. How are the dead going to play football and do cheers? There's no homecoming court like a dead one, though. One of them walks too closely to her. Flies and maggots all over its decaying flesh. She grimaces. "Hey, Walter. Can I read you something dirty?"

"I-I'm not gonna say no to that."

No one else hangs out behind Graphic Arts. The parking lot is empty. They sit down, facing the early Friday afternoon traffic. Gold and rust colored leaves scatter onto the concrete, blow low in the cool October air. Across the street, a tree with fiery leaves looms over the white steeple of a church. Kim luxuriates between Joey and Walter in her black chiffon dress and black cardigan. One of them's gleeful. Judging from the erection rising beneath Walter's jeans, the other is quite hopeful.

She takes out a crimson paperback. On the cover, a black and white photograph of a guy with someone else's skin stretched over his face. It's the unholy trinity of *My Mother, Madame Edwarda,* and *The Dead Man.* She flips towards the back of the book, to *The Dead Man.* Finds "Marie Pisses Upon the Count."

Walter sits so close that she tastes his skin on the tip of her tongue. "Go ahead. Make my day."

Kim reads in a slow, sultry voice. He listens with raised eyebrows. His mouth scrunched sideways. Joey rolls around on the concrete, laughing so hard he's sobbing. His dress hiked up his pale, smooth thighs. Kim starts reading the next section, "Marie Sprinkles Herself With Urine." She keeps looking and smiling at Walter. He sits with his arms wrapped around his legs. His shoulders hunched over. Repeatedly shaking his head. Her grin spreads so wide across her face that her cheeks burn. She takes a deep breath to keep herself from laughing.

"Okay, I'm done." She closes the book. "Did you like that?"

"W-When we go out tomorrow night, c-could you wear nothing but a garter belt a-and stockings under your clothes?"

"What?"

"What did he just say?" Joey asks as he's lying on the concrete.

Walter grins. Reveals straight teeth with a gap between the upper front ones. "You heard me."

"Where did you learn to talk like that?"

"You make me that way."

Kim punches his arm. "Shut up!"

"Oh, Kim. Do that again. You're turning me on so much."

"Fuck you!"

"T-Tomorrow night?"

She punches him again. "Ugh! I didn't mean it that way!"

Walter nods at the grass. "How about r-right now?"

Joey sits up, looks at him incredulously. "He's like a

rash that won't go away!"

Kim twirls a strand of hair around her finger. "But Walter, wasn't it awful to hear me read that?"

He shakes his head. "Oh, Kim. I-It was so tr-traumatizing." He sneers at her. Her blood erupts.

Joey gasps. "Nuh-uh. That did not just happen."

"Please tell me you're not fucking with me," Kim whispers.

"I sure am. And now you have to m-make out with me," Walter stretches his legs out in front of him. There's still a bulge where there's supposed to be one. "I knew you were trying to trick me all along."

"No!" Joey yells. "One-upped by a Tard!"

"How did you know?" Kim asks.

Walter's fingers graze her right cheek. They're warm and soft. No guy has ever done that to her before. "I-I know your face pretty well."

Joey puckers his lips. "I'd make out with him, but I'd probably wake up dyslexic."

"I'm not gonna make out with you." She's hot and tingling as she looks at Walter. Her heart races so fast it's pushing its way out of her bones.

"You have to." Walter says over the sound of Joey's smacking lips. "Consider this payback for the first day of school." His gaze makes her dissolve into the concrete.

"Consider this payback, asshole."

She pulls him towards her by his hair. Presses her lips to his. She forces them open. She feels him, feels the tip of his tongue. They kiss hard and deep, his fingers on her face and in her hair and stroking the side of her neck. Her center of gravity collapses. She's in the twilight between sitting and lying down and pulls him closer, her nipples so hard they hurt against her bra. His hands slide up and down her back, hesitating right above her ass. Not daring to turn the corner towards her breasts. She slips her hands past the hem of his shirt. He kisses her neck, his fingers on the side of her right breast when her palms touch his bare back.

"Oh my god! Kim! Walter?" Someone yells.

They break apart, sit back up. Joey sticks his tongue out at Kim, and does the universal *shame-shame-shame* motion with his index fingers. Mr. Wu stands in front of them. A lit cigarette in his right hand. Petrified. Two shades paler than usual. His dark eyes are saucers.

"Sorry, Mr. Wu," she pulls down the hem of her dress. Inhales. His cigarette is too green and pungent. Walter eyes their Graphic Arts teacher suspiciously. There's no filter on the rolled white stub burning at the end.

"See no evil. Hear no evil." Mr. Wu takes a drag of his joint before disappearing around the corner. A door squeaks and slams.

Walter wraps his arms around Kim. "That was amazing."

"Yeah, it was all right."

Joey points at Walter's lap. "His tightie-whities are soaked!"

She rolls her eyes. "Did that turn you on, Joey?"

"I don't get turned on, Kim. I'm a good girl. Unlike you."

She flips him off, then looks at Walter. His eyes glazed. His mouth wet. She rests her hand on his thigh. "Did you ever do that with a girlfriend before?"

Walter smiles, kisses her cheek. "I just did."

"Huh?"

"Y-You're my girlfriend, Kim."

She stares at Joey with horrified eyes. He shrugs and laughs.

💣

While Kim takes her SATs, Joey does vulgar cheers in front of oblivious test-takers. High kicks. Spread-eagle jumps. Flashing his frilly pink bloomers. Sticking his ass into the air and shaking it. *Go, Kim, go. Do it for your freedom. Do it for your sanity. Fuck your parents. Fuck them. Fuck them.* She's fueled by rage and hatred as she fills in the Scantron blanks with her number two pencil. She needs to get away from their rules and traditions. Their smug control over her. At the end of the exam, she slams her pencil onto the desk. Hard. The kids around her are taken aback.

After the Scantrons and exam booklets are collected, Kim and Joey saunter out of the classroom hand in hand. Their Docs scraping the cement, kicking up dirt. Dried yellow leaves cover the grass. Above them, shades of russet and gold block them from the gray sky. As they bask in the first chill of fall, he reminds her she can live however she wants on campus. Even if her parents are paying for her education.

Kim's dad waits for her on the sidewalk in front of the school parking lot. "Our investment in you must pay off." He gives her three hard pats on her shoulder.

Joey's palm rubs her shoulder. "You'll be out of there in less than a year."

She grimaces, moves away from her dad. "Yes, Daddy. Will I still be able to drive if I get at least a 1300?"

He looks away, nodding towards the parking lot. "We better go."

"No, Daddy. When I got my license, you told me I wasn't allowed to drive until I turned eighteen or got a 1300 on my SAT. You'd be a terrible businessman if you don't keep your word. When we go home, I want a contract from you."

He waves his right palm up and down. "Kim, that is not..."

She glares. "No, Daddy. I want it signed and dated. And that is final!"

He steps back, stares at her. "Wow! You are even worse than a loan shark!"

"You may go to Tower Records." Kim's dad gives her a hard
pat on her shoulder after a food court lunch at the West
Covina Mall. "But you must meet us on the first floor of
The Broadway in an hour."

Kim is tempted to put her hands together and bow. She
just nods. "Thank you."

She and Joey take long, quick strides towards the
escalator. Pushing past other shoppers. Nearly knocking
over a handbag display. He's already outside when she does
a slight jump, shoves open the glass doors. The square
brick building beckons them.

They rush across the street, flitting across the asphalt,
and glide onto the sidewalk. He's already inside the store
when she opens the door. They absorb the plastic-scented
air, bathe in a dissonant punk rock song about dead hearts.
The fluorescent lights ethereal. The scarlet EXIT sign
letters brand into her flesh.

She blinks. Her legs wobble. The back of her skull
throbs. Her head swims in sharp, colorful circles. She
staggers to the end of the newsstand, an empty white space
she can lean against. Her head falls backwards. Her eyes
squeeze shut. She wraps her arms around herself. Wishes
she could feel the skinny, hazel-eyed boy against her.
Inhale the scent of his skin. His fingers on her cheek, the
side of her neck. His erection pressing into her belly as they
kiss.

"Walter," she hears herself whisper.

"No!" Joey grabs her shoulders, angry blue eyes pummeling hers. "Joey! Joey! Joey!"

She's breathing hard. The lights too bright. The music too loud. "Shit." She looks around. People pretend not to see.

He huffs. "I never heard that."

Her head is pounding when she meets her parents twenty minutes later than promised. They don't mention it.

"I buy present for you! See! Your parents love you!" Her mom opens a white paper Broadway shopping bag. Shows her a black chiffon dress with silver buttons down the front. A black lace shift dress. A black lace blouse. A black velvet knee-length skirt. A stretchy black boat neck top with long sleeves. A black mohair cardigan. All cut slim and in her size. None of them like anything her mom usually buys her. "I see you looking at them, know you love them! I so glad they in your big size!"

"Thanks, Mom."

17

Kim and Joey tiptoe out of her bedroom. They're bombarded with melancholy violins, women sobbing in Mandarin. Joey's features scrunch together, and he pretends to cry. On the family room TV, a woman unleashes her high-pitched wail. Squealing violins tear at Kim's eardrums. The thought of living at UCI, even with a roommate who stinks, snores and likes Counting Crows, doesn't sound so bad after all.

Kim's mom jumps up from the couch, holds her arms out at her sides. "Kimmy-ah! You must change! No looking like that!"

Joey rubs at his chin. "Your mom needs tranquilizers."

Kim tries not to laugh in her new black dress and old leather jacket. "But Mom, you bought me this dress today!"

Kim's dad cocks his head to the side. "Kim, you would look much prettier if you started wearing more color."

Joey steps on her foot. "Agree with him."

"You're right, Daddy."

Kim's mom points at the ornate cross around her neck that hangs from black velvet. "What if your little friend choke you?" A glint of fear mixed with excitement in her mom's eyes.

"What if you poke her eyes out instead?" Joey suggests.

Kim rolls her eyes. "She'll bitch about my looks even when she's blind!"

But she can't get over that slick layer of sweat on her mom's face. Her eyes bulge from her glasses. She breathes through her mouth. Her chest rises and falls at an uneasy speed. Does she need medical attention? Kim turns to her dad.

He shrugs. "Mommy is excited because we are letting you go out with a boy." He chuckles. "See, we are cool parents. Cousin Jessie is not allowed to go out with boys until she graduates from college."

Kim's mom shakes her index finger at her. "You no pretty! All woman from Daddy's side of family disgusting!"

"Huh?" Kim's jaw drops. She looks at Joey. He throws his pink-manicured hands into the air.

Kim's dad rushes to his wife. Grabs her hand, swats her palm. "Yan, you shut your mouth right now!"

Her mom tries to pull away. "But Kimmy look like-"

"Not another word from you!" He says firmly. Her lower lip sticks out. A reprimanded little girl.

"Mom," Kim says, "what in the world are you talking about?"

Her dad lets go of her mom. He digs a twenty from his wallet, hands it to Kim. "Just in case."

"Thanks, Dad. But why did…"

The doorbell rings. Kim's dad turns off the TV, puts an

arm around her as they walk to the front door. Kim's mom sidles up to her. Unknowingly pushes Joey out of the way. He walks backwards in front of Kim, pinching his features together. He always does the best impressions of her mom. Right when Kim opens the door, he lets out a whooping laugh. An equally loud thunder crack of a fart. The cool October air rushes onto her face. She smells butter cream frosting and angel food cake. So sweet. So overpowering. Her temples throb, her mouth waters.

"Hi, Kim. Y-You look nice." Walter's eyes flicker. She tries to ignore the warm buzz igniting beneath her skin. Tries to ignore the memory of making out with him yesterday.

She smiles. Blocks out the sound of Joey smacking his lips. "Thank you."

"Oh, Walter!" Kim's mom laughs as she looks him up and down. "You wear a lot of black, just like Kimmy!"

"Yeah, w-we called each other and planned our outfits in advance," Walter says with a straight face.

Joey gasps. "What a Tard!"

Kim's eyes widen. She can't believe he just said that. He smiles, tilts his head from side to side. The mischievous glint in his eyes says, *Believe it, Doll.*

"Really?" Kim's mom asks. "You like twins!"

Neil pats Walter's shoulder. Walter makes a face, and scoots away. "My son can be quite the comedian."

"Does he like rock music, too?" Kim's mom asks. "You

know, Kimmy play piano since she was four! I don't know how she like such loud music when she classically trained!"

"W-We should get going, Dad," Walter says.

Kim smiles at her parents. "Yes, we should."

"I'll bring her back by ten," Neil says.

"Ten?" Kim's mom complains. "She must be home at nine!"

"When we live at UCI, we can stay out all night!" Joey says.

"Yan," Kim's dad says, "Kim is allowed to have one more hour."

It's a miracle they even make it outside. Joey skips ahead of them, his dress swishing from side to side. Kim smiles at the shining white sickle of a moon. The sky above purple. Dried orange and gold leaves on the driveway crunch beneath their feet. Her palm aches for his, but it's not a good idea. Not when she looks back and sees her mom at the window.

💣

Neil drops them off at the corner of Yale and Second in the Claremont Village. The moment he drives away, Walter takes Kim in her arms. She feels better when their lips touch. The warm amber flame grows into an inferno. She thinks she hears Joey protesting. A horn honks. Time floats away. They break apart. He looks at her with glazed eyes.

Shadows fall onto his face. "I-I've been waiting to do that to you all day."

All Kim can say is, "Yeah."

Joey tugs at her arm. "Come on, let's go!"

During burgers and milkshakes at a diner, Joey spaces out as he shoves candy into his mouth. Then they stroll past dark storefronts with tiny orange lights framing the windows. Paper pumpkins and cats taped onto the glass.

Joey walks backwards in front of her, making fun of Walter. For the first time, Kim wishes Joey weren't around. He huffs, then turns. His hair a short golden whip in the dark. He flits a few feet in front of them. Doesn't look back. So she follows him across the street to the grey building with the burgundy awning. Rhino Records.

The windows are covered with band posters. A group of boys on the sidewalk check out every girl who walks by. Walter holds Kim's hand a little tighter. They look past her. But she doesn't care. Not like she would've before.

The store is crowded with Saturday night browsers. A storm of conversations. The constant clacking of CD jewel boxes bumping into CD jewel boxes. A group of waifish teenage girls in baby tees and miniskirts looks at Kim, then at Walter. Whispering and giggling. She sneers at them. Then gets five dirty looks back. Joey points his rear end in their direction, lifts the back of his dress, lets out a loud, angel food cake fart.

"If they saw me," he twirls a strand of hair around his finger, "they'd want to take me home and dress me up in their clothes." He sticks his tongue out at her. "Unlike you."

"So go make them see you." Kim's grateful that Walter is looking at the imports inside the glass counter. He'd so not want to be with her if he knew.

"That's right!" Joey spins around in front of her. "Tard would be so jealous of me that he'd leave! But at least those girls would appreciate me. They'd put ribbons in my hair, and make me up with blue eye shadow and pink lip gloss. I'd be their perverted little baby doll." He twirls one last time before flouncing away.

She's glad Joey's gone for the time being. "Hey, Walter, how big is the Amoeba Records in San Francisco?"

He turns from the import CDs. "Way bigger. You'd love it there."

She laughs. Kisses him. "Would you kidnap me and take me to San Francisco?"

"In a heartbeat. I-If I had a car and money."

They look through the new releases. Hang out in the corner between the two shelves of music magazines. Handbills cover the wall behind them. Joey is on the short gray stage at the far corner of the store, dancing to the oblivious. Suddenly she's quiet. She stands up straighter. Her fingertips tingle. She listens closely to who's playing. It doesn't sound familiar.

The man has a high, feminine wail. Raw and manic. Heavy with liquor and nicotine. When he sings in a lower register, she feels the dirty rumble from his vocal chords. She tries to make out what he's singing. Taking someone sleeping up the street, taking them very softly. Taking them right under the parking lot. Holding them so softly.

The guitar and bass rake back and forth in a blues riff, lurking in the background until it's the chorus and they do their distorted attack. The music and the voice course through her veins. Mix with her blood. She thinks of sweaty outdoor sex. Bourbon. Voodoo. Her body graceful as she twirls around in the desert. Her hair wild in the breeze. Her fingers vibrate, ache to feel strings and a fret board. Making random shapes, moving them up and down until she gets them right.

For the first time in six months, the urge to play and sing is back.

Then the song's over. Replaced by Elastica's "Car Song." Back on earth, Walter is nowhere to be seen. *Shit.* Her eyes comb the store. *Skinny boy in black, where are you? Please tell me you didn't run off with those girls.* But it's all pointless worry, especially as he rushes towards her with something in his hand. "Here. I-I asked who was playing."

She melts, staring. "Seriously?"

"You looked exactly the way I did wh-when I was twelve and heard 'The Mercy Seat' for the first time."

"You mean, when you were at Amoeba and you just froze? And someone placed the CD into your hands?"

"Yeah."

"Shit! You're so fucking wonderful!" She grabs him and kisses him.

He turns red. "N-No one's ever told me that before."

Joey, who's been pretending the store is his personal catwalk, struts over. His hips sway from side to side. His purse a heart-shaped pendulum swinging from his wrist. "I'm the prettiest one in this room, Baby. The rest of the girls here would love to have me as their imaginary friend. Unlike you."

Kim looks at the CD cover. *Miami* by The Gun Club. Two palm trees in a dark blue sky. Three forlorn yet menacing men. The one looking down, with the messy blond hair, has to be the lead singer. When she scans the track listing, she knows *Sleeping In Blood City* is the song that made her feel alive again. "I'm gonna go pay for this. What do you want to do next?"

Walter pulls her to him. "Go somewhere quiet."

She laughs. "Okay."

Joey pouts. "No!"

Kim is the one who leads Walter into an alley. She unbuttons her jacket. Unbuttons her dress to her navel, pulls her tits from her slip. The soft breeze tickles her skin. In Walter's eyes, her twin reflections are sultry. Wild.

"Oh, no! No!" Joey yells. "Put them back!"

Walter's eyes widen. "N-Nice jugs!"

If her tits could cock their head to the side and raise an eyebrow, they would. But what does she expect from a teenage boy? She just smiles and says, "You can touch them, if you want."

He slides his fingers up and down, barely touching her. Joey shakes his head, turns away. She braces against the wall. Walter cups her in his hands. Then he leans down. Nuzzles them. Sucks on her nipples. Gently, unlike the other two. Her fingers in his hair, on his face. The moon grinning above. Their eyes meet. She pulls him up for a kiss. His mouth renders her breathless. She feels how hard he is. Wraps her right leg around his waist.

They move together, kissing passionately and groping until his entire body goes stiff. From the way he moans into her ear, taken by surprise and not wanting it yet, she knows he's coming.

He collapses into her. "I'm sorry." Hugs her tighter to him. "That was rude of me."

"I'm just so hot you couldn't help yourself." Kim's eyes widen when she realizes what just came out of her mouth. It's the first time she's ever said something like that. And felt it.

"Whatever. I'm still hotter than you," Joey says, "and we both know it."

Walter strokes her right cheek. "You are. I-I can't stop thinking about you."

"I'm sorry." She laughs. "What do you think about when you think of me?"

His gaze so intense. A surge of heat rushes through her. "I think of feeling you against me." His hands slide underneath her jacket, strokes the small of her back. "And your hair and your skin a-and how fucking sexy you are." He kisses her neck. She tilts her head back, closes her eyes. "And the way you'd sound."

In black time, they're in bed. Naked and intertwined.

She feels his beating heart. Her skin on fire as she trembles uncontrollably against him. Her eyes flicker open. For a split second, they're downcast. Hot liquid blinds her. She blinks. Joey touches her arm, tells her it's PMS. There's a stab of finality in his voice. Kim smiles at Walter, but she can't bring herself to say anything. She buries her face in his shoulder.

18

Evil Aunt Tai answers the door with a tight smile, looking at Kim's feet. "Take off your big, ugly shoe! You no ruining my carpet!"

"Keep your pants on." Joey eyes Evil Aunt Tai, then Kim's mom. "And never take them off!"

Kim unlaces her new fourteen-hole purple Docs. Rests them onto a mat with geese wearing pink ribbons around their necks. She steps into red slippers neatly lined up against the wall. Follows her mom and aunt into the living room.

Joey wrinkles his nose. "Oh, my Hell! This place is scary!"

Kim's always despised the interior of Evil Aunt Tai's house. Everything is polished. Spotless. Dust and stains the mortal enemy. The beige leather couches uncomfortable by default, because Evil Aunt Tai acts like her fat ass is wrinkling the upholstery. Sheer white curtains with embroidered hearts that shouldn't be possessed by a woman so heartless. A shiny wooden coffee table with a large ceramic swan wounded by imposter red carnations. A wooden armoire with an obsessive compulsive amount of Precious Moments dolls on its shelves. Kim believes Evil Aunt Tai keeps them to compensate for the lack of precious moments in her own life.

"Guess what happen last weekend?" Evil Aunt Tai grabs Kim's mom, leads her to the sofa. They sit together on the couch. Kim and Joey sit across from them on the love seat, Joey has his legs crossed, Kim slumped, her legs slightly spread.

"What happen?"

"I sitting on couch, watching soap opera, when I see this white mama cat and her baby cat in my backyard. I get broom, then I do this!" Evil Aunt Tai pretends she's holding a baseball bat, takes a swing. "I scare those lazy cat away!" She cackles. "They no pay rent!"

Kim and Joey look at each other, shaking their heads.

Kim's mom shrugs. "I have better news. Kimmy get 1460 on SAT."

Swords slice across the room. Joey scoots closer to Kim. Holds her hand. Smiling, Kim's mom nods triumphantly.

Evil Aunt Tai scowls. "Kimmy cheat on SAT!"

"Besides Japanese boy at school who get 1510, Kimmy have second highest score."

"Do you call test center, ask if they make mistake?"

"They no make mistake." Kim's mom sits up and looks her younger sister in the eye.

Besides her parents, Walter, Neil, Mr. Wu and his Graphic Arts class, Diana, and Melinda, no one else believes she earned that 1460. In Intro to Calculus, gnats and flies buzz around undead Chinese kids lamenting their perfect math scores and pathetic verbal ones, then shoot Kim dirty looks. In the halls, zombies accuse her of cheating, since she's obviously dumber than them.

Evil Aunt Tai shakes her head. Her hair doesn't move. "But Kimmy have large breast, and girl with large breast no smart! My Jessie have small breast, but she very smart! You can have large breast and stupid brain, or smart brain and small breast! Not both!"

Kim's mom crosses her arms over her chest. "Kimmy have large breast because Chao make more money and we feed her good."

"You rich, but Jessie get high score without expensive class! Kimmy stupid and need extra help!"

"Mom. Aunt Tai." Kim stands up. "Please excuse me."

She and Joey rush into the family room. More Precious Moments figurines on the shelves. The TV, like every other TV set in Kim's extended family, is cable-free.

They stand in front of the wooden shelf of framed pictures. She picks up Cousin Jessie's senior year portrait. Her signature forced smile, upper teeth pressing into lower lip. Blank eyes.

"You can lose the weight, but Cousin Jessie's always gonna look like a bunny rabbit taking a shit!" Joey says.

Kim's mom and Evil Aunt Tai's voices get louder, but their rapid-fire Mandarin still isn't loud enough to decipher over slamming cabinets, plates hitting the counter, and running water. The smell of roasted turkey flesh is sickeningly heavy, so heavy it cancels out Joey's sweet flatulence.

There's probably no foul turkey smell at Walter's house right now. The Riordans are getting their dinner catered from Boston Market. She imagines them sitting across from each other at their mahogany dining table. Thanksgiving dinner clashing with fine china and silverware. Walter will tell Neil how he wishes she were there. It's not fair of her mom to force her to spend the holiday with her evil aunt. Neil will tell him life's not fair. To please have another cornbread.

Kim wishes she were with Walter, too. She misses him. Kind of.

Joey sticks out his tongue at her. "If you were there, you'd probably have to have sex with him after dinner! Eww!" He giggles. Peers at a photograph of Evil Aunt Tai in her mid-twenties. She wears a paisley mini dress, tights, with boots. Her hair long and flowing. Her smile genuine. Nothing like the woman Kim is used to despising. An equally slim and short Chinese man stands with his arm around her. The sky overcast. The ocean calm. "Who's he?"

She grimaces at the smell coming from the kitchen. "Evil Aunt Tai's dead husband, Uncle Liang." She breathes from her mouth, fans her hand in front of her face. "When she was a few months pregnant with her perfect spawn, he got sick and died. That's all I know. Oh, and I don't think she's been involved with anyone else since."

"Like anyone wants to get involved with her!" He presses his lips into a line, narrows his eyes. "Hey, I don't see any wedding photos. You think she'd have them up everywhere, like your parents do."

"You have a point." Her throat closes. A pang of nausea sways in her belly. Why's everything in front of her dark and blurry? Her eyes burn. She blinks, and tears seep out. She gags, then coughs. "What the hell?"

Joey's unfazed by the strong charred smell. He points towards the kitchen, where blue smoke wafts from the doorway, making its way into the family room. "You know how you hate Evil Aunt Tai's cooking? Well, you might not have to eat it tonight."

The smoke detector starts beeping. Kim's mom and Evil Aunt Tai scream. Windows open. The night air rushes in. After the smoke detector stops, Kim's ears ring as she continues to cough and rub at her eyes.

"Kimmy-ah! We eating now!"

She glances at Joey. "Oh, joy."

The seating arrangement doesn't surprise her. Herself on one side, her mom and evil aunt across from her. Powder blue and yellow place mats with matching napkins. Forks, knives, and spoons placed in a straight row onto them. The turkey is burnt to a crisp on a platter, between plates of blackened candied yams and shriveled green beans.

"Chao say you poor loser, Tai! He right!"

"But my Jessie be doctor! Kimmy only be computer science!" Kim tries to keep a straight face as Joey picks his nose and flicks an invisible booger at Kim's mom.

"You sell yourself to rich man, but he still don't make enough for you to have better house, car, and clothes!"

"You shut up! He give you money for six years after you have Jessie!"

Kim's stomach clenches and growls. Both her mom and evil aunt take small bites, their lips puckered, foreheads wrinkled. Kim picks at her food. She'd have no problem eating whatever's served at Walter's house. No one there would make rude comments about her weight, either.

Joey rolls his eyes. "If you spend Thanksgiving with Tard, it means you'll have to marry him!"

"Kimmy!" Evil Aunt Tai slaps burnt turkey onto Kim's empty plate. "Eat! My food very good!"

Kim's mom wrinkles her nose. "Is not as good as mine."

"No, thanks, I'm not hungry," Kim says.

Evil Aunt Tai keeps piling burnt food onto her plate. All of it swimming in cranberry sauce. The pile grows, no matter how much Kim tells her to stop.

Joey squeals like a pig. "Come on, Fatty! Eat!"

Evil Aunt Tai nods at her plate. "Are you on diet?"

Joey leans over and squeezes her hand. "Oh my god, this is your chance!"

"Do you really think I'm that stupid, Aunt Tai? You want me to eat your burnt food so you can make fun of me later. Well, too bad. I'm excusing myself." Kim gets up, shuffles her chair backwards. Her mom and evil aunt stare as if she just did a striptease on the dinner table. Joey high fives her, and they rush back into the family room, giggling and holding hands.

"That's where Uncle Liang's ashes are, right?" Joey points at a white vase on the second highest shelf.

"I think so. Why?"

He puts his hands on her shoulders. There's an evil gleam in his eyes. "Tip it over."

"What the fuck, Joey? I'm already in enough trouble!"

"Come on! Please?" He widens his eyes, does his sad little girl pout.

No voices come from the dining room, only silverware tapping onto plates, stemware clinking onto the tabletop.

"I hate you." Kim stands on her tippy toes. Squeezes her eyes shut as her right palm grips cold, hard porcelain. When she slides it towards her, it squeaks in protest. She holds her nostrils to its hard mouth, expecting to snort ashes up both nostrils. All she gets is this slightly musty scent.

"Tip it over!"

"Okay, you jerk, I'll tip it over." She tilts the vase. Her hands shake, waiting for ashes to rain onto Evil Aunt Tai's pristine beige carpet. But nothing comes out. She quickly puts it back onto the shelf, porcelain clonking against wood.

Footsteps. "Kimmy!" Evil Aunt Tai yells. "What you doing in here?"

She shrugs, smiles innocently. "Nothing, Aunt Tai."

Joey looks at Uncle Liang's vase. "Nothing is right."

"I see you touch something on shelf!"

"You're just imagining things."

Kim's mom rushes to Evil Aunt Tai's side. Her face

battered by panic. "Kimmy-ah! What you touching on shelf?"

"Nothing." Kim pushes past them, picks up her Docs. "None of this would've happened if you let me spend Thanksgiving with Walter!"

"You apologize! Now!"

"No! You're a selfish mother and you know it!"

"Yan, is all your fault!" Evil Aunt Tai snaps as they close in on Kim. "If you let that dirty Jia go with her stupid friend, then she no ruin my Thanksgiving!"

Kim slaps the side of her own head. "What the hell, Aunt Tai? My name's Kim, not Jia!"

They stop just feet away from her. Bugged eyes. Pale faces. She gives them one last dirty look, shakes her head before pushing open the front door. Once safely outside, she and Joey hug each other. After she laces up her Docs, they laugh hysterically. Do a sloppy waltz on the driveway. Their voices melt the chill of the night air. The sky is starless and foggy. Lights in windows abruptly switch on.

The front door squeals open. Slams shut. They rush to the driver's side of Kim's mom's car, and stand up straight. Seconds later, her mom appears in front of them. Guarded. Pensive.

"I'll drive." Kim holds her hand out. Her mom hands her the keys. "Just relax." Joey's already sitting in the backseat.

The engine is on. The stereo to KROQ. *Interstate Love Song* by the Stone Temple Pilots. A song Walter considers romantic. "Do you mind, Mom? It'll help keep me awake."

"That song is not so bad. Kimmy-ah," she pats her right thigh, "no matter what Aunt Tai say, I believe in you."

"Thanks, Mom."

"We no spend Christmas with her and Jessie this year. I ask Daddy, maybe he no work that day, and we take your little friend and his daddy to lunch. The Chinese restaurant and store all open Christmas Day."

"Really, Mom?" When was the last time her dad spent Christmas with them? Or Thanksgiving, for that matter? Every time, he uses work as an excuse.

"Yes. Tomorrow, you and your little friend can go shopping, too." Her mom smiles. "I imagine it very hard to grow up gay and have learning disability, like Walter. He must get so much discrimination, even more than us. You be good friend."

Kim nods, eyes bulging. "Okay."

A succession of farts burst out of Joey as he laughs. Sweetness fills the car. "Oh, my god! She did not just say that!"

"I never meet gay boy before, but I like Walter. He dress funny, but he is good person." Kim's mom surveys the garage doors and lawn, shakes her head. "If Mommy let you go today, then Aunt Tai not make you throw temper tantrum. You don't have to call her and apologize. Is her fault." For once, her face isn't pinched.

Kim blinks. Looks a little closer. Swears she can see the smiling young woman with hair cascading to her eighteen-inch-waist. She remembers her mom showing her the miniskirts and colorful blouses she wore in her youth. Telling her she could borrow them if she weren't so fat. But how the hell did her mom become who she is now? "Okay. Thank you."

"Something's up." Joey says as Kim pulls out of Evil Aunt Tai's driveway.

19

"I'm dying to meet your boyfriend!" Melinda tells Kim. They sit at their usual seats in the concert hall, fidgeting. Jerking from side to side in their swivel chairs.

"Could you please be careful in front of my parents, though? We have to pretend we're just friends in front of them."

"Of course! You seemed so down right around the time Kurt died, and it's like you're so much happier now that you've found Walter."

"It's because of me," Joey says, "but you just don't appreciate it."

Kim fights back tears. "Yeah. Thanks."

"My parents are lame, too. I'm not allowed to date anyone unless they're from church." Melinda wrinkles her nose. Tugs at the bodice of her green velvet dress with short, puffy sleeves. "They use the same excuse when I want to hang out with you."

Joey gasps. "Shit! It's Evil Aunt Tai and Cousin Jessie!"

"What?" Kim had been counting on them not to show up. They hadn't called since Thanksgiving.

Her head jerks towards the entrance. Her parents are holding hands. Walter's laughing with her dad. They wave.

She waves back. They sit down at the last row, directly facing the stage.

Kim pats Melinda's shoulder. "Excuse me."

While Joey stomps besides her, Kim saunters to her parents and Walter. Thanks them for coming. Then she looks at her boyfriend. Nods towards the exit.

In the lobby, a folding table has been put out for refreshments. Wreaths and silver garlands hang from the brick walls. She waits at the back exit, the one her dad slips out through. Brisk footsteps approach. She braces herself against the glass. It's Walter, in a charcoal thrift store suit and a tie. Joey rolls his eyes. Golden hair blows upwards. Kim pushes the door open. They step out into the cool evening.

Walter takes her hand. "They think I'm using the bathroom." They make a beeline to the side of the building, then to a dark corner hidden from people and traffic.

"Mr. and Mrs. Ho," Joey says, "p-p-please excuse me. I-I need t-to go jerk off in th-the b-b-bathroom."

Kim laughs. "They believed you?"

Walter backs her into a door accessible only to authorized personnel. His embrace keeps her warmer than her black velvet shrug. "O-Of course. Why would their daughter mess around with her retarded gay friend?"

"I'm still trying to figure that out," Joey says.

Kim pulls Walter closer by his tie. "You look like a Young Republican."

"Do not."

"Do too. I doubt you can handle me."

Joey nudges her. "Get him turned on, then ditch him!"

Walter's eyes glaze. Enamored. "Y-You shouldn't tease me like that. It's dangerous." His mouth touches the delicate skin of her throat. She leans back into the door. Her hands run up and down his back as he moves lower, kissing her collarbone, then her breasts through black velvet.

Kim's fingers hesitate on the waistband of Walter's nice boy pants, feeling Joey's hand on her arm. "How dangerous?"

"Very dangerous." His hand slips beneath the flared velvet hem of her dress. She sneers at him. His hand explores her thighs, from where they're covered in black stockings to where they're bare. He stops at her panties, eyes glistening when he feels how wet she is. His fingers dart into her underwear. Stroke her in small, gentle circles. Not like the others, who touched her like they were rubbing away a stubborn stain. "D-Do you like that?" When he looks at her, she can't feel her legs. But she feels her right knee bend, the bottom of her black heel pressing into the door.

Joey takes his hand from her arm. "Ewww! What the hell?"

"Yeah. Yeah." Her heart flips when Walter kisses her. She forces herself to remain standing up, even though she'd rather fall and pull him along with her. He holds her gaze as he sucks on his fingers. When he kisses her again, she's clean. Slightly salty. Like she had never met Kevin.

"Ewww!" Joey squeals. "Tard is so depraved!"

"Y-You taste so damn good," Walter tells Kim, his breath fast and heavy.

She stares. "I do?"

"Yes."

"Come on!" Joey says through clenched teeth. "You've teased him enough!"

Kim strokes Walter through his trousers as he slides his hand up her skirt again, He slides a finger into her and her entire body recoils.

Kevin. His calloused fingers with dirty nails. He'd fingered her like she was the button on a vending machine that wouldn't dispense his can of soda. And she pretended to enjoy it. She felt like she had to.

"It never happened!" Joey's back is to her. Leaning sideways against the wall, his hands over his ears.

"Are you okay?" Walter's finger is still inside her. Firm. Unmoving.

"Yeah."

"C-Could you tell me how you like it?"

"I don't know. Like, move it in and out. And...and...go easy." He doesn't hurt her. She pushes her hips towards him as he kisses her mouth, her throat, her neck. Her hands fumble at his belt buckle. Pulling it tighter before she unbuckles it.

They fumble with the button on his pants. Pushing in the wrong direction before it's undone. She has no trouble unzipping him. He sucks in his breath. Her hand slides down his underwear. The moist pearl at the tip. Hardened tissue. Soft, searing skin. Longer than what she's had before. She imagines him swollen red with protruding veins.

She gasps when he slides another finger into her. He asks her if she likes it. She nods. He starts fingering her a little harder.

"If we were in bed together, I'd touch you and kiss you everywhere." He jerks in her palm as his lips find hers again. "A-And I'd eat your hot, sweet pussy and make you come."

"You'd do that to me?"

"You're my girl. I'd do anything for you." He grimaces and breathes heavier. "Oh, oh god, Kim. I-I want to make love to you."

"Oh, Walter. I want you to make love to me."

When she realizes what she had just said, she's a statue. Her last words echo in her head. Tremble in her heart. She stares at the boy in front of her like she's never seen him before.

Joey grabs her arm. "Let's get the fuck out of here!"

"I need to go!" She pulls her hand out of Walter's pants, pulls his hand from her. Pushes him away.

"D-Did I do something wrong?"

"No!"

Kim and Joey leave him alone in the dark with his pants undone. Diana, who's greeting guests at the door, blanches at the sight of her. Points at her own hair and lips, then towards the bathrooms. Kim nods. They dash into the ladies' room. While Joey laughs his ass off, the mirror confirms her smeared lipstick and disheveled hair. Her eyes moist, on the brink of overflowing. She wipes at them with the back of her hand, reapplies her make-up, pulls her hair back into place. Uses the bathroom while Joey admires his pristine beauty under fluorescent lights.

"Why did you run off like that?" Walter asks when they come out. There's an uncomfortable look on his face. He's got his jacket draped over his right forearm, covering his crotch.

"I can't be late to my own recital."

Her right palm is warm. She's open and wet, the ghost of his fingers inside her. She still hears the words they exchanged before she pushed him away. Especially *love*.

"Tard asks too many stupid questions," Joey says.

With that, they walk towards the auditorium. At the entrance, Diana gives her the once-over. "You must be more discreet, dear one."

Kim's so distracted that Melinda has to nudge her when it's her turn. Under bright lights, she plays Manuel de Falla's *Ritual Fire Dance*. Joey leans against the side of the grand piano, licks a rainbow lollipop as her fingers stretch out into chords. She doesn't care if they're the right ones. She spews out sixteenth notes and doesn't care if they bleed together. She throws her body into it and doesn't care how ridiculous she looks. When she's finished, she rests her hands on her lap. This has to be her most haphazard performance ever.

When she takes a bow, Joey takes one with her. The applause reminds her that it's safer back at the piano.

20

"You're not mad at me?" Kim asks after Walter gives her a brief hug.

"How can I stay mad, Doll?" He hands her a bouquet of irises. "These are for you."

Nearby, her parents are talking to Melinda's parents, a conservatively-dressed African American couple, so Kim kisses him on the cheek. "Thanks." Her eyes water as she takes them. No one's ever given her flowers before.

Joey steps on her toe. "Bullshit. I always give you flowers."

"Aren't you going to introduce me to your boyfriend?" Melinda asks.

Walter smiles at the word. Kim stands closer to him. "Walter, this is my friend, Melinda. Melinda, this is my boyfriend, Walter."

They shake hands. "You make such a cute couple!" Melinda says.

"Thank you!" Walter puts an arm around Kim. "I-I think so, too." Her parents walk towards the lobby. The kiss Walter gives her is longer than the one she gave him.

"Come on, let's get some cookies before my dad eats them all!" Kim says.

Melinda laughs. "He better be considerate and save

some for the others!"

"Kim!" Diana exclaims as soon as they're in the lobby. "This was your best recital ever!" She winks, then lowers her voice. "It definitely made up for your diva-like behavior."

"Really?"

"Yes!" Diana looks over at Walter. "It's so good to finally meet you, Walter! Could I get a picture of you and Kim?" She's got a Canon Point & Shoot, its lens the diameter of a golf ball. Kim stiffens, looks down at her feet.

"Just pretend it's a toy," Joey says.

She looks warily at its lens looking at them. Closes her eyes when the shutter goes off.

"Kimmy-ah! I want picture, too!" Kim's mom takes out her own camera, the edge of the lens level with its body. No zoom. She points it at them. Kim's features tighten. She has to look at the camera. She has to smile, whether she likes it or not. The corners of her mouth sting. Walter still has his arm around her. "You and your little friend so cute! I take film to Costco tomorrow and give you copy!"

Once her mom goes to talk with Diana, Kim sighs. Wipes the sweat from her forehead. Joey curtsies before disappearing into the crowd. Walter still has his arm around her. They're silent as they look at the night through the glass entrance. She's back in their dark corner before the recital. Repeating their words. Deciphering their meaning. Their eyes meet. There is one answer as he leans closer.

"Kim. Walter." Her dad says at their backs. They break

apart and greet him. He holds a paper plate, looks his usual stoic self. "Would you like to share these with me?" He pats his hard, flat stomach. "I have the body of a teenager and must maintain it."

Her smile is uncomfortable. "Okay, Daddy."

"Once school starts again, Mommy will let you have the keys to her car. You will also get a gas card, so you won't need to worry about having enough cash. You and Walter will drive to the library every day after school, so you can do your homework and help him with his reading."

"Really?" She and Walter say simultaneously, then look at each other.

"Yes. This year, you have gone beyond your expectations. It is responsible of you to help someone with a learning disability." Kim's dad nods at Walter, pats him on the shoulder. "I am so glad you are my daughter's gay best friend."

"Um, so am I, Mr. Ho."

💣

"Hey, Dad," Walter says after he opens the front door, "we're back."

Neil looks up from reading *The New Yorker* on his leather armchair. "Sorry I couldn't make it to your recital, Kim. I just got back from a convention I was at all weekend."

"That's okay. What do you do at those things, anyway?"

"Pretend I'm Keith Richards." He gets up, in slacks and a sport coat. Loose tie and wrinkled shirt underneath. "May I take a picture of you two?"

Walter glances at Kim. "Sure, Dad."

The only light in the living room is the one over the armchair. Shadows hide the wooden shelves of records and art books, the framed desert photographs on the wall. Neil comes back into the living room. More lights flicker on. His camera hangs from a strap around his neck. Its cyclops eye appraises them while he adjusts the aperture and shutter speed.

"Lemme get some pictures of you."

"I wanna go home!"

"Just a few pictures. I'll take you home after that."

Kevin is why Kim didn't get her senior portrait taken.

She feels a hand on her shoulder. "Are you okay?"

"You're okay," Joey says as he stands in front of her, "it's just a fucking toy."

She blinks, slaps her right cheek. Looks at Walter. "Yeah."

Neil steps closer to them. "Are you okay, Honey?"

"Yeah, I'm okay, thank you."

The pictures will capture her uneasy return to a memory that won't fade.

Joey plops down onto the tan leather couch. Shakes his head. Walter leads her into his room, shuts the door, turns on the lights. Neither of them go any further than a few feet behind the door.

"C-Could you please tell me what's going on, Kim?"

"Nothing's going on!"

"Y-You've been acting weird all night!"

"No, I haven't!"

"C-Could you please just tell me?"

She shakes her head. "I told you, I'm okay. Why do you keep asking?"

He looks at the carpet, then back at her. "Because I-I love you."

Her chest tightens, shoulders shake. Tears roll onto her cheeks.

"Kim." Walter hugs her. "I'm sorry. I-I didn't mean to make you cry."

"I'm not crying."

He holds her tighter to him. Kisses her. "I'm sorry. I-I..."

"I should go."

Joey's already waiting at the front door. Fidgeting. Tugging at the white lacy hem of his dress. Neil puts a hand on Kim's shoulder. "Is everything okay?"

She nods. "Yeah, thank you."

She knows he doesn't believe her.

In her bedroom, her shadow clings to the wall, darkens the edge of her bed. Joey's is nowhere, his reflection absent from her dresser mirror as he sits on the other side of her bed.

"Joey, why does Kevin keep coming back?"

He twirls his hair. "I can't wait for the after-Christmas sales. More new dresses for me!"

"Goddamit! Why does he keep coming back?"

"You should take a hot bath and go to bed."

She hurls a barrette at him. "Why aren't you answering me?"

He waves a dismissing hand. "I'm definitely putting sedatives in your tea tonight."

"Get the fuck out of here, Joey. I don't want to see you right now."

"You'll regret it."

"I don't give a shit."

He blends into the tense air of her room. She reaches out to where he was sitting, but doesn't feel a thing. She looks around her room. Yellow bookshelves. The papers and books on her desk. Her dresser. Bottles of perfume oil from Uncle Rod.

She should've spent Valentine's Day with Uncle Rod.

21

Kim rubs her tits into Rodney's chest. Inhales dryer sheets and patchouli. His gray sweater prickles her forearms and face in a comfortable embrace, an old black leather jacket a girl keeps going back to.

"You brought a porno with you, right?"

He chuckles, warm breath on her right ear. "A lesbian one, just like you wanted. And Christmas presents, too."

"But I haven't gotten you anything yet!"

"Don't worry about it. Wanna have lunch and go to Tower?"

"Nah, I'd rather stay here."

They sit next to each other on the family room couch, in front of the thirty-inch TV set and black entertainment center. What would porn look like on such a large screen, anyway? She rubs her calf against Rodney's as he unzips his backpack, produces a red gift bag. "Merry Christmas, my favorite niece."

She lifts up the iridescent tissue paper. Underneath a plain brown wrapper, its contents are legal-sized. Some sort of periodicals. She tears it open. "Oh my god!"

They're magazines Kim can't buy yet. *Women Who Administer Punishment. Bitches With Whips. Taste Of Latex.*

"Look deeper. There's one more thing."

She reaches around until she feels something square and hard. A CD jewel box. She pulls it out, stares at the cover. "No way!"

"Yes, way."

It's the Sonic Youth CD she's had trouble finding. The SST reissue of their eponymous EP from 1982.

Kim drops the CD into her lap, hugs Rodney. "You're the best uncle ever!"

"I'm glad I can make you happy, especially since your parents are forcing you to go to UCI."

"At least I won't have to live at home anymore." She runs her fingers through her freshly-dyed burgundy hair. "Like my hair?"

"Yes. You are so my girlfriend once you turn eighteen."

Kim nods at Rodney's backpack. "Wanna watch some porn, then?"

"Can't say no to that." He winks. Produces an oversized video box. An oversized box with a glossy finish that won't let you forget it's a porno. And if you lose it, it'll be relatively easy to find. As long as you don't have a hundred others.

Two buxom blondes with empty eyes absently bump pink tongues on the box cover. *Lesbian Seduction*. She looks deeper into the girls' eyes, but can't find anything in those shallow rivers.

After the red FBI warning screen, then a message about how the company's records are available for inspection, the screen turns black. *Lesbian Seduction* flashes in white capital letters. Eighties synthesizer music. A kittenish collision of feminine wails and moans. Bare flesh on pink satin. Harsh studio lights magnify every freckle and blemish on the actresses' skin. Those women look as they would look if they were in front of her.

A blonde and a brunette in various shreds of black lace and stocking and heels. Their slender bodies writhe against each other as the camera shoots from a bird's eye view. Tongues start flicking at each other rhythmically. Butts shake as red Lee press-on nails run up and down smooth backs and flat stomachs. Bras unhook. Panties slide down tan legs.

"Your pussy's so beautiful!" The brunette croons after the blond lies down and spreads her legs, revealing shaved lips and a swollen clit.

"It's totally beautiful." Rodney's grin is carved from ear to ear. "Would you ever go down on another girl, Kim?"

She doesn't rule out kissing or feeling up another girl, but she's not so sure about going down on one. The idea's never turned her on. Maybe, just maybe, it would if it were the right girl. But as she looks at Rodney, she sees that's not the right answer.

"Of course."

The brunette's tongue makes delicate circles on the blonde's clit. A close-up of the shaking flesh of her thighs. Faint jagged pink marks at their highest, softest point. Rodney shifts in his seat. His breathing gets heavier. Even though the heater's not on, Kim's clothes stick to her.

"You wanna have some real fun?" She whispers into his ear.

"What about Walter?"

"I won't tell if you don't."

In his hands, Rodney cups her chin. She blinks. Their eyes shift down to each others' lips. Mouths meet. She turns cold, arms at her sides. The arms of a dead girl, stiff and heavy. She needs to float away from the heaviness of her body.

"Kim?"

All feeling in her body, gone.

"Kim?"

The lead keeps her in place.

Hands on her shoulders, shaking her. "Are you okay?"

Her eyes focus. Rodney's sitting next to her. "I think I should go now."

She wants to get up. The backs of her thighs are glued to the couch. His footsteps rush to the front door. It opens and shuts. She lies on the couch in a daze, extremities tingling. The engine starts up. Rodney's truck squeals into the pavement as he drives away. She understands he's not going to call again. No more care packages from him.

The faintest trace of him on her skin. She tastes his saliva. Feels his hands. A short silver hair on the beige leather couch. On top of her dresser, in a porcelain vase, the irises Walter gave her last night. Her heart and stomach sink through the cushions. Fall to the carpet. She begins to sob in breathless convulsions, hugging herself tightly. Wishes Walter were hugging her. Kissing her. Telling her she'll be okay.

The realization of what she just did to him is a blow to her chest.

Her nostrils clogged, blocking all traces of Rodney as she breathes through her mouth, she wishes she could lie there forever, but the phone starts to ring. She lets the answering machine get it.

"Kim?" Walter's concerned voice sounds like it's right next to her. "Are you there? I just...I-I love you, Kim. I really do." There's a pause. "I wish I could see you right now. But could you please come over after our parents leave for work tomorrow? I'll make you breakfast a-and we can hang out before the show. You probably don't want to walk or take the bus in your concert clothes, so I-I can call you a cab and pay for it when you're here. Okay? I love you."

She keeps playing back the message. Every time she hears him say "I love you," she cries a little harder. Trembles a little more. The words hurt, yet feel so good. She wants to make sure he's really saying it, wants to feel how much he means it. It kills her to do it, but in the end, she has to erase Walter's message.

She trudges to the living room. The beige carpet jerks back and forth. Joey's on the couch, with his arms and legs scrunched together. In a white dress with puffy sleeves and strips of pink ruffles on the bodice. Unsoiled. Crisp cotton like fresh snow. White knee socks and black Mary Janes. Kim steps towards him uneasily. His head tilts up. He looks at her with red eyes.

She sits next to him. "Where were you?"

He grabs her arm. "Don't go to Tard's place tomorrow!"

"But Joey, I want to!" Kim thinks for a moment. Yes. She truly wants to. She can feel it.

"No!" He shakes her head. "You can't!"

"Why not? He's my boyfriend!"

"That's what you keep telling yourself." Joey tugs harder at her. "Please? You don't want to be trapped there all day! Stay here and we'll have the best tea party ever!"

She wrenches away. "Stop telling me what to do!"

22

The next morning, Kim bursts into tears as soon as she's in the Riordans' living room. "I'm sorry, Walter. I'm so sorry."

Joey flicks his index finger onto the back of her head. "So it takes only a twelve-dollar cab ride for you to spread your legs? You make me sick."

Walter hugs her tighter. "Here, let's sit down."

"I'm just not...it was stupid of me and-"

Joey stomps his foot. "You're only with him because you can't get anyone else."

Walter kisses Kim's forehead. "It's okay. You can cry in front of me."

She shakes her head. "But I don't deserve..."

"Yes, you do, Doll." He leads her into the kitchen. Pulls out a chair. Joey sits Indian style on the far end of the table, smoothes his frilly pink skirt over his thighs. He eyes Walter, his glossy pink lips curled in disdain.

"I still can't believe my parents think we're gonna go to the library every day after school! How can they not suspect anything at all?"

Walter hands her a Kleenex. "I know why, a-and don't want to say it."

Joey laughs. "The retarded kid won't go for you

because he's gay, and you're so fat and ugly that no one wants you, anyway."

Walter goes to the kitchen counter. "Your dad's cool, but your mom makes me cringe." Mugs are placed onto the counter. Coffee poured into them. A spoon swirls around. "Are pancakes, sausage, and scrambled eggs okay?"

Kim cries even harder when she sees he knows she takes coffee with milk and sugar. "Are you sure you wanna make me breakfast?"

"It beats cooking for my right hand."

The fact that her boyfriend cooks a breakfast her parents would never let her have makes it taste even better. After they're done eating, she kisses him. Joey makes retching noises as Walter pours them more coffee.

"May I ask you something?"

He sits back down. "Sure."

"Please tell me you're not asking Tard to have sex with you." Joey doesn't look at her as he plays with a mint-green My Little Pony Unicorn with pink hair.

She stares at the sleek metal refrigerator. "How far have you gone, Walter?"

"A-All the way." His coffee mug hits the polished tabletop. Some of it splashes out. "I-I've never told anyone this before. It's gonna sound sick."

"Ooh, I gotta hear this!" Joey brushes his My Little Pony's mane with a small pink plastic brush.

She looks at Walter. "Try me."

"Okay." He lowers his head. "I lost my virginity to m-my cousin."

Joey wrinkles his nose. "Eww!"

"How old were you?" Kim asks.

"W-We started fooling around when I was nine, b-but that happen when I-I was eleven." Walter doesn't look at her. He's slumped over, his arms pressed into his sides. "Like, w-we've given each other hand jobs. A-And she's blown me. This one time, sh-she slipped it in, but I pushed her off. I didn't wanna be an eleven-year-old dad to a two-headed fr-fr-freak baby." Kim studies his face. She swears a younger Walter sits next to her, his eyes empty.

Joey shakes his head. "We should really leave. Now."

"Do you still talk to her?" She asks.

"I have to 'cause she's family. I-I've told her about you. The first time, she yelled at me and hung up. Now sh-she gets bitchy every time I mention you. I thought she'd be happy for me."

"Okay." Kim closes her eyes, rubs at her forehead. "Thanks for telling me."

"I hope y-you don't think it's too gross o-or wanna dump me."

"Dump him! Dump him!" Joey cheers.

She puts her hand on Walter's. "No." She takes a deep breath. "But you should know that I'm not a virgin, either."

He begins to show signs of life again. "I figured, when you pulled up your dress and y-you were wearing those stockings a-and see-through panties."

"Are you telling me I'm slutty?"

Joey laughs. "Yes!"

"No. I-I mean you were so comfortable with your body and knew what you wanted." Walter looks at her. "S-So how many, then?"

"Two."

"D-Did you love them?"

"No."

"Did they at least get you off?"

She shakes her head, takes another sip of coffee.
"One of them gave me Chlamydia and a bacterial infection earlier this year."

"What a fucking asshole! A-Are you okay?"
"I was prescribed antibiotics and I've been okay since June."

"A-As long as you're okay now. I'm glad you told me."

"Do you have any rubbers?"

"Dad bought me a big box from Costco. But are you, um, on the Pill?"

"No. We're gonna to have to use a condom every time."

"Do you think w-we could do it without one day?"

"I'll think about."

"Like, will you, please?"

She swats his forearm. "Jesus, Walter. Even though I've had an STD?"

"It's not like you have AIDS."

"Gee, that makes me feel better."

Joey takes another My Little Pony from his purse. A lilac Pegasus with blue hair. The Unicorn's horn disappears between the Pegasus's hind legs as its head moves rhythmically against its ass. "Oh, Tard! Fuck me! Oh, yeah!"

"Stop it, Joey! It's not funny!"

The Pegasus stops getting it from the Unicorn. They fall sideways onto the tabletop. "You're no fun today."

Walter puts his hand on Kim's thigh. "I-I kind of wanna smoke after telling you all that."

A cigarette sounds like a great idea. "Have you ever smoked before?"

"I tried one of my uncle's when I was ten, and felt like I was gonna cough up a lung. You?"

"No, but the liquor store across from school won't card you if you look eighteen." Kim smiles at him. "Should we see if it's true?"

Joey glares. "If you smoke, my dresses will turn yellow and stinky!"

Walter nods. "Let's go."

The rumor turns out to be true. They leave with two packs of Lucky Strike Lights, two plastic lighters. Kim's glad Joey stayed behind, and wonders how to get rid of him for good. She hears him huffing inside her head when she thinks that.

She and Walter stand on the driveway. Bare branches. A gray, cloudless sky. Dormant Christmas lights. Holiday decorations garish in the daylight. They stick cigarettes between their lips. Light up. Cough after the first inhale. Look at each other and laugh. It gets easier. Holding it in isn't so uncomfortable anymore. The best part is blowing out smoke. Every time Kim does it, bullshit disappears into the air. It soothes her. She feels lighter.

Walter's smiling, sixteen again, his eyes no longer lifeless. He speaks normally and stands close to her. Glances are exchanged at regular intervals. Particles and waves whirl and hiss. When Walter looks at Kim, her hips tingle.

"Um..." He blushes and looks away. Looks at her again. "D-Do you wanna go..." He nods in the direction of the house.

She touches her palm to the back of his hand. "Yes."

23

"No!" Joey walks backwards in front of Kim. "If you go in there, you can't change your mind! It'll be all your fault!"

She sighs. "You're not coming along."

"Whatever. I'm not welcome in other people's bedrooms, anyway"

Walter shuts his bedroom door behind them. A faint streak of sunlight escapes through the drawn white shades as they sit on his unmade bed. Faded forest green sheets. Two pillows side by side. The framed picture of Harry on the nightstand, along with his battered red collar and doggie toys. Maroon and gold canister of his ashes. Small shelf of battered *Dirty Harry* paperbacks. CDs stacked in no particular order. Kim's own music collection is first filed alphabetically by band, then titles, in chronological order.

Once their boots are off, he's in white tube socks. Her feet are encased in black fishnets. They look at each other. There's only one way to make up for yesterday's indiscretion.

She lies back, pulls him on top of her. Reaches up the Germs shirt he silkscreened in Graphic Arts. Her fingers on the map of his vertebrae, on his warm skin. His kisses soft and searching. They lie there for an indeterminate amount of time. She has to force herself not to cry from the innocence she feels.

They strip down to their underwear. He's pale and hairless. Concave belly, protruding ribs and clavicle.

Spindly arms. He's the first one who's seen her in a black mesh bra, matching panties, and fishnet thigh-highs. Not her cute widdle girl undies. From the way his eyes widen, she knows he's enthralled.

"Y-You're perfect."

"No, I am!" Joey yells from the other side of the door.

Kim's eyes water. "No one's ever told me that before."

Walter kisses her. "Fuck them. You are."

His mouth on her right nipple. She stares at the ceiling. Her fingers reach for his hair. Soft and fine. He moves lower. Kissing his way down. Her fingers dig into the mattress. He kisses through her panties. She freezes. Feels his fingers hook into the waistband. Forces herself to raise her hips. There's nothing left to hide behind. He kisses her inner thighs. Her outer lips. Inhaling her. She thinks she hears him moan with pleasure. Did he? She shakes her head. The white ceiling washes her question away. He spreads her open. Her knuckles white.

"Oh, Kimmy, lay down and let me lick your little pink muff."

Walter touches his tongue to her.

A few minutes later, Kevin takes his mouth away. He straddles her shoulders, beats himself against her chin. Crushing her. "Suck it."

There's gentle tapping on her right hip. "Kim? Kim? Are you okay?"

White floats above. "Huh?" She lifts her head. Sees

herself stark naked, her legs spread, Walter's face between them. She plops back down. "Shit!"

He moves back up, lies besides her. She glistens on his chin. "W-Was I doing something wrong?"

She shakes her head, ruffles his hair. "No. Do you want a blow job?"

"Maybe later. L-Let's just lie together for a while." He moves closer. Drapes his limbs across her. "Come here."

Even though the door separates her from Joey, she hears him giggling, like he's right beside her. Kim grits her teeth. Wishes Walter could hit her in the head so she won't hear Joey anymore. But his voice gets louder and he starts taunting her.

Fat. Ugly. He doesn't even want you. See? You made him soft. Your pussy stinks like rotten tuna. Tastes like crap. He's only with you so he can make up for losing his virginity to his cousin. He's gonna dump you for someone skinnier and prettier after Christmas break. Just watch, you twelve-dollar whore.

"Kim? C-Could you put your arms around me?"

Shut up, Joey. Shut the fuck up. "Yeah."

He's still running his mouth as she wraps her arms around Walter. They're face to face. Skin on skin. His heart beating into her. She listens to him breathe. Fights to stay there with him in the moment. Tries to block out Joey as much as she can. *Shut up. I don't need you anymore.*

Even though Walter's narrower than Kim, she begins to feel safe in his embrace. His warmth burns away some of the bad things. This feeling is all she ever wanted. Needed. She tried so hard to find it on party lines, in mosh pits, always failing miserably. It's more profound than fucking. Stronger than the most mind-blowing orgasm.

"Oh, my god." Kim feels like she's having a seizure. The tears pour out. "Oh, my god."

Walter kisses her wet eyes. "Wh-What's wrong, Doll?"

"I just, I don't know…I've never been with someone I loved before."

"Y-You love me?"

Joey pounds on the door. "You love me!"

Kim wipes her eyes. Looks at Walter and nods. "Yes. I love you."

An anguished howl. More pounding.

Walter sighs, a deflating balloon. Holds her tighter to him. "Oh, god. I-I was so scared y-you didn't, especially after I told you about Lisa. I mean, m-my cousin. And wh-when I went down on you, it was like y-you didn't care."

"I did!" She shakes her head. "It's just that, I don't know, no one's ever done it to me for that long! I was expecting you to shove your dick down my throat a few seconds later!"

"Lalalala!" Joey sings. "I'm the most perfect little girl! The most perfect little girl in the whole wide world!"

Walter's wet eyes widen. "Wh-What the hell? I'm not

an asshole!"

"I know you're not! But," she exhales though clenched teeth, "you think I'm sexy and all that, but I've never had an orgasm with a guy before!"

"Well, I-I wanna give you bunch of them, b-but you're gonna have to tell me what you like and wh-what feels good! H-How am I supposed to know? How am I supposed to feel wh-when you just lie there like that?"

"Well, no one's ever fucking asked me what I like or what feels good! I don't even know!" They're both still in tears. Holding onto each other.

The doorknob rattles. "A tea party! Running through the field! Playing with My Little Ponies!"

"I don't know, d-do you know what you don't like, then? That would really help," Walter says.

Kim glares. "What? So you can do it, anyway?"

He lets go. His fingers on her cheek. "J-Jesus fucking Christ, Kim. D-Did someone hurt you?"

Something hard drives itself into the door. Joey's shiny black Mary Jane. Repeatedly and methodically, like chopping down a tree. "It's 1992! I'm a virgin! I've never been kissed!"

Kim tries to breathe long, relaxing breaths. All she gets are short, shallow ones that fray her nerves even more. Her shoulders shake. Kevin pushes in further. "Ow! You're hurting me!"

"No! Just leave with me and you'll be okay!"

It burns so much. She can't even pretend she's having fun.

The hinges are about to break off. "Kim! Put your fucking clothes back on and get out of there! Come on!"

He straddles her chest. Crushing her. The fur on his ass and thighs prickles her skin.

"No! You're crazy, Kim! It never happened!"

It did, too.

"Kim!" Walter shakes her gently. "D-Did someone hurt you?"

She can't move, and so she dies. So she wouldn't have to feel it.

She nods slowly. "Yes."

Tears run down his face. "Shit! D-D-Did someone r-rape you? I-Is that what happened?"

Joey screams. "Nonono! He's putting words into your mouth!"

She cringes at the word. It's so fucking ugly. The true four-letter word. A blunt blow to her spine. Rape. Her throat closes. Joey's voice rings in her ear. She hears how futile he sounds. It's pointless to deny it ever happened. Rape. Kevin never held her down or hit her or even put a gun to her head, but she had been so scared. She didn't want it. She said no and she's never been the same. She said stop. He didn't listen.

"Yeah." Kim gulps. Wipes her eyes before looking at Walter. "Someone raped me."

24

Joey howls, a sound from deep within his lungs ripping through his delicate throat. Then *BAM!* A gunshot? An explosion? Her ears ring. She snuggles closer to Walter. Whatever happened, she feels better. No knots, limbs soft. The silence comforting. She'd be breathing fine if she weren't so clogged with snot.

Joey's gone. He's not coming back.

"I-I'm sorry, Doll." Walter says.

"Thanks." She laughs bitterly. "You shouldn't be apologizing, though."

Rage slashes through his wet, red eyes. "True. W-We should make him."

Why's she laughing even harder? "I wanna shove a huge dildo up his ass and fuck him until he does."

"Oh, ow!" He wrinkles his nose. "O-Or, maybe a loaded gun up his ass and threaten to pull the trigger if he doesn't? Then pull it, anyway?"

"How the fuck are we gonna get a gun?"

"Too bad Dad doesn't own one." He kisses her, strokes the small of her back. "Shit. Both of us are totally sick."

"It's why we're together."

"W-We're like Bonnie and Clyde, all the way."

They get out of bed, walk to Walter's desk. Papers, writing instruments, and books scattered everywhere, but he always finds what he's looking for. Her parents would kill her if her desk were in such disarray. They blow their noses. Laugh when they miss the wastebasket, tissues sticky as they drop them in. He lights candles, burns sandalwood incense. Kim forgets she's even naked until she and Walter lie back down. By then, it doesn't matter.

"Since I don't have a gun, is there anything else w-we could do?" His pale face red. "I mean it."

"Yeah." She closes her eyes. "Love me."

She feels his mouth on hers. Soft sheets against her skin. She's not allowed to die. She has to stay in her body. When she catches herself drifting, she imagines Walter breathing life back into her. Candle light flickers on the walls. White wax drips while they kiss. He pulls her on top of him, hard through his underwear. Looking up at her. It's a little easier to stay alive in this position because she's never been in it before. He touches her gently, fingers sliding up and down her back. Stroking her ass. Time turns meaningless. She feels herself getting wet, rubs herself into him.

"You want to?" Kim whispers. She's covered in goose bumps, expecting Joey to yell something. But he can't anymore.

Walter's heavy eyelids tremble. "Y-Yes. Do you?"

"Yeah."

"You sure?"

"I'm sure." She moves down. The fuzzy trail of brown hair beneath his navel disappears into the elastic waistband of his tighty-whities. The bulge beneath them arouses curiosity and apprehension.

"You ready?"

"Yeah."

She slowly pulls them down. "Jesus Christ! How big are you, anyway?"

Walter laughs nervously. "E-E-Eight inches. Um, Kim, do you think that's why I'm slow? Like, does the blood rush there, a-and not to my brain?"

She laughs so hard she snorts. "I don't know!"

"God probably felt sorry for me."

"Um, yeah."

When he's all the way inside her, he's a good kind of pain. He holds her tightly. His lashes flutter. All he can manage to say is her name. She tentatively rocks forward, watching his face. From the way he looks and sounds, she guesses she's doing okay. She does it again. Her hair falls around them. He gets even harder, holds her tighter as he tells her he's coming. They lie together and it's the safest she's ever felt.

💣

Kim opens her eyes. Yawns. Her limbs stretch in opposite directions. The candles still burning. She turns onto her side. Face to face with a rumpled hair boy. His hand on the small of her back. Right when Walter's about to kiss her, the phone rings.

"It's probably Dad." He picks up the phone. "Hello? Oh. Hi." The beginning of a laugh crumbles into a cough. He rubs at his eyes and sits up. She stifles a giggle. "Oh, yeah...I'm doing good." He twirls a strand of her hair between his fingers. She sticks her tongue out at him. "She's already here." She turns onto her stomach, buries her face into the pillow. Smells detergent and her boyfriend. "Oh, Mom called?...how is she?... fine, we'll see you soon." He hangs up. "He's on his way."

She peers at him through her hair. "What time is it, anyway?"

"2:10, It takes him about half an hour."

She gets up, turns on the lights. Walter's eyes on her as she digs through their pile of clothes on the floor. She moves slowly but surely. Meets his gaze as she walks back to his bed. Sits next to him at the edge. Indifferent to her round belly and thick thighs as she puts her underwear and thigh-highs back on, then her black dress. He steps into his underwear and black jeans. In front of the full-length mirror, she smoothes out her hair, touches up her make-up. He stands behind, arms around her waist, his chin on her shoulder.

"You know that photo booth at Taang! Records?" Kim asks. "I want us to go in and take pictures together."

He raises an eyebrow. Turns his head to her in the mirror. "I thought you hate having your picture taken."

"I do, but it won't be so bad since I'll be with you." She

smiles. "What do you say?"

"Okay. Do you wanna go to that store with the taxidermy and dead animals in jars? And that weird place with all those dark-colored flowers and carnivorous plants?"

"Of course."

"A-And Retail Slut, so you can try on sexy outfits for me?"

She swears that this one time, two of their punk rock salesgirls gauged her and agreed she was too fat for their clothes. "I don't know, Walter. Maybe."

He pouts. "Please, Baby? Y-You'd look so fucking hot in that stuff."

"You think?"

"Hell yeah! You're a goddess!"

After they kiss and he puts his shirt back on, the garage door hums open. They grab their jackets. There's a cloud of pink smoke in the hallway. Baby powder on the carpet and walls. Rotten strawberries and dead roses. Strands of faded golden hair scattered everywhere.

Kim takes a deep breath. She's not sad. Not regretful. Joey's gone, and it's better this way. She casually appraises the carnage as she and Walter go into the living room. Not looking back. They sit on the couch. A key rams into a lock and it twists. The door opens and slams.

"Walt?" Neil calls. Walter squeezes her hand. He doesn't let go as his dad walks into the living room. The top button of his shirt and his tie already undone. Keys jangle from his fingers. "Mom called. Jeff and Matt got arrested for breaking and entering last weekend."

Walter's hand goes limp. "Wh-What's gonna happen to them?"

"It was their first offense so probably juvie for little while." Neil fixes his gaze on her. "Kim! How are you, Honey?" He sits next to her, puts a hand on her shoulder. She scoots even closer to Walter as Neil studies her face. Is she wearing too much black eyeliner and eye shadow? Is her lip-gloss too dark and shiny? Is her dress too low and transparent? Can he smell his son on her?

Kim smiles, then looks away. "I'm fine, thank you."

"Th-They can't be tried as adults, right?" Walter puts his hand on her knee. Her shoulders twitch.

"Any kid could be tried as an adult, if the crime was violent enough." Neil sighs in relief. "Thank god we're not living in Hayward anymore. Your grades have improved and your girlfriend's an honor student." He takes out his wallet, counts two twenties and a ten, hands them to Walter. "You guys go somewhere better than Rock and Roll Denny's for dinner. It's almost Christmas, you know?"

"Thanks, but a-are you sure? This is thirty more than usual."

"Yup. I'll drop you off in front of Mann's Chinese and meet you at the Palace later."

"Dad? Wh-What do you do in Hollywood wh-when we're not around?"

"I hang out. Why the interest all of a sudden?"

"Why are you being so secretive?"

"I'm not being secretive." Neil's expression is placid as he gets up, nodding towards the hallway. "We should get going now."

25

On the first day back from Christmas break, Walter's leaning against the wall with his hands in his pockets, shoulders slumped. As soon as he sees Kim, he stands up straighter. "Hey, Angel Tits."

She laughs, punches his arm. "Angel Tits?"

He hugs her. "That's right, Doll. You've got the tits of an angel. And only an angel would b-bust them out on a date." His erection presses into her belly, but there's dark circles under his sad eyes.

Blood rushes to her face. "Okay."

After Joey combusted, she knew her classmates would no longer be zombies. They're the same assholes they've always been. No more maggots. No more flies. But they're too busy doing their own thing to make fun of them.

Walter kisses her deeply. "I-I'm just so happy to see you."

She reaches up the back of his shirt. "Even though we saw a lot of each other these past two weeks?"

"Yeah."

"Are you okay, though?"

He pouts. "I want my Mommy." Even though he's being sarcastic, Kim detects the pained edge in his voice.

"What happened?"

"Mom called last night. I found out Dad in-intercepted a Christmas card. It got there Saturday afternoon, when your parents took you a-and your gay best friend to Huntington Library."

"What the fuck? Did you finally get to see it?"

He nods. "He gave it to me with the envelope already opened. At least he didn't keep the check. When I called her, I heard him pick up the other phone. He pretended he wasn't there when I called him on his shit. We yelled at each after I hung up and god," he sighs and hugs her tighter, "if it weren't for you, Doll, I-I'd probably go live with Mom."

The tardy bell rings. "Shit! We should get to class!" But it's so hard to let go of Walter, too.

💣

At lunch, they sit across from each other in the field behind the gym. Poke at their chicken fried steak and mashed potatoes, make sure the wind doesn't blow away their napkins and sporks. The sky gray, about to spill. Seagulls cry and fly in circles.

"How's your mom, anyway?" Kim asks.

He smiles, leans forward. "She's really happy at beauty school."

"That's cool. Is she doing hair? Or nails?"

"Hair. Sh-she really wants to meet you." He doesn't look the least bit fazed after saying that. "She says we can come stay with her."

"Really?"

"Yeah. Next time I go, I wanna take you. But Dad doesn't like the idea, because he thinks I'm gonna see Jeff and Matt." Walter takes a bite of chicken fried steak. "Just because they got busted doesn't mean they're bad guys, you know? Th-They're really fun to hang out with."

"That's cool." She sees two swaggering boys with slightly mocking expressions. Baggy clothes and chain wallets. They're the kind of boys who'd pick on her. She just knows.

"Mom doesn't like them, either. Sh-She says living here is for my own good, but it feels like sh-she doesn't want me around." He looks absently at the grass, yanks out a handful of blades. "I think it's because she wants to spend more time with her new twenty-eight year old b-b-boyfriend."

Kim shakes her head, stabs her spork into her mashed potatoes. "Walter, I bet your mom misses you, but maybe she's right about you living here."

"I mean, she sent a picture a-and he looks like one of those guys from those lame romance novels she always reads!"

"Yeah, but he is good to her? Does he make her happy?"

He shrugs. "I guess."

The bell rings. They trudge back to the main campus, holding hands but not talking, and barely make it on time to Graphic Arts. Still not talking much as they tape clear blue stencils over screens, position them onto black T-shirts. Run squeegees back and forth over blood red ink. Kim does it in smooth, firm motions. Walter does it harder and faster, his jaw clenched.

He remains in his own world as they hold their shirts under the drying lamp. Mr. Wu walks past them with a raised eyebrow, then looks back twice before he goes into the supply closet. Sure, they've got matching Cramps shirts now. But they're not gonna wear them at the same time. If they're even staying together.

"Walter? What's wrong?" Kim asks as she folds up her shirt and slips it into her backpack.

"Just some shit, Doll." He stuffs his own shirt into his backpack. A strained smile, faraway eyes. "Y-You know I love you, b-but I've been homesick a lot lately."

She nods. "It's the holidays."

"Yeah, it is," he tosses his backpack onto the concrete floor, "but Lisa's there, too, a-and I don't miss that bitch."

The venom in his voice is assuring. She doesn't want to show how relieved she is. "It's probably good that you're away from her."

He glances at her as they sit down at their work bench. "I-I don't wanna see her ugly fucking face." He kisses her. "I'd rather see your sexy one."

"Walter! Kim!" Mr. Wu barks, slapping the tabletop. "No kissing in class!"

After school, he waits for her in front of Physics. They kiss passionately in front of her repulsed classmates and instructor. Of course they're not going to the library. On the drive to Walter's house, The Gun Club purifies her mom's car stereo. Kim sings along to random verses, loud and off-key. Her fingertips throbbing around the steering wheel, wishing for guitar strings. But where the hell is her guitar?

"I couldn't sing after what happened," Kim says as they smoke on the driveway.

Walter shakes his head, narrows his eyes. "That piece of shit." His free hand forms a fist. "God, I-I just wanna bash his fucking head in."

She shivers beneath black leather. Even the bare tree branches are nervous. "With what?"

"A tire iron? A baseball bat? Anything that would crack his skull open."

She imagines a wet cracking sound. Broken skull. Seeping blood. Her heart races. Oh, god, she'd love to witness that. Or even do it herself. "Mmm." She takes a drag of her cigarette. Smiles after she blows out smoke. "You know what else sounds good? Punching him in the face until it's a bloody pulp."

"Like, breaking his bones with your bare hands?" He blows out smoke, then leans closer to her.

"Yeah. Just thinking of him lately has made me wanna hurt him." Her lips go straight to the filter, inhaling right when they connect. Kevin's been visiting her in her dreams again. They've been too vivid. Too close to reality. As soon as she realizes it's just a dream, she forces herself to wake up. Thinks of Walter until she falls back asleep.

"I know. I totally wanna to hurt him, too."

They throw their cigarette butts into the road. Go inside and wash their hands, brush their teeth. In Walter's room, they kiss and help each other out of their clothes.

"Y-You mind if we just lie together today?" He asks.

"No. That would be nice."

"It's not that I don't like fucking you, Doll. I don't know, I just want to do this instead."

She curls up on her side of his bed. "It's okay. We don't always have to." Swears she hears Harry panting and barking when she sees his picture on the nightstand.

Their chests touch. She sighs happily when she feels his arms around her. She inhales the scent of his skin, touches her mouth to his shoulder. "S-So do I. But I-I've been reading up on stuff, too."

"Like what?"

Walter laughs. "What else?"

She spanks him. "What did you find out this time?"

"I read that w-we should try just being with each other and not really think about coming, you know?"

It's so nice not to have Joey yelling shit or banging on

the door. "Well, you're the first person I've ever loved having inside me, so that's a start."

"Th-That's good. D-Do you feel pressured to come when I go down on you?"

"Kind of. But I know you're not gonna sit on my chest and shove your dick down my throat."

"I guess w-we should work on enjoying it instead. But c-can you keep telling me what you like and what feels good?"

Her eyes water. "Of course."

An hour later, they do their homework in bed. Kim wishes they could just lie there like that all afternoon, but her freedom counts on her GPA. They remain in bed as Walter reads from *Dirty Harry: The Killing Connection.* He can now read for longer periods. He doesn't need to sound out as many words. Sometimes he gets letters and words mixed up, but she touches his shoulder. Tells him it's okay to mess up. She doesn't want to be a tyrant like her mom. She doesn't want to end up like her or Evil Aunt Tai. Bitter. Miserable. She wishes she could just be with Walter. The happiest she's ever been. When they get dressed and kiss each other goodbye, her chest burns. She understands what they've got is important. Precious. And if her parents find out, she'll lose everything.

26

When the bedroom walls were pink and there was childish white furniture, Kim never touched herself. Joey would've gotten pissed at her for messing up his fancy white sheets. But now she can do that in her own bed. Back in her own room. White walls, wooden bedroom set she's had since she was seven. The door closed. She touches her tits, her belly, then between her legs. Imagines Walter teasing her with his fingertips.

"You're doing great, Kimmy," Kevin says after she plays a sloppy rendition of "Smells Like Teen Spirit" over the phone. "Pretty soon you'll be able to play all their songs."

Kim's hands go dead. "Oh, fuck."

"I thought about you and jerked off last night. We had just played The Palladium and we did it in our suite at the Sunset on Hyatt. It was so hot."

Her head rolls from side to side. "Oh, no. No you don't, you fucker."

"Did you put your fingers up your pussy and pretend my sausage was inside you?"

You piece of shit. Stop it.

It's been almost a year since she's masturbated. She feels like Kevin's holding his hand over her mouth and nose. Her heart palpitates. Her limbs immobile. Is she just going to stop breathing? Die in the damn twin bed with the same Strawberry Shortcake sheets and comforter she's had since she was seven? What if she dies in this incriminating position, leaving her mom to discover her corpse and yell at it for disgracing her family?

It goes away as fast as it comes. Her heartbeat slows. She stops shaking. Kim takes long, slow breaths. Moves her hand lower. She's still wet. The inside of her bird-flipping finger moves in small, gentle circles. The sensation familiar. Bittersweet. Her legs spread wider. Walter slips inside. No condom. Bare skin.

Every time Kevin comes back, she makes him go away. He can't win. It's her fucking body.

She swells beneath her fingertip. Rubs harder. Walter's fucking her in earnest. Her knees up, hands on his ass, she pushes him deeper, almost in tears when she's at that sorely missed threshold. She knows she's about to come and it feels so good, but she doesn't want to just yet. She wants to keep touching herself, keep fucking Walter. Her muscles clench. She clenches around him. Hips bucking. A wild buzz at her core spreads and every part of her contracts. She says his name. Imagines him making her come like this. Imagines him coming inside her.

She wipes her fingers on her sheets, laughing and crying. "And I'm gonna win every time, you fucking asshole."

💣

"You know what I did last night?" Kim whispers after she pulls Walter into the Graphic Arts supply closet. She switches on the light, pushes her back into the door. Cans of paint and solvent on the wooden shelves. Stacks of screens and squeegees. Reams of paper.

Walter lowers his head, raises his eyes. His hands on her shoulders. "What?"

Her lips on his earlobe as she giggles. "I got my self off and thought of you."

"Jesus fucking Christ! I almost creamed my pants!"

The closet is small. No cushioning anywhere. The air heavy with chemicals. She puts her left heel against the door, pulls up her dress. Touches herself through her underwear. "Too bad I can't really show you in here."

Walter watches her, dumbfounded. "Y-You're killing me!"

She squeezes his erection through his jeans. "I know."

"Wh-When we go to my place today, c-could you show me? And make yourself come?"

"I could." Kim pulls Walter to her by his belt loops. "We should do something about that hard-on of yours."

She's about to undo his belt when someone knocks at the door. "Open up!" It's Mr. Wu.

They look at each other. Stifle their laughter. Walter covers his eyes with his palm, shakes his head. Kim grabs a squeegee and opens the door. "Sorry, Mr. Wu. We were looking for extra squeegees."

"Yeah," Walter adds, "the ones out there just didn't cut it."

Mr. Wu tilts his head to the side. "Kim, if you didn't have a 4.0 and a high SAT score, both of you would be getting two Saturday detentions in a row." He steps out of the way, waves his arms towards the work area. "Out!"

💣

"There's something else I want to show you," Kim says as she picks up Walter on Lincoln's Birthday.

The mountains beyond the strip malls and one-story homes are capped with snow. They're on Arrow Highway, closing in on the wooden buildings and Western fonts of Downtown San Dimas. She's having trouble breathing again. But she wants to, needs to, do this. A wagon is permanently hitched on the blacktop between McDonald's and Kentucky Fried Chicken. The Motel 6 is on the other end of the block. For the first time, she doesn't look away. Walter puts his hand on her knee. Both of them silent. The stereo off.

The closer they get, the faster her heart beats. "I want to bring you to where it happened, okay?"

He nods. "I-If it doesn't freak you out."

They make a right. Bypass the Denny's parking lot. She keeps looking at the Motel 6 until she sees a space that faces room 216. Fuck driving straight into it. Kim makes sure the coast is clear, switches into second gear, jerks the wheel towards the opposite lane. Her mom's poor Camry skids in that direction and makes a complete turn. Tires squeal. They stop right at the edge of the parking space, rear bumper first.

Walter gasps. "Damn! That was scary! A-And kind of cool."

She's slightly dizzy from the sheer speed of her maneuver. They back into the parking space. Kill the engine. She unbuckles her seatbelt, rests her forearms on the dashboard. The knots come back.

Kim exhales through pursed lips. "Well, here we are. Room 216."

Walter blinks, then looks to the green door, left side of the building, the second floor. "Y-You're too beautiful for this place."

Her fingernails dig into her palms. "He was unemployed and lived with his mom. Probably too cheap to take me somewhere nice, anyway."

"Fucking asshole!" The side of Walter's fist hits the glove compartment door.

She jumps. "Shit!" She tilts her head back, takes a deep breath. "I thought it was my fault for not leaving while I still could. But I couldn't fucking move. All I had to do was push open the door and go. I still don't know why I couldn't. It's like my body screwed me over."

"I wish we knew each other back then." Walter covers his head with his hands. "I would've been there for you then a-and on the day Kurt died. You wouldn't have had to be so scared."

"Walter, it's too late for that shit."

He wipes at his eyes. "I know." He throws his hands up in the air, shakes his head. "I just, I just love you. I wish I could've done more."

"It's okay." She puts her hands on his cheeks. Kisses him. "Let's go have a smoke."

They lean against her mom's car, his arm around her, her head on his shoulder. Cars speed past them on Arrow Highway. The crisp air smells of dirt and gasoline. Room 216. The shades drawn. The lights off. She keeps standing against the wall, watching the dead girl on the bed. She can't look away. She keeps fighting it. Stares at her faint reflection in another car window. Scratching at the paws that grip the dead girl's thighs while Kevin pumps away at it. She takes a cigarette out of her square. It slips through her fingers, lands into a puddle.

Kim looks at Walter, then begins to cry. "Shit!"

"It's okay, Doll. Here." He sticks a cigarette of his own square into her mouth. Lights it before he lights his own. Holds hers with his left hand, his own with his right. Listening to her inhale, he takes it out after each one.

She smiles at him, wipes at her eyes. "There's no way I'd press charges. I might as well get gang raped by the entire courtroom, then murdered by my parents."

He blows out an angry stream of smoke. "We can take care of him ourselves."

"You really think so?"

"Just because I'm retarded doesn't mean I don't know how to plan." Walter stares at the building, leans closer to her. "H-He deserves to die in the shittiest motel room we can get."

Kim nods. "It should be somewhere out of the way." She takes one last drag of her cigarette, tilts her head back. A combustible fairy when she blows out smoke.

He tosses their spent butts onto the blacktop. "How do you feel?"

"Like hanging out for a while."

"Put on your sunglasses. I'll put mine on, too. We'll hang out at Denny's as long as you need."

Kim glances at room 216, then back at him. "Okay. After that, I wanna get the hell out of San Dimas. I don't know, like go to Long Beach or something. It's a nice day for that." And by nice, she means overcast and cloudy.

"Okay. I mean what I said, Doll. For now, I-I'll grow a moustache and beard. Then I'll send out for a fake ID. It'll be easier to check into a room that way. We should figure out what we're gonna use, then make sure we destroy the receipts a-and don't get our fingerprints on anything."

"It's a good start." She squeezes his hand, looks around. Everyone else hides in their cars. "But I'd rather just be with you right now."

💣

That evening, she stops in front of the guestroom. Touches her hand to the door. It's still there. It's always been there. She hasn't stepped inside for a year. What does it look like on the other side? What does it smell like? Then she remembers something.

She goes into her bedroom. Digs beneath the oversized tops in muted colors. There it is. That Valentine's Day package from Kevin.

Her parents are watching Chinese soap operas. She sneaks through the garage. Out the door that leads to the concrete walkway. The green stems of her dad's dormant roses dark metal in the night. She opens a trash can. It's filled to the brim with plastic bags. She takes out a few bags, tries not to gag as she sets them down by her feet.

Tiny creatures with wings hover and hum. She wrinkles her nose, takes a step back. The Patti Smith cassette is thrown into the trash. Then the Valentine. She rips up the yellow envelope with their names and addresses before throwing it away. Buries the evidence with trash bags. Her hands shaky, soiled. The garbage is scheduled to be picked up tomorrow. She opens the gate, wheels the two trash cans out onto the curb.

The next morning, she parks in the Riordans' driveway. Her red dress billows in the breeze. It reminds her of Long Beach yesterday afternoon. She and Walter had clam chowder in bread bowls. He read her Anais Nin while they were curled up together on the waterfront. But that was because she put her foot down. While they were at Denny's, she told him she was sick of talking about Kevin. They couldn't mention him for the rest of the day, along with the next. It's their time together, and he doesn't have the right to haunt it.

Walter opens his arms to her. Dark circles under his eyes. A regular occurrence now. "You okay?"

She falls into them. "As okay as I'll ever be. You?"

"Last night, Lisa called and gave me shit when I told

her we were ditching together." The tiniest bit of brown stubble on his cheeks and chin. "I wish that bitch would just fucking stop."

"Really?" Her back tightens. "Does she hate me that much?"

"I tell her sh-she'd like you if she gave you a chance, but she won't listen. She's just mad she doesn't have anyone to spend today with."

She kisses him. His face slightly scratchy. "But we have each other."

He smiles at her. Sadness at the sides of his mouth. "That's right, Doll. So fuck them."

They exchange gifts. Kim gives Walter a Zippo with a she-devil on it. A black leather belt with two rows of metal grommets. He fastens a black leather wristband with a dangling silver heart around her wrist. "Hold your hair up for me," he says. She gathers her hair into a messy bun. He gets behind her, clasps something around her neck. An asymmetrical necklace with multiple chains that drape over her collarbone. It's the very necklace she coveted beneath the counter at a shop in Hollywood.

She turns around, pulls him to her. She can barely stand up straight when they kiss. She stumbles backwards, braces herself against the wall. "This is the best Valentine's Day ever."

His lips touch the side of her neck, and she tilts her head back. Throws her right leg around his waist as his mouth finds hers again. Every part of her on fire. "I know. All I've ever wanted was to have a girlfriend on Valentine's Day."

They should be in school, but she's straddling him on his bed. Kissing and grinding. Her hair tumbling around them. She unbuttons his shirt. Kisses her way down his bare chest, inhaling the sweat of his milk-pale skin, touching her lips to his sharp hipbones. She unbuckles his belt, then his jeans.

Their eyes meet. He's watching her with parted lips. The only guy she's ever enjoyed blowing. The only one who deserves it. She takes her time, kissing and licking him before taking him in her mouth.

When he's about to come, she stops. He whimpers. Tells her she's awful. She laughs and starts again, doing it with a ferocious hunger that surprises her. He's moaning, "Oh, fuck. Oh, fuck." His fingers constrict hers when he comes the loudest she's ever heard him come. He trickles down her throat. Tells her it's her turn.

She undresses, then lies back down. Relaxes beneath his lips and tongue. He moves in small circles. The corners of her mouth stretch upwards. The undersides of her calves graze his biceps. She strokes his hair and his face while he asks her if she likes it. She loves it. She fucking loves it. He makes her feel so good. So alive.

He squeezes her breasts and he sucks her, moving his head from side to side. Her legs clamp around him. Clenching in small spasms as she hears herself squealing. His mouth relentless on her until she starts giggling from being too sensitive. She pulls him back up, kisses him hard and deep. Tasting herself on his breath, licking herself off his face. Her legs trembling, heart beating in her clit. Alive. Every bit of doubt and fear in her released.

Take that, Kevin.

Walter looks down at her, grinning. "Not bad for a retard, huh?"

She spanks him. "You're not retarded, Dummy." Then she looks up at him, touches his left cheek. Starts to cry. "Thank you. No one's ever made me feel this way before."

27

Kim's not looking forward to scoping out motel rooms. Why can't she and Walter spend their Spring Break like a normal high-school couple? When normal high-school couples aren't fucking, they'd watch movies, hang out at the mall, go to Disneyland. Their conversations would never entail plans of premeditated murder.

She sighs. Her overnight bag-of-tricks slung over her shoulder. Her purse dangles from her wrist. A seventy-percent chance of rain today. The sky already gray. Maybe she can use the weather as an excuse. She drops the note onto the kitchen table. A page torn from a yellow legal pad in her neatest handwriting.

> *Dear Mom and Dad,*
> *Mary Chong, a Chinese girl from Intro to Calculus, is having a slumber party tonight. She invited three other Chinese girls and me from our class. There will be parental supervision. Sorry this is such short notice. Mary invited me last week and I was so excited about getting into UCI that I forgot. If you need anything, Mary's number is (818)555-0303.*
> *Love,*
> *Kim*

As soon as Kim parks in the Riordan's driveway, Walter rushes to her. Looks like he's in his early-twenties with his beard and moustache. Hair now longer, softer. Hiding his pointy chin. He taps on her window, cigarette dangling from his lips. Two distressed taps to match the lines crinkling his forehead. He shakes a white sheet of paper in his hand. She raises her index finger. Kills the engine. He moves to the side so she can get out.

"What's that?"

He hands her the sheet of paper, slips his cigarette out of his mouth. Slumps into the side of the car. She sits beside him on the driveway. "I-I found this on the kitchen table before Dad left for San Diego. Now I know what he does after h-he drops us off in Hollywood, and when he claims he has to work late."

It's Neil's Visa bill. The words are a foreign language at first, even though it's all printed in English. She glances at Neil's name and address at the top. Looks away. She can imagine Neil standing in front of them. Clucking his tongue. *What do you think you're doing, kids?* When she refocuses, she sees how much Neil owes.

Walter tosses his cigarette butt into the street. "C-Could you look at the individual charges?" He asks in a shaky voice. "I'll show you which ones."

The billing cycle is from the middle of February to the middle of March. He points. The paper trembles every time his fingertip strikes it. The charges range from thirty to three hundred dollars. Two of them from Fantasy Escorts in Pomona. Another two from Motel 6 in Glendora from the same dates.

Kim takes out her Hello Kitty datebook. All made on weekdays. Probably the two times when Neil had to work late and her parents took them to Chevys for dinner. The charges on March 11th are from Hollywood Bad Girls and The Hollywood Downtowner Inn.

The Saturday night they saw Morphine at the Palace.

The day they bought tickets, she had written Morphine into that calendar square in large black letters. Then she had kissed Walter before drawing two small hearts beneath it.

He kicks at the grass. "I-I am so fucking pissed at him right now! Y-You don't even know!"

"No, Walter, I do know. Instead of scoping out motel rooms, maybe we should..."

"I know he's not in San Diego on business! He's only staying there so he can have more time to..." The veins in his forehead and his neck pulsate beneath his flushed skin. Dirty air accumulates in her lungs. Their eyes meet, but it's like he doesn't really see her at the moment. Above, dark clouds drift. Almost as dark as the sky.

She tugs at her hair. A white van slowly drives past them. Speeds away. Otherwise, the streets are empty. "God, I wish the stupid fucking judge gave Mom full custody, s-so I wouldn't have to live with Dad!"

His words leave a long, slow scratch across her heart. Her shoulders slump. A tear slides down her cheek. She hugs herself, wishing it were him instead. But now is not the best time to touch him.

"She agreed to let me move here because it was supposedly for the best! Th-They just didn't want me to see Jeff and Matt anymore!" Walter's arms fall to his sides and his head drops forward, eyes in another time and place. "Those guys never made fun of me for being in special-ed, a-and talked shit to the assholes who did! Maybe they got in trouble a lot, but they were my friends!" He lights another cigarette. Groans and tilts his head back after he blows out smoke. "Dad should just marry Evil Aunt Tai. Maybe they'll end up killing each other."

Kim's laughter is quiet, nervous. "Not if I tell her what we found in that photo album my parents hid in the back of the cabinet."

"I want to be there when you drop the bomb. Do you think there's any way y-your mom would let me come along?"

"Possibly." She sighs. "Lately, they've been bitching about us spending too much time together. I keep telling them we're just friends, but they're always telling me to make new ones at UCI." She lays a tentative hand on his shoulder. "Walter. Do you really wanna go live with your mom?"

His mouth quivers as he shakes his head. "I-I miss her and my friends, but you're here."

She sniffles, wipes at her face with the back of her hand. She's appalled at how much she's crying. "If your dad didn't have to move for his job, then we never would've met."

"I-I'm sorry, Doll. I didn't mean it like that. Sometimes I just get so pissed when I think about Dad making decisions for me and not caring if I'm happy."

Kim stares at the sunless morning sky. "I know we're supposed to go scope out motel rooms, but maybe we should cheer you up instead. Want to do something before it starts to rain? It's supposed to get really bad later."

Walter nods. "We'll just do it tomorrow." He takes the fake Florida ID out of his wallet. They saw the ad for it in the back of a magazine. All it took was twenty bucks and a small photo. "You think they'll let me check in with this?"

"Of course." She smiles. "It looks pretty real, you know?"

Harry Peralta, born August 6, 1973. Name of his first pet coupled with the name of the street he grew up on. Five nine, a hundred and thirty pounds. He's glaring at the camera, color picture taken at a photo booth. It resembles a mug shot, chestnut beard and moustache clashing with the dyed black hair on his head.

He puts his fake ID back. "I-I'm totally fine going by myself to check in."

"Okay. But I don't want to park my mom's car in front of wherever we go." The murder weapons will be waiting with her. Baseball bat for Walter. Knife for Kim. Both bought at the newly opened Walmart next to the freeway. The items paid for separately in different lanes. Receipts destroyed. Their fingerprints probably on them already.

"Maybe we can find a motel near a Wal-Mart or a grocery store."

Maybe the person behind the desk will see that ID and tell Walter it looks fake. They'll confiscate it and threaten to call the police. Or maybe, just maybe, Walter will run back to the car. Then they can call the whole thing off.

She musses his hair, wishes he'd get rid of his beard and moustache. "Yeah. Maybe."

They drive around, listening to Medicine's *Shot Forth Self Living.* Layers upon layers of glorious feedback. Swirling guitars underneath sleepy vocals. They end up at the park across the street from school. Dubbed Pervert Park by their classmates, because a certain U.S. History teacher supposedly cruises for gay sex there.

The air is cool and clean. No trace of people.   Even the stoners, who deserve recognition for showing up every day, are nowhere in sight. They hold hands, the soles of their Docs sinking into the damp grass. The sun's absence turns leaves black and shadows fall around them.

They push each other on the swings, chains wailing uncomfortably. They go down the slide. Kiss on the rickety wooden bridge before they jump up and down, rattling chains beneath. Everywhere is rust and chipped wood and litter. The bathroom, where all the gay sex supposedly takes place, is a small grey square building in the darkest area of the park.

Kim lies back onto the bumpy surface of the merry-go-round, as Walter spins her as hard as he can. Its old steel heart creaks, and she closes her eyes, laughs. Squeals when he jumps on. The merry-go-round spins slower, grows quieter, devolves to a halt.

He lies next to her, his hand on hers. Dark clouds above them move faster. Leaves rustle. The air thickens with impending rain. A lone crow sings its atonal song. She wishes they could stay there forever.

He cups her chin, kisses her. His hot mouth cinnamon sweet. The merry go round jerks slightly as she pulls him on top of her and he kisses her earlobe, moaning her name as he presses into her. Showing her how he wants her. She's spread out. Aching. Wishing she were on the Pill. Wishing he could take her right then and there.

He tells her he wants to make love to her without a condom. Feel her hot, wet pussy wrapped around his cock. It sounds so fucking right as they're kissing and moving together. They ignore the cold drops of water falling onto them.

She's drunk on the smell of his skin laced with the ozone, rusted metal, and moist dirt. Right before Walter is about to move lower, thunder pummels through the sky. It begins to pour.

He groans. "Damn rain. We should go."

Kim looks at him knowingly. "Let's go find a box of those sponges, so we won't have to spend our allowance money on an abortion."

This will definitely take his mind off killing Kevin.

They buy the last box of Today Sponges at Albertson's, along with groceries and a blue plastic ashtray. If Neil pays for sex, they can smoke in Walter's room. Back at his house, he watches her insert the sponge in the bathroom. It's surprisingly easy to get the thing in. It opens up, the indented side protecting her.

Walter grabs Kim's hand. He's dragging her, she's dragging him into his room. Kissing and groping and pulling off each others' clothes.

He lies her down on his bed. "Th-This is a big deal to me. It means w-we're gonna be together forever." A pang of sadness in his voice.

She looks into his eyes. He's behind bars. They're separated forever. "It means you're the one I love the most."

When Kim feels Kevin feels slip inside her without a condom, she screams. Pushes at his shoulders. "No! Put on a rubber!"

"But Kimmy, I can't make babies! When I was thirteen, I went to the doctor and they told me that I had only one

functioning testicle." His movements are slow yet forceful. She hates how exposed she feels. The feeling of skin on skin almost sickening. "Just a few strokes, okay, Kimmy? Then I'll put on a condom."

She's paralyzed.

"But I'm not on anything right now!"

"Come on, don't you trust me?"

Her arms fall to her sides. "Y-Yes." Her voice is small.

"Kim? Are you okay?" She hears Walter ask.

A few strokes turns into twenty minutes. She lies there and takes it. Afraid he'll get mad if she tells him to stop. He's not going to stop. She pretends she's on a tour bus, absently strumming her guitar. Stares out the window past miles of brown flatlands to their next show.

Kim sobs at discovering the distinction between wanting it and not being given a choice.

"Kim?" Walter hovers above her, his erection pressing into her thigh. "You okay?"

She sniffles, then reaches for him. "Yeah. It's kind of weird, especially after what happened." Ignoring the flash of anger in his eyes she kisses him. "But I've wanted this for a long time."

He nods. His features soften. "M-Me too."

Please, please make it right.

His warm back trembles beneath her palms as he slips

inside. Bare, hard heat fills her. The tip of him at her womb. She blinks away more tears. Tiny aftershocks erupt in her limbs. The two of them lie still and gaze at each other. She wants to stay like that as long as they can. In the safety between him and his mattress. Her fingers stroke his cheek. His heart beats into hers. She can taste every loaded emotion in his kiss.

Kim wraps her legs around Walter's waist. "Come inside me."

Raindrops fall with her tears for what she lost to Kevin, for him corrupting what should've been saved for her real boyfriend. She imagines water leaking through the roof and trickling down on them, flooding Walter's room as they move together in earnest. She grabs his ass, pushes him deeper. Her entire body trembles into his. Crackling thunder in her bones. His last violent thrust holds her in place, face buried in her shoulder as he comes. Cleansing her. Purifying her.

They curl up together, smoke in bed. Kim's limbs tingle as she feels Walter seep out of her. Her body so light it levitates. He's all that keeps her from flying away, from hitting the ceiling. After they put out their cigarettes, she buries herself in his warmth, closes her eyes. Wishes he'd never let her go. The raindrops coax her into a comforting void, and before she's completely gone, she hears herself humming.

💣

When they wake up, it's still raining. The shadows that covered his bedroom remain. They kiss lazily, his erection greeting her hipbone. It's the perfect time to pull something out of her overnight bag-of-tricks.

"I have a surprise for you," Kim smiles, stroking Walter, "so you have to face the wall, and you can't peek."

He grins. "What if I can't help it?"

"Then it won't be a surprise."

As Walter faces the wall and pulls the sheet over his head, Kim unzips her bag and slips out into the hallway. Leans against the wall as she puts on stockings, hooks on a garter belt and bra, steps into a thong and shiny black heels. One of the many things Walter circled in the Frederick of Hollywood catalog. A black lace ensemble labeled "one size fits all." Um, not quite all.

She sucks in. Her belly still hangs over her garter belt. The band of her bra digs into her ribcage. She's not used to having scratchy fabric in her butt crack, nor does she feel the least bit sexy. More like a truck stop hooker on a Monday afternoon. But it'll make her boyfriend happy, and anything that take his mind off killing Kevin helps.

"Now you can look," Kim says as she walks back into Walter's room.

He sits up, eyes widening. "Whoa! Y-You're so fucking sexy, Doll!" He scoots towards the edge of the bed, his erection saluting her.

"You can call me Kimmy Danger."

"Like the song?"

She looks away, tries not to shake her head as she

lights the candles on his dresser. "Yeah."

She wanted him to tell her that he liked being in danger.

Pushing away that thought, she puts on "Gimme Danger" by The Stooges. The music dark. Sleazy. Her hands all over her body. Hips circling. Tossing her hair. She struts towards him. Candlelight projects her shadow onto the wall. Gazes held as Walter's hand moves up and down. She crawls onto the bed, then leans backwards. He doesn't make it to the end of the song before he grabs her, kisses her. Pulls her panties to the side.

The rest of the afternoon, they fall into a cycle of fucking, resting, fucking. Then resting. And fucking again. Pissing is the only reason to get out of bed. She doesn't die beneath him. Or above him. Or beside him. Her pleasure is better than Kevin's death.

They finally put on clothes. Walter, black jeans. Kim naked beneath her dress. He chops tomatoes at the granite counter. She can't stop groping him, kissing his shoulders and back. They end up fucking on the kitchen table. Resume making dinner. He hasn't mentioned killing Kevin all afternoon. Doesn't mention it when they have tacos by candle light. Coke in Neil's champagne glasses. Kicking and stepping on each other's feet under the table. Listening to the rain.

"I wanna show you a picture Mom sent the other day," Walter says.

She follows him into his room. "Your dad didn't steal them?"

"Nope. Her plan to mail out stuff on Saturdays works,

because I can get the mail before he does."

They sit next to each other on the bed. Walter takes pictures out a lavender envelope, hands them to Kim. Formerly Debbie Riordan. Now Deborah Kelly. She looks younger than late-thirties. Slender, with long blonde hair. A wide smile. Standing on the pier beneath the sunny sky in jeans and a brown leather jacket. A seagull wandering behind her. Kim peers closer. Sees Walter's nose and bone structure.

"You look like her!" Kim's mom shoves a photograph of a young Aunt Jia in front of her face. "See? Both of you fat!"

Kim looks down at her bare feet. Her mom's words ring in her ears. Walter put his hand on her shoulder. "Are you okay?"

"Yeah." She smiles. "You look so much like her. What color are her eyes?"

"Blue. Dad's are brown, so that's probably why mine turned out like this." He puts the photograph and letter back into the envelope. "Do you think that's why Dad's such an asshole to me?"

Kim's mom shakes her finger at the image of the short and round, yet jovial, Aunt Jia. "She even worse than prostitute! You must lose weight and listen to your parents, not be like her!"

"I wouldn't be surprised. It's kind of like how Evil Aunt Tai and my mom gang up on me."

"They've got no right to, either. You can't fucking help it."

"I want to wait for the right time, you know? Maybe this summer, if Cousin Jessie's home from Berkeley. They should all suffer."

He kisses her. "No shit. And if you look the way your Aunt Jia does in her forties, then I-I'm definitely marrying you."

She can't help but say, "If so, I want us to be married for real. No conjugal visits."

"Don't worry." He laughs. "We'll be fine. I'll shave off the damn beard and moustache soon. But here," he shows her his mom's letter, "we're welcome at her place any time, even if Fabio's living with her now."

"There's no way my family would let me go." She lights a cigarette. Shakes her head. "I'm almost eighteen, too. It's bullshit."

"We can go after you turn eighteen, if you want." He puts an arm around her. "I just love imagining us together in San Francisco."

"Me too." But she doesn't want to meet Jeff and Matt.

"It'll be romantic."

She laughs out loud, punches his arm. "True."

"Hell, Doll, wh-when I saw you the first day of freshman year, I was like, I'm gonna marry that girl. And all day, I've been pretending you're my wife, 'cause stupid Dad's gone."

"Oh my god!" She hits him again. "You are such a dork!"

Secretly, she loves it. Kim Riordan just sounds right. Since they've had the house to themselves, it does feels like they're married. Living in an apartment in San Francisco. They stayed out late, decided to spend most of their day in bed. Fucked in the kitchen before making dinner. It feels so real that she expects to see the Golden Gate Bridge when she opens the shades. As they cuddle on their bed, their dead golden retriever smiles at them from the nightstand. Rain continues to fall onto the rooftop as she lies in her husband's arms.

Kevin can keep living, for all she cares.

28

Sunlight sneaks through the shades. Shit. Kim squints, turns away from the window. Walter is fast asleep, his messy facial hair erasing every trace of the boy inside. He breathes warm air onto her face every time he exhales through his mouth. Last night, he snored while she tossed and turned. Dreading the morning.

She doesn't feel like driving to the shady parts of Alhambra and El Monte, two cities halfway between them and Kevin. The more she thinks about it, the more she doesn't want to call Kevin to lure him into a motel room. She doesn't even know if she can speak to him, but she already feels the trap door shut in her throat. The knots in her back and chest.

The idea of telling him she wants to fuck him again makes her feverish, nauseous. She'll have to do a lot of sweet-talking. *Oh, Kevin, I'm sorry I was such a bitch to you when you taught me how to play guitar. Really. I shouldn't have been so mean.* She grits her teeth, tries not to punch the mattress. Why the fuck should she apologize to *him*?

They're going to fuck up. She knows they will. One little mistake will send them down the river.

She wakes him up by spitting into her palm and stroking him. His lashes flutter open. He moans, his smile halfway hidden by his beard. A kiss undeterred by morning breath. "It's so nice to wake up next to you." He pulls her to him. They go slow, still raw from yesterday.

"I have an idea," Kim says after they're done, "why don't I call Planned Parenthood and see if I can get an appointment this afternoon? Wouldn't it be great if I were on the Pill, and we could do it without rubbers all the time?"

He nods slowly, grinning. "That would be awesome. But w-we should go scope out motel rooms first." He glances at the window. "It's nice out."

Why can't there be another thunderstorm? "It is, but since we're killing Kevin at night, we should go later. That way, we can get used to the area after dark."

He kisses her. "Y-You're so smart."

She needs a second cigarette right after the first. Jarring sunlight as she makes breakfast and they eat at the kitchen table. Outside, the birds chirp loudly, begging her not to go through with it. Maybe Neil will come home early. Maybe she'll suddenly remember a homework assignment she forgot to do. Walter has three cups of coffee instead of his usual two. His kaleidoscope eyes hell-bent, gold and green flecks of a minefield.

"I know, why don't we go to Disneyland today?" Kim takes her last bite of syrup-drenched pancake. "Since it's a weekday, it won't be so crowded. All the other times I went was with my family, and believe me, my mom knows how to make Disneyland a punishment." She smiles. "It would be nice to go with you."

Walter makes a face. "Disneyland sucks!"

"What about Magic Mountain or Knott's Berry Farm, then?"

"No!" His fork lands onto his plate. "All those places will be full of st-stupid kids on Spring Break!"

She sighs, rests the side of her head against her palm. "What about the mall, then?"

"W-We can always go to the mall!" He stares at her. "Y-You don't wanna back out, do you?"

"No." She looks away, presses her lips together. "But it's such a nice day, and we should do something fun." Their eyes meet again."I know, maybe we can go see *Tank Girl*."

"I'm not in the mood. L-Let's just chill here until tonight." He takes another gulp of coffee. The bottom of his mug collides with wood. Dark liquid splashes. "D-Do you know what you're gonna say wh-when you call that fucking asshole?"

She's seasick. The kitchen sways back and forth. "I don't know." She picks at what's left of her pancakes, slips a lukewarm bite into her mouth. "I'll probably say that I miss him and want to see him again." It's so sweet she can barely swallow. "I...I'll tell him it's always been my fantasy," she wipes at her forehead, laughs nervously, "to dress up like a schoolgirl, in pigtails and my cute widdle girl underwear and wait for him on the bed." The birds are now shrieking. "And for me to keep the motel door unlocked, so he can just come in and do whatever he wants to me." Her voice quavers. She rests her chin in her palms.

"That'll probably work."

He slaps the tabletop. "What? I-I don't want you talking to him like that!"

"How else are we gonna get him in there?" She wipes at her eyes. "And I know I'm going to have a nervous breakdown when I call him!"

"W-We can kidnap him, so you won't have to go through all that."

"What?" She bursts out laughing. "How the fuck are we gonna do that?"

"I dunno, w-we'll figure it out."

"But Walter, kidnapping is a federal crime! They told us so in Civics!"

He shoots her an impatient look. "We'll be okay, Doll. Trust me."

She stares at him. "I can't go through with it!"

"Fine. I'll do it myself."

"But I was the one who was raped, not you!"

"D-Don't you want th-that son of a bitch to suffer?" He leans forward, nostrils flaring. "Fuck the system! W-We need to do it ourselves!"

"But don't you see?" Tears stream down her cheeks. She wipes at her eyes with the back of her hand. "I can actually come now! I have you! It's all the justice I need!"

"B-But he's a sick ass pervert wh-who needs to die!"

"Walter! Stop it!" She gets up, chair squealing behind her. "I'm leaving!"

He follows her into the living room. "Wh-What do you mean, you're leaving?"

"It means that I'm fucking leaving!"

"W-We're not gonna get caught," Walter hugs Kim, "it'll be okay, Doll."

His embrace is oppressive. She wriggles away, looks at the front door. She can't bring herself to leave just yet, and ends up sitting next to him on the couch. "Walter, I've been thinking. Maybe you should go live with your mom for a while."

"Wh-Why? Are you trying to get rid of me? Don't you love me anymore?"

"Of course I love you. I just think..."

"W-We're like Bonnie and Clyde a-and now you do this?" He presses her hand to his chest, squeezes his eyes shut. His heart palpitates into her palm. "I-I know you're scared, Doll. So am I. Kind of. But I am gonna destroy him." Tears drip hot onto her knuckles, run down her hand.

"But he didn't rape you!" Kim yells. "Why does it matter so much, huh?" She pictures Kevin's lifeless body. His blood on their hands. On their boots.

"Y-You know you want him dead as much as I do."

His head swims in a pool of blood. "No! I don't!"

"H-He's a fucking predator, Kim! People like that are never gonna change! W-We'd be doing the whole world a favor!"

Walter crouches down in front of Kim. The two of them tremble and hold each other at the scene of the crime. Barely able to stand up. His gaze so unnerving that she looks at her lap. Her legs pressed tightly together. They ache to fall apart, pull him towards her. But he's so far gone that her love is useless.

She turns away, presses her legs together even harder. "I had no idea that killing Kevin means more to you than us."

"What do you mean? He hurt the only person I love!" Walter wipes at his eyes before he puts his hands on her knees. "It's okay, Doll. I-I'm the retard who flunked third grade. You're the girl who gets straight A's and a 1460 on the SAT. If we're caught, I'll take the fall. It's not like I have much of a future, anyway."

He might as well have punched her in the tits. "I'm sorry, Walter." She pushes him away.

"No!" They get up at the same time. His hands clamp down onto her shoulders. Her teeth clatter. She doesn't want to look at him. She doesn't want to see mocking dark eyes and too many white hairs. "You can't leave me like this!"

Kim opens her mouth. Only futile air comes out.

"Open your mouth wider, or I'll fuck you with it." Kevin *drives himself deeper into her. She hears herself gag. Even deeper. She gags again. Her lower back tightens. Water*

oozes from her eyes, nostrils and mouth. Her jaw begins to shake, then

Her scream tears her vocals chords. "No! I don't want to!" Walter's grip tightens. He presses his chest into hers. "I-I-I didn't mean to scare you! Please stay!"

"Let go of me, you fucking rapist!" She shoves him to rescue herself. The room teeters, brown and light blue and floating white. Birds drown out the sound of Walter sobbing. She practically flies towards the front door, and slams it behind her.

When she gets home, her dad's car is still there.

29

Kim's parents wait at the kitchen table in their work clothes. Her mom leans forward, smirking. Her dad sits up straight, hands folded in his lap.

"Sit down." He points at the wooden chair between them. "We need to talk."

"Sure, Daddy." The mini-blinds shut out the sunlight. She sits down, realizes she needs to remove her sponge soon.

"Last night, we called Mary Chong and found out it was a disconnected number." Her parents scoot towards her, chairs squeaking. She shrugs, crosses her legs. "Where were you and who were you with? Tell us the truth."

Kim smiles, looks her dad in the eye. "Oh, I'm sorry, Daddy. I saw a concert in Hollywood and ended up staying at a motel there, because it was too late to drive home."

"You no allowed to go to Hollywood without supervision!" Of course her mom narrows her eyes. "Why you lie to us?"

She tries her hardest not to laugh. "It was a band I really wanted to see, but I felt like going alone. I'm sorry. You would've said no, anyway. I had no other choice."

"So you have to lie? That stupidest thing I ever hear!" She looks at her husband. "We must ground her!"

"You are right, Yan." Her dad clears his throat, crosses his arms. "You will not be allowed to drive until you graduate from high school. Mom will be giving you a ride every day from now on."

Oh, god. Kim's so sick of her mom's triumphant nod, too. "You must give back key!"

"Fine." Neither of them know she's made a copy. It hides in the coin pocket of her Hello Kitty Wallet. She pulls her mom's key off the ring, hands it over. "Here you go, Mom." She gives her dad three gentle taps on his shoulder. "Since mom is making me take Public Speaking at Mt. Sac, is she going to drive me there every day, too? It is a morning class that gets out at noon."

Her mom is about to nod, but her dad shakes his head. "You may drive yourself to summer school, as long as you maintain your 4.0." He studies her face. "For a young lady in trouble, you appear awfully rational."

"Well, I lied to you. I deserve to be punished." Kim gets up. "May I be excused?"

Her mom glares. "Why you no cry, huh?"

Because it beats getting charged with murder. "Because I agree with you."

Kim's dad stands up and reaches for her shoulder. She moves out of the way. "We will go to work now. You are not to leave the house. We will call you at any time, and you are required to answer the phone."

"Fine."

●※

After dinner, Kim's dad hands her the phone while she's practicing piano. He walks away without saying a word.

"Hello?"

"Hi, Kim." Neil's voice is grave. "We have a problem. When I came home, I found three hundred dollars missing and a note from my son that reads, *I'm not so retarded that I don't know how to take a bus to Hayward. Too bad for you, Dad.*"

"Wow." She stares at the black and ivory keys. Her tailbone tingles. She hadn't wanted to talk to Walter all day. Not after he tried to hold her back like that. "He actually did it." The ivory keys turn bright, blinding, along with the sheet music. She turns off the fluorescent lamp on top of the piano, rubs at her forehead. Her parents are silent in the next room. One of them has switched off the Chinese soap opera.

"Is that all you have to say?" Neil's voice becomes louder. She holds the receiver away from her ear. "Do you have any idea what the hell you just did to my son? Huh?"

At first, his words cause her heart to go into overdrive. The trap door in her throat slams shut. Cold sweat seeps through her pores. Then Kim exhales hard. Remembers the hypocritical things other grown-ups have said and done to her. "Yeah. I've just reunited your son with his mom."

"You also reunited him with Matt and Jeff! We moved because they were a bad influence! He was constantly getting suspended and in danger of failing! With you, his grades had improved and he rarely got in trouble at school! Why'd you do that to him, huh?"

She chuckles as she fights back tears. "I didn't do anything to him! We got into an argument today!"

A quiet gasp. A few seconds of silence. "Shit. Look, Kim, I shouldn't have yelled at you like that. Do you know if he had plans to go up north?"

"No!" The tears win. There's a hollow ache in her chest. She wishes she could feel Walter's arms around her. "He didn't say anything!"

"Then what happened between you two that made him want to leave town, then? Do you remember saying or doing anything that would make him react so drastically?"

All the lights are on, but it's still dark in room 216. All the lights are on, but it's still dark in the guestroom.

Kim forces herself to exhale, but the knots are more powerful. "I-I don't know." It's way too warm in the living room. All the weight from her head slips down to her limbs. "I'm sorry, Neil, I don't know. I need to practice piano." She jabs her index finger into the power button. The phone slips from her fingers, lands onto the pristine beige carpet. Her head drops forward as she begins to bawl.

"We heard what happened, Kim. It is for the best," she hears her dad say.

What? They're listening in on her phone conversations now, too?

Her parents stand together next to the piano bench. Her dad's unaffected by her red eyes and tear-stained face. Her mom's got her hands on her chunky hips, a wide smile stretched across her face.

She nods, wipes at her eyes, can't bring herself to say anything polite.

Her parents are relieved. Almost happy. What was she expecting from them, anyway? Sympathy? She silently curses herself for not knowing better by now.

"Kim, you and Walter have been spending too much time together, anyway. Mommy and I discussed forbidding you to see and talk to Walter outside of school, but he has made the situation more convenient for us." Her dad gives her three hard pats on her back. "You cannot cry. He is not a good person, and did you a favor."

She itches to take a swing at his stomach. She lifts up her ass, sits on her hands. "I'll try not to."

"Kimmy-ah." Her mom touches cold fingers to her cheek. Stigmata on her skin. Kim presses her lips together. "You spend so much time with Walter, you forget about your parents! Now you spend more time with us before you go to UCI!"

They'll probably make her come home Friday afternoon and not drive her back until Sunday evening. Monopolize her so she won't get to see Walter. If he ever comes back. "Okay, Mom."

"I know! We taking you to Hollywood this weekend, go to your favorite restaurant and store!" Kim's mom shakes her shoulder. "That so nice of us, huh?"

Yay. Happy Rape Day to her. She takes shallow breaths through pursed lips. Wishes she could knock her mom onto her ass, the back of her head hitting the wall, the smirk smacked from her face. Kim's sweaty palms melt into the piano bench. Her forearms quiver into her sides. Gunshots go off inside her head. Why was she so scared of killing Kevin? Why did she have to chase away her Clyde?

Fingers snap inches from her face. "Kimmy-ah! What you thinking about?"

She forces herself to exhale and says, "Nothing."

"This is for your own good," her dad says. "Even though Walter is gay, I have suspected that he was in love with you, and possibly bisexual. Your friendship was becoming inappropriate, and I was worried you were giving him the wrong idea."

She knows she's pushing her luck, but can't resist asking, "Yeah, but what if he comes back?"

"You no allowed to see him or talk to him ever again!" Kim's mom says.

She laughs to herself. "I'll be eighteen soon. You can't dictate whom I can and can't see."

"We your parents and we paying for your education!"

"O-kay."

"Mommy is right!" Kim's dad says. "You must stop crying right now! It makes you look lazy and weak! You may think your life is hard, but ours is harder! We need to work and make sacrifices so you can have a good future!"

Her mom hugs her. She's suffocated with White Shoulders. Every muscle in her body stiffens. "No one love you as much as us! One day, we die and you regret not spending enough time with us!"

"I need to practice piano now," Kim says through clenched teeth.

💣

Kim's mom answers the phone during dinner on Saturday. "Hello?" She narrows her eyes. Her dad puts his chopsticks down, looks at her. "Walter, my daughter no want you anymore! She too good for you, and she look forward to making new friend at UCI! If you call again, I call police!" Her mom hangs up, nods triumphantly. "I do good, huh? Now he never call again!"

Kim stares at her mom, dumbfounded. Her hands shake. The contents of her stomach swirl. She pokes at her food, doesn't know if she can bring herself to finish her salmon, boiled cabbage, and rice.

Her mom waves her own chopsticks. "Kimmy-ah, your finger too low! You must hold it higher!"

"It is a shame that you are Chinese, yet cannot hold chopsticks properly!" Her dad shakes his head, then turns to his wife. "That was very effective, Yan," Kim's dad says.

"On Monday, I will call the phone company to have our number changed."

"That very good idea!

He smiles. "What would you like to do tomorrow, Kim? Your wish is our command."

"We go to UCI, then Fashion Island!" Kim's mom says. "We go eat there, and I take you shopping!"

"Yes, we will walk around campus, so you can get some exercise!"

Kim touches her hand to her mouth. Sour liquid seeps from her throat. There's no way she can continue eating. No way she can survive five more months of living at home.

30

april 14, 1995
hey doll,
    tried calling you saturday but your mom
told me you didn't want to talk to me anymore.
that's not true is it? now your numbers
disconnected. your parents did that didn't
they?
    i wasn't trying to rape you. i just wanted
you to stay. im sorry. the more i think
about it, the shittier i feel. i shouldn't
have held you like that and gave you a
flashback. i hope your ok. that's why i try
calling and i'm so worried because we weren't
able to talk. yeah i went to live with mom.
she took one look at me with my facial hair
and started to cry. said i looked like a
serial killer and made me shave it. you can't
be a serial killer if you just wanna kill one
person right? now i have sideburns. it looks
pretty cool. i do miss her and its nice to
spend time with her. i thought her boyfriend,
brendan would be a total asshole but he's
pretty cool. he runs his own auto shop and
says he's gonna teach me the basics of auto
repair soon. she looks so happy. like she's 25

again. we all help cook and do household chores.

dad calls every night and tries to pick fights with me. i told mom he sees hookers and she says he's a pig. it felt so good to be able to get onto that 480 to the claremont transit center and buy my ticket. you really were the one thing keeping me in town, even freshman year. did you know last year was the first year i got perfect attendance? i even got a certificate and a coupon for applebee's. i dunno seeing you every day at school made me feel better. it gave me something to look forward to. i've never met anyone like you before and hearing that you were raped killed me. it made me want to kill. i just love you and felt so bad that it happened. i still feel like if i could turn back time i would've talked to you earlier. but i didn't have the balls. steve perez kept telling me to all freshman year and i finally got the nerve after kurt died.

it just felt like life was too short and i had to. its weird i never wanted to leave after i saw you but now that im living with mom i realize how much i miss having a mom. but i miss you too and as soon as you want me to come back i will.

how's school? they put me into continuation school but oh well. at least i won't have to see lisa because she always follows me around whenever we go to the same school. if i didn't flunk the third grade, we would be in the same grade. she annoys me so much and i hate being seen with her. i think my school district must really hate retards, though, you know? jeff and matt are out of juvie and we hang out a lot. those two are so fucking funny. we mostly get drunk and high. we don't really do

anything bad, you know? like i said, they're
not bad guys. they like to pick on me for
having a smart girlfriend who's going to
college, but they're just jealous because
they're never gonna get in. and don't worry,
they do it in good fun. every night, mom
makes sure i do all my homework and i read to
her, too. hope you're not too mad at me. hope
your parents don't hide this letter. i love
you and your always gonna be my girl.
   -walter

April 17, 1995
Hey, Walter:

   I'm so glad I got your letter this Friday.
My mom's been driving me to and from school
every day. I think grounding me turns them on
and it's their substitute for sex. Of course I
still love you and want to talk to you! It
pissed me off so much that my mom put words
into my mouth like that. Yeah, they changed
our phone number, too. Just to make sure
you'll never get ahold of me again. You
should've seen how proud they were. But they
still let me get the mail when we come home.
I just hide the letters. They have their heads
so far up their asses that they don't think
you'd actually write me.

   Yeah, you gave me a flashback. I know you
didn't try to rape me, but it didn't make me
happy. Sometimes I just don't know when it'll
happen. It's so unpredictable. But trying to
restrict my movement or make choices for me
always pisses me off. I'm glad you realize
that. But I'm as okay as I can be. Haven't

really had much of an appetite lately. Mom's been piling food onto my plate and begging me to eat. I just can't bring myself to. I have a little here and there, but my appetite's mostly gone. Yesterday, mom brought back this huge cake with lots of frosting and encouraged me to have much as I want. Dad got so pissed at her and told her it was her fault I was so fat in the first place. Then he congratulated me for having self-control. At that moment, I knew exactly what she was doing. This is the bitch who made me clean my plate, yet always gave me shit for being fat. I really believe she's trying to fatten me up even more. She's hoping I'll get so huge that no guy will ever want me. I bet it's her dream for me to stay the fat Chinese girl forever. It's the only thing people will ever know me as. Always the friend, never the lover. I think my mom secretly loves having a fat daughter because it makes her feel superior, even though she's heavy herself. I used to stuff my face to comfort myself from her shit. Now I'm practically starving myself to spite her. But god, I get so hungry in the middle of the night. I smoke a lot during lunch. Wish I could do it all the time. Can't do it at home because mom's always breathing down my neck. All I want is to get the hell out of here. They take me to Hollywood, take me out to dinner and shopping. They get me all this stuff but it feels so fake. I'm so sick of them telling me that they're cool parents. They think we're so close and everything's perfect. Yeah, right.

I'm always alone now at school. Now that you're gone, people just talk shit right in front of my face. There's a rumor that you skipped town because I aborted our retarded baby. I didn't even feel like telling them it wasn't true. They can believe whatever they want.

(By the way, the sponge worked. I got my period yesterday).

Why are you in continuation school? You were doing so good, too. I was so proud of you when you made the honor roll for the first time last fall. It's great your mom is helping you with homework and reading.

Walter, I really am flattered that you feel that way about me. Every time my parents tell me that no one loves me as much as them, I cringe. You're the only one who's truly loved me and made me feel fine the way I am. But when I think about it, I just don't think I'm comfortable murdering someone. And when you told me that you didn't have much of a future, anyway, it hurt me so much. What do you mean? What about our future together? I really did feel like we were married that night. It was so nice. Do you know how terrible it would be if we were in jail and couldn't see or talk to each other anymore? Neither of us belong there, too. And you know what guys do to each other in jail, right? I don't ever want that to happen to you.

Even if we weren't caught, we'd always have it hanging over our heads. You've seen that shit on TV. People get arrested for crimes they've committed decades ago. Please just think about that. My dad sounds like a broken record, always telling me to be rational and

to think before I act, but it's important this
time.

I miss you, too, but these past few months,
it really felt like you wanted to be with your
mom. I love being with you and I really mean
it when I say that you're the first person
I've liked having inside me. All those
magazines say sex is better with love and
they're right. But I know how much you miss
your mom and for now, maybe it's good that you
stay with her for a while.

-Kim

P.S. Our new number is (626) 555-8923.
Don't actually call until I tell you it's safe
to. I'm rarely home alone now. My parents are
that paranoid.

31

Finally, graduation day. Kim puts on a long black lace dress with a corset back and fluttery sleeves. It's the most expensive one she owns. She's still surprised her parents bought it from the Betsey Johnson store on Melrose Avenue. She reluctantly puts on her blue graduation gown. Emphasizes her sad eyes with black eyeliner and eye shadow, three coats of mascara.

"Kimmy-ah!" Her mom bangs on her bedroom door. At least they're nice enough to let her shut it. "Let's go take picture!"

She rolls her eyes, puts on her cap. "Jesus Christ."

In the front yard, Kim is forced to pose under the late June heat. Her fake smile cuts into her skin. But it's not good enough for her mom. She's not smiling right. Her eyes are too small. Her face is too round. She keeps smiling, her hands behind her back. Trying not to grab the camera and smash it to pieces. She sighs, watches a black car drive past them.

"Kimmy-ah!" Her mom screeches. "Look at camera!"

When she does, her eyes narrow. Her lips press into a line.

"You must smile! I no want ugly face in my photo album!"

"Speak for yourself, Bitch," she mutters, forcing herself to smile again.

There are twelve family photo albums. In each and every picture, everyone's smiling and looking at the camera. But it's all a façade.

"Kim! Yan!" Kim's dad dangles his car keys in his hand. The sight of him wearing a white polo and jeans is oddly reassuring. "We are going to be late!"

She tries not to jump up and down.

When they arrive in front of the football stadium at her soon-to-be alma mater, her dad says, "We are going to pick up Diana and bring her to the ceremony. Congratulations, Kim. I am very proud of you."

"Thanks, Daddy," she says.

Kim's mom turns around. "When you go to UCI, you must be more normal like Cousin Jessie! She have very good Chinese friend her own age, and they already studying for MCAT!"

"Good for her. I'll see you guys later."

Kim tries not to slam the door. She doesn't look back at as she walks into the stadium. Walter's letters are hidden in the lining of her purse. He wanted to come back for graduation, but she insisted it wasn't the best time. Made some excuse involving schoolwork and living in the Forbidden City. As much as she misses him, she's happy to be alone, and there's no hurry for him to return.

In the field, there are rows of metal folding chairs. The same field where beefy boys in tight, shiny pants prance around and catch footballs. In the distance, a podium on top of a wooden platform. Kim scans chairs and classmates' faces to find her row and seat. She's stuck between Dave Hicks and Sean Hoberman. Who are they again? Her soon-to be former classmates keep filing in, sides and asses slide dangerously close to her face. They're all chatting and squealing and hugging. She drowns them out by re-reading Walter's letters, trying not to cry.

A marching band plays something more appropriate for a funeral. Kim wishes she could pull off her gown. Get that thick, flammable polyester off of her. The school principal begins his speech about how the graduating class of 1995 is part of Generation X, but no one at this school is a slacker and everyone's going to succeed. Kim presses her lips together to keep herself from laughing. And how dare the Valedictorian ramble about working hard and living sober when Kim's heard her brag about being a speed freak?

People begin to fidget in their seats. Finally, the principal begins to call out names. "Hold the applause until all diplomas have been distributed, please." Traci and Michelle are never called. When Kim's name is called, two girls whisper about her aborted fetus. She sighs and gets up. Makes sure no one's trying to trip her as she walks towards the platform. The principal gives her a firm handshake, hands her a blue vinyl folder with the school's horse and shield logo embossed in gold. The actual diploma isn't even in there. No one gets one until they return their graduation gowns.

After everyone gets their fake diplomas, they're instructed to turn their tassels the other way. A collective cheer roars throughout the stadium. Kim's classmates get up, tossing their caps into the air. She removes her cap, flings it onto the grass. Shoves past her now-former classmates.

Her parents and Diana are nowhere to be found. Of course, it's her mom's shrill voice that cuts through everyone else's excited chatter. Laughter. Stares. Kim wants to disappear, not bothering to hide her displeasure as she walks up the bleachers. She hugs Diana a little longer than she hugs her parents.

They go to Hometown Buffet for dinner. Get their first plates of food from the salad bar. After they sit down, Kim's dad raises his glass of milk. "I would like to wish Kim a bright future at UCI."

"Thanks, Daddy." She's relieved he's not asking her if she's drinking Diet Coke. Because she's having regular.

They clink their plastic cups together.

"I am so proud of our daughter. This year, she has shown so much improvement by maintaining her 4.0 and getting a 1460 on the SAT!"

Kim's mom points at her own chest. "But if I no push her, she no get 4.0 and 1460! How come nobody thank me for my hard work?"

Kim grits her teeth, watches Diana oh-so-subtly shake her head. "Thanks, Mom."

Kim's dad chuckles. "Yes, Yan. Thank you." He clears his throat. "I am also proud that Kim used her free time to help a boy from special-ed with his reading."

"That boy better not come back!" Kim's mom glares at her.

"I thought you liked Walter, Yan," Diana says.

Her mom shakes her head. "He steal my daughter from me! But now she can spend more time with her parents!"
Kim's about to roll her eyes, but her dad's watching. She sits up straight. Picks at her food with a lowered head. She's hungry, yet the thought of shoveling food into her mouth still repulses her. If she doesn't eat, her mom is going to give her shit. But if she doesn't eat something low in fat and sugar, her dad is going to give her shit. She grimaces after biting into a tomato. Its sourness overwhelming.

"It's normal for teenagers to spend time with her friends, Yan."

"But we no accept Walter! I so afraid he bad influence!"

"She needs to find her own way. The culture here is quite different, and she's torn between two worlds. Besides, she's such a unique girl."

"She must respect our heritage! And what unique mean?"

"She is a very original and creative girl."

"I no want original and creative daughter! I want thin and obedient daughter!"

Kim doesn't want a yapping Chihuahua for a mom, either.

"Diana," her dad says, "I want to thank you for being Kim's friend. She needs good friends, especially since we no longer approve of Walter, and never liked Traci and Michelle."

"I am glad to be Kim's friend, Chao."

"I want her make friend her own age!" Her mom says. "You forty-one, why you no marry or have children?" She stares at Diana pointedly. "Are you lisbon?"

Kim's dad gives his wife one hard pat on the shoulder. "Yan, that is not your business."

Kim gets up. "Excuse me, I'm going to get more food. Want to come along, Diana?"

"Yes. Please excuse us." Diana smiles politely at Kim's parents.

Once they're out of earshot, she touches Diana's arm. "I'm so sorry. My mom had no right to say that."

"Well, you handled it well," Diana says. She glances back at the tables of people eating plates piled high with food. "I noticed you haven't been eating much. Are you okay?"

They're in front of the hot foods cart. Even her usual favorites, like potatoes au gratin, and macaroni and cheese, don't sound good. "I think I've been eating too much just to deal with my mom's shit, and it doesn't sit well with me anymore."

"Well, you need to eat, just to keep yourself going." Diana leads her to the meat cart, where a guy in a green apron slices up ham and roast beef and slaps them onto people's plate. She nods at the salmon and steamed vegetables. "Why don't you have some of those, at the very least?"

Kim bites her lip as she reaches for the metal tongs. "Okay." She raises an eyebrow. "Diana, I don't think my mom's even congratulated me today. I mean, she's complained about my looks and disobedience, but it's like she doesn't even care that I just finished high school."

"I do, and I'm very proud of you, because I know how much you hated it." Diana gives her a quick squeeze. "Have you heard from Walter lately?"

"Yeah. He sent me a stuffed kitten and some candy jewelry yesterday."

"I hope he comes back soon and you can start seeing each other when you move out."

"Me too, but sometimes, I think he's even more fucked-up than I am." Kim looks at Diana. "Too bad we can't have dinner by ourselves."

💣

Saturday night, Kim's dad finally returns minutes before midnight, reeking of booze and smoke.

"Daddy, where did you go?"

"I was at the office." Since when was smoking and drinking allowed there?

"Did you get a lot of work done?"

He nods. "I always do."

Kim's mom puts on her pitiful mask. "Chao, why you go out so late? Is it because I bad wife and mother?"

He laughs, gives her three soft pats. "Of course not. I work late so I can provide for us."

"Are you cheating on me? Is that why you spending so much time away?"

"Do not be silly, Yan." He walks towards the bathroom.

Kim's mom blocks her path to the hallway. "If he with other woman, is all your fault!"

"Whatever." Kim forces herself to breathe, pushes past her. "Good night, Mom."

An hour before they go to LAX to pick up Cousin Jessie, Kim changes the sheets in the master bedroom. Grumbling under her breath as her mom watches Chinese soap operas. Then she changes her own sheets before walking into the family room. "I'm done."

"You must do guest room! When Aunt Tai and Cousin Jessie stay overnight, they no sleeping in dirty bed!"

Her hands shake. "I already did it."

"You lie!" Her mom gets up. "Since you lazy, I change them myself!"

She stomps down the hallway. Kim trudges to her room, sits on her bed. Holds her head in her hands and sighs. After Kevin left that day, she just remade the bed. She should've changed the sheets and did the laundry. A year and four months have gone by. Why didn't she take advantage of all those opportunities?

It's time for her to take it like a man.

The guest room door creaks open. There's rustling. A gasp. Her mom rushes into her room, grabs her by the crook of her elbow, yanks her to her feet, pulls her into the guest room. The lights are on. Her shoulders tighten. A fist presses into her heart.

A hard slap on her upper back. "Look at the sheet!" Her mom yells.

She feels Kevin's palm over her nose and mouth. Her sternum throbs. There's nowhere to run. The tingle in her lower back spreads down to her ass. She's simultaneously overheated and freezing, sweating and trembling. Her own mom is going to kill her in the guest room. She just knows it.

"What's that?" Her mom points at the bed as she blocks the door. She's heaving, red-faced. But the corners of her mouth are pulled upwards.

On the ivory fitted sheet, there are brown and maroon stains.

Kim closes her eyes.

32

A stinging slap lands onto the back of Kim's head. "You open eye, or I hitting you again!"

She pries her eyes open. The spots are still there. No need to look closely to know what they're from.

"Come on, Kimmy, just a little more, okay? Then I'll stop if you want. Most guys would totally go crazy when they're fucking your poopie, but I'm being gentle. Doesn't it feel so good?"

Suffocated by shit and lube mixed with Pantene and dryer sheets. The knot in her chest pulled tight. On the verge of splintering and bursting her lungs.

Her mom stomps her foot. "What's this on bed? Huh? Huh?"

"Come on, just a little more. You love it, don't you, Kimmy?"

Kim tries to breathe long, relaxing breaths but all she can get are short, shallow ones that fray her nerves even more. Her shoulders shake uncontrollably as Kevin pushes himself into her. "Stop it! It hurts!"

"Just a little more. It won't hurt so much if you relax."

"Kimmy-ah! Do you lose your virgin on bed?" Her mom's eyes are a smoldering line of coals she'll never be able to walk over. An unnerving grin across her face. "Answer me!"

She looks at her mom, tries to open her mouth. Nothing comes out.

Her mom slaps her across the face. She topples to her knees. Her mom delivers a blow to her upper back. "You pretend to be good girl, but you fake!" A punch to her left arm, a freight train crashing into brick. Kim falls sideways onto the carpet. "You think we never find out, huh? How dare you think we stupid! You make us believe Walter gay so you can sleep with him after school!"

She stands in front of the window. Fallen princess blocked from the early summer breeze, watching herself bent over the edge of the bed.

Kevin stands behind her, his hands on her hips. Her face buried in the mattress to hide the humiliation. She can't even scream. Inhaling shit and lube. Fabric softener. She breathes through her mouth. Sucks the comforter against the O of her lips. Hoping her shit sprays all over Kevin, so he'll get the fuck away. But it doesn't.

"Why you no say anything, huh? I thought you rebellious, willful daughter! You coward!" A hard kick to her left buttock. Kim lurches forward into the Pacific. Her body flailing in ribbons of seaweed. Icy saltwater fills her lungs. Blinds her. She wants to swim to the surface, yell Walter's name into the sky. Tell him it's time to come back.

But she's already sinking towards the bottom.

Her mom kicks her again. "I only doing this because I love you! Is for your own good!" Kicks her again. Kim digs her heels into the wall, braces herself against the windowsill. "You have sex because you think it will hurt me, but you only hurting yourself!" Her mom kicks her over and over. Her laughter is a fork scraping metal. "I teaching you lesson so you never have sex again!"

She's barely breathing through chapped lips. Sprawled out on the ocean floor in a shroud of cold, black water. Fish with distended jaws and bulging eyes poke and prod at her.

"Nobody ever love you more than me! Boy will leave you, but Mommy love you forever!"

Kim's entire body convulses. Shit and lube and fabric softener and shampoo spin around in her head. Kevin's greasy palms clutch her hips. A colony of ants cover her body. All she sees with closed eyes is a patch of wet mud wriggling with earthworms.

Kevin pulls out. "I wanna come on your face."

Kim turns around slowly, not wanting to see him. Wishing she were made of stone. She's on her knees, scrunched arms hiding the rest of her. She can't even bring herself to say no. He's going to, no matter what.

"I doing this so you no get pregnant, embarrass entire family! I give you everything and sacrifice so much! You think you so good, huh? Daddy say it all my fault if you have sex before you marry!"

From Kim's safe place at the window, streams of tears shine on her mom's cheeks. Her lips contort into a frown as she keeps kicking her. "We so close when we grow up! This how you thank me? Who you think you are? You think you so special, huh? You no special! You stupid, selfish prostitute! You think you skinnier and prettier than me because handsome man want you, but look what he do!"

Kevin grabs Kim by the chin. His other hand moves up and down. She tries not to gag from the smell of shit and lube. "Here it is!" Greasy skin squeezes greasy skin, followed by his animalistic growl. Hot liquid scalds Kim's right eyeball.

"And you think because you have big breast and pig lip, you can have any man you want? How dare you! You ruin my sister, and my daughter, too! She only seventeen, but she already worse than you!"

Kim's not sure who her mom's insulting anymore as she rips the sheets and mattress pad off the bed. She stomps out of the bedroom, soiled bedding in her hands. Kim keeps standing in front of the window. She watches herself yowling and rubbing at her eye. A sweaty Kevin chuckles as he apologizes.

Her mom returns, keys jangling from her hand. Her brown leather purse slung over her arm. "I go to Leaner to buy new sheet! For rest of year, you no getting allowance! You no allowed to drive or go to Lullupalooloo! I no care if you just buy ticket on Saturday! You throw yourself and your stupid ticket into trash!"

33

She doesn't know how much time has passed, but someone's on top of her. A solid, unfamiliar heaviness. A drop of warm liquid falls onto her forehead. A man's loud, rhythmic breath. She can't feel her arms and legs, but she can feel his thrusts, hear herself scream. He's hurting her. He's making her feel good. She thinks her eyes are open, but all she sees is black. Then, a sharp, stinging pain on her cheek. Bright white cuts into the darkness.

She gasps. The light shining onto his short blond hair gives him a deceptive halo. In his cold blue eyes, her twin reflections cower, but can't look away. Trembling beneath his wolfish gaze as he fucks her brutally. His cheekbones and jaw line sharp enough to cut. She's too weak to resist. Her arms and legs coil around him.

In the distance, the mirror surrounded by light bulbs reflects images of nude women with automatic weapons, creatures with exaggerated mouths and deadly claws.

The smell of blood in the air. Whiskey, and something bitter, on her breath.

"Rise, Angel, rise." His voice is deep and scratchy, with a German accent.

"Who are you?"

"Your lover."

He kisses and fucks the life back into her. Her twin reflections are stronger, more radiant. When she comes, she screams with pleasure and rage.

He gets up. "We must hurry! You cannot be late!" He's pale and defined. A polished statue. She watches him button up his starched white shirt, pull up his black trousers tucked into heavy black boots.

"Huh?" Hot liquid seeps out of her as she sits up, smoothes out her black silk dress. Lethal toes on her glossy red heels. The floor is a checkerboard. She spots an empty white bottle, picks it up. It's unmarked. "What's this?"

"You do not remember?" The man raises an eyebrow as he puts on his black jacket. Its lines are sharp. Authoritative. Gold buttons down the front. Badges and medals for every act of violence he's ever committed. A red armband. "You were to perform for the first time in a year, but your ex-lover paid you a visit." He slips on his officer's cap. A pair of crossed metal scythes at the center.

Kim cocks her head. "And?"

"He begged you to leave with him. You got into an argument. He tried to make you leave, so you killed him and tried to kill yourself."

The bottle slips through her fingers, clatters onto a white square. "Bullshit!"

He puts on black leather gloves. "He is still on the couch."

She shakes her head, over and over. "You're lying!"

"Let me show you." In a single motion, he lifts her off the floor. Black leather gloves on the bare undersides of her thighs. She flies, colors spin. The smell of blood is stronger.

On the old leather couch, Walter is lifeless. The handle of a knife sticks out of his chest. Red covers the front of his shirt and the couch, begins to flood onto the floor. He died with his eyes wide open. Anguish twisting his mouth. Even as a corpse, he wants to know why she killed him. It all comes back to her.

She starts screaming, tries to escape, but the man won't let her go. He's indifferent as she scratches and shoves at him. Silent as he cradles her in his arms. Inside her head, the sound of Walter crying. He loved her. How could she do that? She just did. She held the knife in her hand and rammed it through his heart as hard as she could. Then she took twenty sleeping pills and washed it down with a bottle of Jack.

"Who are you?" She slaps the man hard across the face, but he doesn't even care.

"I told you, I am your lover, and you have a show to play. You cannot be late."

"No, you're not!" She nods at Walter, who stares at them through empty hazel eyes. "He is!"

"No, I am." The man kisses her. "We need to go."

"But I can't go onstage without doing my hair and make-up! I look like shit!"

"You look fine."

"But what am I supposed to perform? I don't know any songs!"

"The songs are inside you. They will come out."

"But I can't even sing or play guitar!"

"Yes, you can!"

She floats through the air as they rush out of the checkerboard room. His boots pummel the floor. She turns in the direction of the couch. Walter's skinny arm dangles over the edge. He faces her with his permanently shocked expression. She looks away.

In the darkened hallway, people wave at her. Call her Kimmy. Congratulate her on performing again. She doesn't recognize anyone.

They go through a doorway. An explosion of lights above them. The wooden stage so bright it turns phosphorescent. The man gently sets her down on her feet, straps a black Les Paul across her. Kisses her forehead. "I will be right behind you."

She shakes her head at the sea of grinning faces in the audience past the drum set and microphones. "No! I won't go on!"

"You must!" He nudges her in their direction. "They are waiting for you!"

They're chanting, "Kimmy! Kimmy!"

"No!" She tries to run away, but he blocks her.

They begin to clap and stomp their feet. "Kimmy! Kimmy!"

"Go!" He kisses her before pushing her forward.

The applause gets louder. She's blinded by the lights, unable to see in front of her. She clutches her guitar, holds it across her like a shield. Her footsteps small, slow. Her back and shoulders heavy as they tremble. Onstage, her shadow is ten feet tall with a long wingspan. But something is dripping from them. She looks back. A trail of blood. She slips.

34

"Kimmy-ah!" Something hard drives into Kim's left buttock. "Why you no getting up?"

Darkness under the bed. Tiny tufts of beige carpet, the same ones that flood the entire house. The pain in her backside is a million pricks of silver. Her upper back and left arm aches. She exhales, balances her hands on the carpet. Forces herself to sit with her back against the dresser drawer handles.

"If we late, is all your fault!"

She bites down on her lower lip, staggers to her feet. Incinerating red stars on her butt. Her mom stands at the edge of the bed, blocking her passage. A large shopping bag from Linens N' Things on the bare mattress. The only way out is across the bed. She heaves herself onto it while her mom demands what's wrong with her.

Tiptoeing across the mattress. Every muscle in her lower body tears and screams. On the closet doors, her shadow struggles to rise from the ocean. When it finally stands up, seaweed is coiled around its bare body, it's the most beautiful she's ever felt. She's the shade of a storm cloud. Her wings soaked, yet majestic.

Rise, Angel, rise.

Except for his wolf eyes, the rest of his face is a blur. She shivers at the memory of his uniform and accent. It was only a dream. It will soon fade away.

"Why you so slow?" Kim's mom yells.

Kim gathers every bit of strength in her aching body. With both her hands, she shoves her mom into the dresser. A muffled banging sound. A blood curdling shriek.

"Oh my gosh! Oh my gosh!"

"I'm going to use the bathroom while you make the bed. Then I'll meet you in the car."

With that, Kim goes into the bathroom, locks the door behind her. Leans back into it, moaning. It hurts to move. Why can't she stay home and rest? Since she's so well-fed, she's obligated to carry Cousin Jessie's luggage. If she doesn't, she'll be called fat and lazy. She'll have to hear about how hard it was for her cousin to grow up without a father. And why can't Evil Aunt Tai leave work early and pick up her own daughter? Kim laughs bitterly.

Well, her aunt doesn't have a rich husband. That's why Kim and her mom are going to pick up Cousin Jessie, then drive all the way to Simi Valley to meet Evil Aunt Tai at work. At dinner, her aunt and mom will praise her cousin, and they'll all gang up on her. On the drive home, her mom will be Ms. Pinchy-Face while she bitches about her disgraceful daughter.

It'll be like this all summer, and summer's barely started.

"Fuck!" She pounds on the fake marble counter. Shakes her head and winces as she rubs the side of her hand.

She expects yelling and pounding on the bathroom door, yet another stupid excuse to make her miserable, but her mom stays away. Kim rolls her eyes, lets cold water fall onto her hurting hand. Laughs. Maybe she should take up boxing. Paste pictures of her mom, aunt, and cousin's faces on punching bags. It would be nice to have muscular arms. If they ever talk shit to her again, she could punch them out.

She's about to wash her face when her palms fall onto the counter. In the splotchy mirror, she's pale. Gleaming. Her cheekbones and jaw the sharpest they've ever been. Her full lips are cruelly curved. Her eyes as black as her hair and eyebrows. At first, she's taken aback by how intense they are. By the pure hate in them.

She smiles. And sings, "I know a secret. A dirty, dirty secret."

35

Evil Aunt Tai smirks at Kim during dinner Sunday evening. "Kimmy," she holds her chopsticks like she's ready to snip off someone's nose, "what happen to your little friend?"

Under the table, Cousin Jessie's toes push against hers. She resists the urge to stomp. "Yeah, Kimmy, why did he leave town?"

Kim's mom nods triumphantly. "I will tell you story!"

"Sure, Mom," she takes a sip of diluted orange juice, "you should, since you're so great at telling them."

Evil Aunt Tai glares. "Shhh! Is not your turn to speak!"

"You're right, Aunt Tai." She smiles sweetly at her mom. "So are you going to tell it, or what?"

Kim's mom leans forward. "He one year younger, mentally retarded, and flunk third grade. One day, his dad call Kim, tell her his son no want to see her anymore!" She pauses. Victory already in her eyes, her smile. "He hate her so much he run away to live with his mom in Northern California!"

Walter must really hate her guts if he's still mailing her letters and presents every week.

Evil Aunt Tai and Cousin Jessie don't bother to contain their glee as they look at each other.

"He leave her for skinnier, prettier girl!" Evil Aunt Tai cackles, nudging her daughter. "Yan, when you tell me Kimmy have little friend, I think she making it up! But this even better!"

Cousin Jessie clucks her tongue. "It must be awful to be dumped by someone in special-ed, Kimmy."

Kim rests her hands on her lap, takes a deep breath. Looks straight at her cousin. "It must be even worse to learn your father is still alive, Jessie." Her heart pounds. Instead of feeling like she's about to die, she's alive and powerful. Bad blood running through her.

Her mom and Evil Aunt Tai gasp. Chopsticks drop from fingertips and onto their plates. Evil Aunt Tai's face is pale, slackened. Her mom is even more disgusted with her, if that were possible.

Cousin Jessie leans forward. "What?"

Kim's mom grabs her by the crook of her elbow. "Kimmy-ah! Shut up!"

She swats her mom's hand away. "Yan-ah! You shut up!" She uses her shrillest voice. Mocks her mom's accent. She was six when she last did that. Yelled at and spanked, grounded for a month. This time, she laughs loudly. Her mom looks ready to throttle her.

"What's going on?" Cousin Jessie puts down her chopsticks. She slowly shakes her head as she looks at Evil Aunt Tai, then at Kim's mom.

Evil Aunt Tai pats her shoulder. "No listen to Kimmy! She jealous of you!"

"She mad because we love you more, Jessie!" Kim's mom adds. "She crazy, making all this up!"

Kim rolls her eyes. "I want to be more like Jessie, but I can't meet your high standards. Maybe I should just kill myself."

Cousin Jessie huffs. "Good idea."

"Not so fast, Baby." She smiles, pulls a piece of paper from her skirt pocket, unfolds it. Hands it to her across the table. "See that man?" She points at the two photocopied color prints. "He's your father. That woman is my Aunt Jia, or Uncle Chao's youngest sister. She and I look alike, because we're both fat and ugly, remember? And those kids are your cousins." She smiles as her cousin breathes fast through her mouth. "Uncle Liang hasn't changed much over the years, has he?"

"No! That can't be true!" Cousin Jessie grabs Evil Aunt Tai's arm. "Mama, Kimmy's lying, right?"

"Yes! He die from pneumonia before you born!" Evil Aunt Tai glares at Kim. "You horrible, horrible person! Why you playing trick on my Jessie?"

Cousin Jessie wrinkles her forehead as she studies the pictures. "I'm the smartest and prettiest one in our family, and you want me to suffer! All you do is spend your parents' money and listen to that stupid music!"

Kim scoffs. "You're the prettiest one because you're a skinny China doll! All you do is get good grades and kiss your mommy's ass! You don't know how to think for yourself!"

Cousin Jessie looks up, but avoids eye contact. Her lips tremble. "I do too!"

"So what do you think, Jessie?" Kim nods and smiles. "Are you gonna get in touch with your dad?"

Aunt Tai slams her chopsticks onto her plate. "You shut up!"

"I kill you!" Her mom's open palm begins its swift take-off towards Kim's face.

But it stops in mid-air as Kim looks her in the eye and smiles sweetly. Remains sitting tall. "Go ahead. We're not in the old country anymore. You won't be able to save face when you're convicted of murdering your daughter." She laughs as her mom's hand crash-lands. "God bless America!"

Cousin Jessie gives an exasperated sigh. "Listen to you! You're a banana, Kimmy! Ever since we were little, you've rejected our heritage!"

"Fuck our heritage! It rejected me, because I don't look and act a certain way!" She glares at her mom and Evil Aunt Tai. "And fuck Confucius, too! If I could go back in time, I'd blow his fucking brains out!"

They're too stunned to yell at her.

"Oh, god. Can you stop trying so hard, for once?" Cousin Jessie rolls her eyes, then wipes at her forehead. "Anyway. Where did you get the pictures?"

"Aunt Jia sent them to my father a few weeks ago."

"Why you so nosy, looking at our stuff?" Kim's mom demands.

Cousin Jessie bites onto her lower lip. Any other time, she'd be a bunny rabbit taking a shit, but Kim can't bring herself to laugh. "Mama," she peers at the paper, "he does look like Baba, but why would you lie to me?" She drops it over her plate, wraps her thin arms across her chest. Fights back tears. "Please tell me it's a joke."

"I wish it were a joke, Jessie." Is that compassion in Kim's voice? She scratches her head. "Haven't you noticed there aren't any wedding or funeral pictures? That's because your mom got pregnant before she got married, and I think your dad left her." Her mom and aunt look down at their laps. Cousin Jessie begins to cry. If they didn't hate each other, Kim would hug her. "They've been lying to us for years."

"No, Jessie. He get sick and die," Evil Aunt Tai says in a weak voice.

Cousin Jessie wipes at her eyes. "Why do I have trouble believing you, Mama?"

"It's true. Kimmy do this because she bad, hateful person."

"I'm doing this because you're bad and hateful towards *me*!" Kim takes another sip of diluted orange juice, wishes she has the balls to light a cigarette.

"Mama, please tell me if Baba's really alive!" Cousin Jessie tugs at Evil Aunt Tai's arm, her eyes sad and pleading.

She swats her hand away. "Jessie! Go to your room!"

"But Mama! Why won't you tell me?"

"Go! I counting to three! One! Two! Th..."

Cousin Jessie sighs, gets up. "Fine."

They listen to her stomp upstairs. Her bedroom door slams shut. "So where were we?" Kim asks.

Her mom pounds her hand against the kitchen table. Glasses and plates tremble. "Apologize! Now!"

She shrugs. "What's the use?"

Evil Aunt Tai glares at Kim's mom. "Yan, do you tell her? Kimmy not smart enough to find out herself!"

"She sure did." Like her mom, Kim pauses. Makes sure all the attention is on her. "She said you had to lie, or our entire family would lose face."

"Yan! How could you do this to me? You my sister!"

"I've known since I was eleven." Kim watches her evil aunt sob. "Mom told me that if I got pregnant, she'd kick me in the stomach so hard that I'd miscarry. She wishes she did that to you when you were pregnant with Cousin Jessie."

Kim's mom stabs her chopsticks into the pliant flesh of her fish. "Are you happy now, Kimmy?"

Evil Aunt Tai narrows her eyes at Kim's mom. "I not happy! You have sex before you marry, too, but you lucky, never get pregnant!"

Kim freefalls through the chair. "What?"

"Your mommy pretend to be good girl, but she have two boyfriend in college! She have fun and get away with it! I had to suffer!"

Her mom's silence confirms it's true. So do her hunched shoulders and tears.

"Jesus fucking Christ." Kim sighs, looks at her aunt and mom. How did two attractive, cheerful young women turn out this way? She shudders at the thought of being a bitter middle-aged woman. She'd never make her daughter her own little pawn. She'd never beat her for having sex. But it's all they know. Their mother was probably just as bad. And so was their mother's mother. It makes her want to cry. But then she remembers what happened in the guest room. "I'll be right back." She rushes to the living room, grabs the empty vase and runs back.

Evil Aunt Tai shrinks back in her chair. "You put that back right now!"

"Kimmy-ah! I counting to three!" Kim's mom yells. "One! Two! Th..."

"How dare you!" Kim screams. She pivots sideways, pulls her arm back, hurls the vase at her mom. They shriek. Duck. Heavy white porcelain narrowly misses the top of her mom's head. The urn smashes into sharp white shards against the wall. A beautiful, cathartic sound.

"Okay, I'm happy now," Kim says calmly, rubbing at her bruised back.

Her mom and evil aunt slowly sit back up. Bits of porcelain all over the table. In the glasses. On top of the food. They dust themselves off. Wincing. Trembling. The sun streams through the open window, casts Kim's shadow onto the wall. It looms over her ineffectual mom and aunt, wings caressed by the breeze.

"You no longer welcome at my house!" Evil Aunt Tai screams. "Both of you! You dead to me!"

"Gee, what a loss. I'll meet you outside, Mom." Kim says before she struts to the front door.

The balmy evening air smells of eucalyptus trees. The setting sun blinding. Her intestines burn, begging for food. She clutches her stomach. Tires squeal in the distance. Her bladder throbs. She crosses her right leg in front of her left, presses her inner thighs together. Laughs bitterly. Of course she made the mistake of leaving before using the bathroom.

The drive back home is an hour and a half. Her mom always refuses to exit the freeway to find her a bathroom. There's no way she could ring the doorbell now and say,

Sorry I ruined your life, Aunt Tai, but do you mind if I take a piss?

She stands over the astroturf doormat, pulls her panties off. Dangles them from her wrist as she crouches down. Her elbows on her thighs. She lets out a stream that forms a puddle beneath her. Some if it splashes onto her legs and Docs. None of it better get on her skirt. She cleans up with a crumpled napkin from McDonald's, tosses it in her evil aunt's manicured lawn, pulls her panties back on. Lights a cigarette as she leans against the side of her mom's car. Might as well. She's already in enough trouble. But at least she won't have to see Evil Aunt Tai and Cousin Jessie all summer.

As soon as Kim hurls the butt into the street, the front door squeaks open. Slams shut. Footsteps. Her mom makes a wet trail of footprints across the driveway. She looks down, confused, before continuing to stomp towards her car.

"Hi, Mom."

"You selfish, want everyone to suffer because your little friend leave you!" Her mom unlocks the car. "When we go home, you die!"

36

"Chao! Sit down!" Kim's mom shrieks as she stomps towards the kitchen. "We need family meeting!"

"You've got to hear it, Daddy!" Kim adds, sauntering behind her, hips swaying from side to side. "It's important!"

Her mom turns around. "You shut up!"

"Why are you so excited, ladies?" Her dad sits in the claustrophobic middle seat. She and her mom are better off sitting across from each other, anyway.

"Tonight," her mom glares, "Kimmy tell Tai and Jessie that Liang not dead and leave her for Jia!"

"Wow! It is very unfortunate that I am not welcome at Tai's home!" She's never seen her dad laugh harder. So hard his entire body convulses. His eyes disappear into his persimmon face. She wishes he'd do that more often.

"Chao! Is not funny!"

"My god, Kim! How did you find out?"

"Walter and I did some research."

He stops laughing at the mention of Walter's name. "Have you no shame?"

"Not really."

"How dare you involve your little friend in this!" Kim's mom yells.

Her dad leans closer. "I want to know what kind of research you did, Kim."

"We looked for Uncle Liang's wedding and funeral pictures in every photo album." She nods at the middle cabinet across from the couch in the family room. Smiles at her dad. "I discovered you were even more handsome when you were younger and had more hair." Winks at her mom. "And that Mom wore the most stylish clothes before I came along and ruined her eighteen-inch waist." She presses her lips together, shakes her head. "Then we found this blue album at the very back of the cabinet. There were a bunch of photographs of Uncle Liang and Aunt Jia, and we were wanting to know why you say he's dead when he's still alive."

His eyes widen. "You are quite smart. Not in the way we wish you were, but still smart."

"You say she smart when she and her little friend destroy my family? Do you know Kimmy lie to you, too, Chao?" Her mom smirks. "I clean guest room, find dirty sheet. Kimmy give her virgin to Walter!"

Kim wishes she could disappear through the wooden slits of her chair. Or fly out into the foothills. She slowly nods to herself, stares out into the night. She had it coming. But she has to pretend she's not afraid.

Her dad just shrugs. "I already know. Neil made me very aware of that."

"But-but when, Daddy?"

"Why you no tell me?"
"I've been seeing him these past two Saturday nights. We have dinner and drinks, talk for a long time. I feel like he truly understands me, and I can tell him anything."

"What? You date other man? Why you no tell me you gay?"

"Eww, Daddy, why are you seeing Walter's dad?"

"I am not gay, nor am I cheating with Neil. Trust me. Daddy likes women. Neil, too."

"But Kimmy and Walter lie to us!" Kim's mom leans forward, her eyes deadly. "And Neil even worse, because he help them! What kind of parent let their child have sex like that?"

Kim's dad shrugs. "An open-minded American father. But I am not surprised that Walter left you. Boys who come from broken homes and have poor grades will do that." He turns to Kim. "You must live with the consequences."

Like write Walter back and wait for his reply? "Yes, Daddy." She lowers her head. "By the way, Aunt Tai told me that mom had two boyfriends in college, and had sex before marriage..."

"This conversation is not about Mom's past..."

"You in trouble, not me!" Kim's mom adds.

"Yes, but did you know that when you married her?" Kim cocks her head from side to side. Smirks at her mom, who looks ready to detonate. "Did you tell *her* to live with the consequences? Or maybe she never told you. Is that it?"

"You not my daughter anymore!"
Kim's dad exhales loudly, closes his eyes, rubs at his forehead. He looks like he wishes he could get the hell away from them. "My goodness! Just stop, okay?" He groans. "I am not surprised you did what you wanted, instead of listening to us. Tomorrow, I will make you an appointment to obtain a birth control pill prescription."

She stares at him. "Are you serious?"

"No!" Kim's mom shakes her head furiously. "You give her pill, you encourage her to have sex!"

"Yan, Kim will turn eighteen in two months. We will not be able to supervise her when she is living on campus. Daddy will feel better if she is protected."

"I have idea! We throw her out! I no want to pay education or living expense for such an ungrateful dog!"

"Do not be irrational! Kim has worked hard to get into UCI, and I will not let her waste this opportunity!"

"But you letting her live on campus without parental supervision and putting her on birth control! You want her to embarrass us, huh?"

"If Kim gets pregnant, she will embarrass us even more!"

"I want you to cut her piano lesson, then! She no allowed to see Diana, even as friend!"

"She is expected to play her last recital in August. We will cancel her lessons after that!"

"But why you want to help this piece of garbage? She no love us!"

"Of course she loves us! She is our daughter!"

Kim looks in the direction of the hallway, clears her throat. "Um, Mom? Dad?"

"And what kind of person are you, laughing when you hear about Tai?"

"I am sick of lying about that for almost twenty years! It is about time someone told the truth!"

"But Kimmy hurt Tai, and Tai is my sister!"

"And Jia is my sister! Liang left Tai long before he met her! Quit blaming Jia for something that was not her fault!"

Kim shakes her head. "Seriously! Mom? Dad?"

"Is her fault Kim already like that fat, dirty pig!"

"Do not talk about my youngest sister like that! She has tried to make peace, but you refuse to accept her! And do not forget that I sent money to Tai until her daughter turned six!"

Kim's mom lowers her head. "Chao, I fail as wife and mother. I no raise Kimmy right. If you want divorce, I will sign paper."

"Oh, god." Kim groans quietly. When her mom first said that seven years ago, she felt like it was all her fault. But since then, she's said it so much that Kim no longer cares.

Kim's dad rubs at his temples. Sighs. "Yan, you should know by now that I am not going to divorce you." He looks at Kim. "I will bring you to the doctor's office myself."
"Oh, one more thing. Mom says I'm not allowed to drive or go to any concerts all summer, nor do I get an allowance until next year." Her mom nods repeatedly. "That is extreme, especially since she had sex before marriage, too."

"But I do in college, not high school!" Her mom says.

"Okay!" Kim's dad no longer bothers to hide his irritation. He waves his hand up and down in front of his wife. "Do not get too excited!" Visions of beer, or perhaps whiskey, dance in his head as he gives Kim one hard pat. "I agree, Kim. You are allowed to go to Lollapalooza, and can drive Mom's car to summer school and piano lessons. Instead of an allowance, I will call my credit card company and make you an authorized user, so I can keep better track of you." He waves dismissively at her and her mom. "Daddy is tired."

37

The next morning, Kim can't stop thinking about Kevin. She's not sure what brought it on. Yesterday, she tasted delicious revenge. Things worked in her favor. But it's still a hollow victory. Something's missing, not quite right. All she knows is the disgust vibrating in her rapid heartbeat and shallow breath. It plagues her during her first Public Speaking class of the summer. She resents being there, walks out thirty minutes later. Drives back home. After she has a cigarette on the driveway, she sits at the kitchen table.

While her parents are at work, she's overcome with the urge to call Dionysus Records and Sympathy For The Record Industry. She already knows the answers, but wants to hear them from someone else. The men on the other line don't know of Kevin's bands, nor have they ever released any of their music. They don't even know who Kevin Ball is.

The guy from Dionysus Records is polite but gruff. The guy from Sympathy talks her ear off about their upcoming releases, and she politely thanks him before hanging up. Then she rests her elbows on the kitchen table, holds up her head with her palms. Kevin has mentioned playing the Anti-Club, Club Lingerie, Raji's. She should call 411 and get their numbers.

A woman answers. "Hello, what city, please?"

Kim's about to say Hollywood, but "Highland Park" comes out instead.

"Name?"

"I'm looking for the Ball residence." The messy handwriting on the package Kevin sent her. She squints, looks through the sliding glass doors. The houses on the hills are much smaller, closer. "I think they live on San Rafael Avenue? May I please have the street address, too?"

Her arm doesn't belong to her as she writes down the information. After she hangs up, she stares at the piece of paper. Then she puts on sunglasses and her dad's tan fisherman hat, grabs her purse. Drives with the windows rolled down.

Legal Weapon's *Death Of Innocence* on the stereo. She sent out for that CD through Insomnia Records, along with *No Sorrow* and *Your Weapon*. Kim's only listened to them a handful of times, but she's already familiar with Kat Arthur's rough, melodic voice. Even though the songs were written when Kim was in kindergarten, it's like Kat knows what she's been through. Like she's her imaginary punk rock auntie who reminds her to keep going, and live for herself.

Judging from the older cars and unkempt lawns, Kevin lives in a neighborhood much more run-down than hers. A one-story beige stucco house with white doors and window frames. His old Tercel is parked on the driveway. She grips the steering wheel tighter. Parks across the street. Presses the button that rolls down all the car windows. There's a white birdbath in the front yard. Kim begged her parents to get one when she was little, but they never delivered. The shades are open, a cat relaxes on the windowsill.

She switches off the car stereo. The unmistakable sound of Kevin playing power chords on his guitar fill the air. The garage door is closed, but she imagines him standing inside it, wearing holey sweats, an old T-shirt, and dark sunglasses. Watching himself play in front of a full-length mirror on the wall. When he stops, Kim rolls her eyes, clapping and cheering like she's had too many beers.

For the rest of the afternoon, she sits in her car and listens. Waves at the neighborhood children and senior citizens walking by. It's a hot, dry day. Sweat runs down the back of her neck, her dress sticks to her chest and stomach. She lifts up her right arm, wrinkles her nose. Should've worn more deodorant. But she can't imagine smelling any worse than Kevin. He has to be sweating inside that garage, even if there's several fans in there. And if there are, the thought of them short-circuiting and blowing up his amp makes her feel better.

He knows nine songs. He's already played each of them twice. At four-thirty, a red Nissan parks in the driveway. The garage door opens. Kevin, in black shorts and a white shirt, stands with his mahogany Les Paul strapped across him. Her throat closes up. She makes a feeble attempt at inhaling hot air.

Her scalp is itchy beneath her dad's hat. Her sunglasses foggy from sweating so much. But she can't take them off. Not when he walks to the driveway. He looks her way. He doesn't nod or wave or make any other acknowledging gestures. Did she ever tell him what kind of car her mom drives? Can he recognize her?

A large, older woman in business casual clothing gets out of the car. He kisses her cheek. He asks how work was. She sighs. Pats him on the back and says, "tiring." Kim's eyes narrow at the woman who bred Kevin. She probably enabled his asshole tendencies. Kim grips the steering wheel so tightly that her knuckles are about to burst through skin. His mom probably cooks for him. She probably does his laundry.

Kevin and his mom disappear into the garage. The door closes behind them. Seconds later, he starts playing guitar again. She drums her fingers onto the dashboard, bobs her head. Two little girls on tricycles giggle and wave as they ride past her. She wonders how young Kevin would go as she howls, *Your cock, my face/baby, what a disgrace/my ass, your lips/gonna take a nasty shit/my gun, your head/gonna shoot you fucking dead.*

Around six o'clock, a Domino's Pizza car parks in front of Kevin's house. His mom probably paid for the pizza and let him pick out the toppings. Her own parents never believed in ordering pizza. Her belly is a starving, bloated monster. Her ass and thighs are sore from sitting so long. Her throat parched from forgetting to bring bottled water. Her bladder burning from not pissing for almost four hours.

The houses and lawns blurred by her dizziness from the heat. And she could really use a cigarette.

"Fuck this!" She pulls her dad's hat off her head. Yanks off her sunglasses. Her hair falls damp into her face.

Kim burns rubber out of Kevin's neighborhood and has dinner at El Pollo Loco. Spanish rice, black beans, and spicy flame-grilled chicken dipped in avocado salsa. Diet Coke. She could go for more food. Another chicken, or maybe dessert. She sits and rubs at her belly. No. Not a good idea. She's not really hungry, but her feeling of disgust is.

The asshole hasn't been in her life for over a year, but he might as well still be. Once again, her needs were ignored for his. Her time and energy drained. Just like they were when she was sixteen and he pretended to be twenty-six. She could've practiced piano, or went shopping. But no. She doesn't even know why she came here in the first place. It's not like she's going to ring the doorbell and ask him why his old record labels haven't heard of him or any of his bands. Or ask his mom to have tea. It's not like she's going to throw a firebomb at his garage, or drive her car through it.

Her brittle laughter causes other diners to stare. She's glad Walter is still in Northern California. She never could've gone through with it. Not on the phone, or in the motel. All that work for a sloppy man who lives with his mom. Kim punches the table with the side of her fist. Her chair squeaks backwards as she gets up. An entire afternoon gone.

But since she's in the neighborhood, she's going to make her trip worth it.

She uses the last of her cash on the cheapest supplies she can find at Ralph's, Home Depot and Office Max. The fiery sun slides down the purple sky as she parks across the street again. Kim hears Kevin playing guitar, spits out the window. For someone who claimed to have been playing for fifteen years, he isn't all that good. She switches on the lights, takes an envelope out of her purse. Eight strips of photo booth pictures of her and Walter. She remembers where each one was taken and which show they were going to.

If Walter were here right now, he'd be in the passenger seat. Insisting they kidnap Kevin, or set his house on fire. They'd be arguing. And with her luck, Kevin would hear them. See them.

She puts the pictures back into her purse. An irritated sigh from her chapped lips. Kevin's mom is probably watching him play guitar. She probably tells him that he's wonderful, and his dreams will come true if he keeps believing in himself. Whatever happened to those dirty pictures he took of her?

She looks over at his house. The lights are on, but the shades are drawn. The knots return to her chest and back. Has he developed any of those rolls? If he has, where's he hiding them? What's the penalty for taking naked photos of an underage girl? The thought of him looking at them makes her shoulders tremble. She punches the dashboard. Growls.

If Walter were here right now, he'd remind her that Kevin is a predator and deserves to die. Look how mad he's making her. She couldn't possibly let him get away with it, could she? But it'll pass. It always does, and it always will. No one needs to get killed.

Kevin begins playing the same two-chord fast melody. Probably the twentieth time she's heard him play it today. Those two little girls on tricycles. What do their parents think of him? They better have taught them about inappropriate touching. The feeling you have when you know something's wrong.

She rolls her eyes and snarls, *Want some candy little girl/let me fondle your curls/banned from the playground/banned from the playground/let me feel your no-no spot/promise you won't tell a soul/banned from the playground/banned from the playground/wanna see my wiggly worm/come touch it and watch it grow/banned from the playground/ banned from the playground.* Then she gets out of the car, has two cigarettes in a row. The neighborhood crickets are better musicians.

The lights flicker off after ten. Kevin's guitar goes silent. Kim puts a fresh blade into the Exacto knife she got from Office Max. Tucks it into the side of her boot. She lifts up her hips, slips off her panties. Places the carton of eggs, can of shaving cream, and bottle of red food coloring into the same shopping bag as the bottle of Grass-B-Gon. The night has cooled off the inferno of a day, but she's still hot and sweaty. Watching. Waiting.

At eleven thirty, Kim gets out of the car. The streetlamps cast her shadow on Kevin's driveway. Her wings flap mischievously. She crouches next to Kevin's left rear tire. His car is so old it doesn't need an alarm. She pulls the Exacto knife from her boot. *Click.* The blade jumps out. It's exactly how she feels. She jabs it into the side wall of the tire, slashes her arm downwards. The hissing noise is a revelation. She can't even blame Kevin for fucking up her first real relationship. She was the one who chose to push Walter away. She pulls it out, does it to the other three.

She slips the Exacto knife back into her boot. Her shadow on the driveway ready to pounce as she takes a piss. Tries not to get her boots wet. Then she hurls all twelve eggs at his car. Her anger gradually slips away as each one cracks against metal. Their yolks drip down the body and onto the driveway. Her shadow's arm pulls back gracefully and shoots forward.

The neighborhood crickets cheer her on as she coats every car window with shaving cream. After she's done, she puts the empty can back into the shopping bag, tiptoes to the birdbath. Whooping. She finally gets to experience the American teenager's rite-of-passage of trashing someone's front yard. It's all her parents' fault. They never let her go Trick-or-Treating without them. She giggles as she dumps the entire bottle of red food coloring into the birdbath, then falls silent.

If Walter were with her right now, there would be a brick thrown through the window. Or a flaming bag of shit on the front porch. Or a lit tampon stuffed into the neck of vodka bottle.

Kim's not even going to tell him she was here.

She scales the lawn, pondering what to spray into it with the Grass-B-Gon. "Rapist" is a no-go. Kevin probably doesn't believe it was rape, anyway. There are too many letters in "pedophile." He'll definitely know it's her if she sprays "poopie" or "suck it." A swastika's effective, but she doesn't want to be guilty of a hate crime. When she makes up her mind, she has to force herself not to cheer.

At the bottom of the lawn, she sprays the outlines of two large circles next to each other. A car approaches. She ducks behind the bushes. When the coast is clear, she draws a long line from the top of each circle. Makes sure they're about three feet apart. The finishing touch is a large mushroom head at the top.

Right when she's done, the living room light flickers on. She sees a dark figure with short, curly hair behind the curtain. Kevin's mom. A taller figure approaches. Kim freezes, sees the curtain opening.

She sprints across the street. Curses herself for not putting her hat back on as she digs around for her car keys. She's covered in cold sweat, her heart pounds. Moaning as she turns on the engine. But she can't resist looking back. The front door opens, reveals a thick leg jaundiced by porch lights. Kim slams her foot onto the accelerator and escapes in a squealing storm of dust.

38

"I'd like to switch classes, please." Kim yawns as she hands her registration form to the woman behind the counter.

She's heavy set, hair dyed red. "One moment." Her long, coral nails batter the keyboard. "Sorry, that section of French 1 is full."

The line behind her gets longer. "Are there any other classes on the same days and times?"

"You should've filled out your alternate choices before coming here." She nods past Kim's shoulder. "Get back in line."

Kim's too tired to argue. She planned on going to French 1 this morning, instead of Public Speaking. Announce that she's learning the language to read Bataille and de Sade *en français.* She had no idea she was going to summer school until her mom told her two months ago. It had already been filled out on her college application. And she was registered for Public Speaking without her consent. At that moment, she hears her mom's shrill voice. *If you no take summer class, UCI kicking you out!* She resists the impulse to destroy random objects.

Twenty people are ahead of her. Her head aches from lack of sleep, and florescent lights. Last night, she parked in the driveway, slept in the backseat. She kept waking up and wondering if Kevin saw her.

The extra-large coffee she had is useless. It's a struggle to stand up, to not drop things. When she flips through the course catalog, the black letters are a continuous ribbon. She can get away with switching as long as she hides her textbooks, takes a class during the same dates and times as Public Speaking. Too bad she doesn't meet the requirements for poetry or literature classes. And photography would entail lots of supplies and darkroom time.

The line moves at a surprisingly fast pace. Even though no one's shouting, voices are amplified. All she wants is to go somewhere dark and quiet. Just to be on the safe side, the other three morning sections of French 1 are her first choice and two alternates. German 1 is her last choice.

The other French classes area already full. German 1 is her only choice.

She rushes to German 1 in yesterday's clothes, her hair pulled back. Finds a seat towards the center. The girl next to her is nice enough to share her textbook. Even though Kim missed the first class, it's easy for her to count to ten *auf Deutsch.* The numbers so similar to their English counterparts. She finds herself more engaged than expected. She doesn't mind braving the crowd to buy her books, looks forward to tonight's assignment.

After class, she drives to the Claremont Village. Has lunch at cafes and bistros. Orders something different every time. Whenever she ate with Walter, he'd finish faster, fidget and tap his fingers until she was done. Without him, she takes her sweet time. Then she goes to Books and Prints, and Rhino Records. Sometimes to Jasmine and Raku, for fancy toiletries and stationary.

She wanders down Arrow Highway, past one-story houses and the TransCenter, where Walter took the bus to Hayward. Her hand never aches for his. She'd rather smoke and listen to Legal Weapon. Walk around Montclair Plaza without buying anything. Two blocks east, there's a cluster of motels renting by the hour, adult video stores with garish triple X marquees. She takes pictures with a disposable camera, then returns to the Claremont Village.

Soon, she's able to walk faster. The sun darkens her skin. She's down to a hundred and forty-five pounds, but her parents don't care that her clothes are getting loose. It still isn't good enough. She's never going to win. Even if she's thin, they'll find something else to pick on.

She does her German homework at the table in front of Some Crust Bakery, accompanied by a cup of iced coffee.

Her favorite part of the afternoon. The warm breeze in her hair. People strolling past her. Her drink sweet and cold. She can't remember when she last felt this peaceful. If she ever did. But her calm disappears once she starts obsessing about Walter.

She no longer looks forward to talking to him on the phone while her parents are gone. Her physical desire for him has run off to Antarctica. The guilt kicks in, and she gathers her things and drives home. Always taking the side streets. At every red light, her guilt is magnified.

She loves Walter. At least, she thinks she does. But if she does, then why does she feel this way? Her head's as smoggy as the sky. She's tired of sneaking around. She doesn't even know how excited she is to see him again. After all that happened, it was comforting to have a high school sweetheart. It made her feel normal. He helped her take her body back from Kevin.

She runs the red light at Allen Avenue, past flat suburban office space and strip malls. Turns, looks for pigs. No pigs in sight. It's hard not to speed down the stretch of foothills and fields that lead to her neighborhood. A downward, winding road. An uncomfortable free fall. She can't feel her foot on the accelerator. Her shaking hands grip the steering wheel.

Every time she's home, she's about to faint. Calling him is an obligation she can't blow off. So is saying "I love you." She sits down on her bed, sighs. Punches in the pre-paid calling card number, then dials. Her dad's roses stare at her accusingly through the mini-blinds.

"Hello?" It's his mom. Scratchy cigarette voice, yet cheerful.

"Hi. May I please speak to Walter?"

"Kim?"

"Yes, this is her."

"It's so nice to finally talk to you! Unfortunately, Walter and Brendan are working late, and won't be back until nine."

"Okay, thanks. I'll call back tomorrow."

"Kim! Wait!" A click on the other line. Slow inhale. Long, contemplative exhale. "Can we talk?"

Her fingers go slightly numb. "Sure, Ms. Kelly. What's going on?"

"Please call me Deborah." She laughs sadly. "It's so nice to see my son again, but I think it's safer for him to live with his dad."

"Why?" Her yellow plastic shelves overflows with books. She's tempted to bring them all to UCI. "Is he okay?"

"Yes, and no. He's gotten better since he started working at Brendan's shop, but on his first day of school, he broke a classmate's nose and ribs."

💣

"Hello?" Walter answers right at five-thirty the next evening, his voice hopeful.

"Why didn't you tell me you beat the crap out of someone?" Kim yells from her concrete throne in the backyard. The roses cower. Blades of grass shrink away.

"Shit." He takes a drag off his cigarette, exhales loudly. "I-I just, I don't know. Y-You were mad that I wanted to kill Kevin m-more than you did. I'm sorry. I didn't want to scare you even more."

"Okay, okay." She closes her eyes, but she can still see the damage she did to Kevin's property. Wonders if she should tell him. Decides against it for the hundredth time.

"Y-You're not mad at me, are you?"
"No." She still needs to tell him she kissed Uncle Rod. "So how's Lisa?"

Walter groans. "Come on, Doll. Don't start. You know I-I hate that bitch!"

"Okay." Biting into her lower lip keeps her from asking if he's messing around with his cousin again. "It was nice talking with your mom yesterday. I'm glad I did, because I found out things you didn't tell me."

Walter still doesn't know about Joey, either. No one does.

"B-But I was gonna to tell you one day! It just wasn't the right time!"

She's not looking forward to telling him, either. "Well, you know what? I was doing just fine until you became obsessed with killing Kevin! I mean, talking about it was cathartic, but even I knew it was a bad idea! And you just didn't seem to get it!"

"Like I said, h-he hurt the person I love the most! H-How else could I have dealt with it?"

"By being a good boyfriend and loving me! And not wanting to kill Kevin anymore!"

"I-It's hard not to feel that way, Doll! Every time I think about him, I-I wanna do it!"

"Well, don't! He raped me, but you helped me get better. I just want to fucking move on, okay? If you can't respect that, then I can't be with you!"

He gasps. She feels how jarring her words are to him. "Okay. Okay. H-He may piss me off, b-but I promise I won't. A-And I won't talk about it anymore. I mean it."

"You better."

"Kim, a-are we just gonna fight today?"

"No, Walter, I'm sorry." She rolls onto her back, clutches her belly. The contents of her stomach are complacent.

"I wanna come home soon, Doll. I miss you."

She winces. "I miss you, too."

39

At sunrise, Kim gets into her mom's car and starts the engine. Even though Walter begged her not to go to Lollapalooza alone, there's no way she's going to miss it. Today is the last day she'll be underage. Her last day of being alone before he returns tomorrow morning. She's got no intention of coming home tonight. A motel room near the Claremont TransCenter awaits her.

There's already a line under the dusty blue sky and blazing heat. Kim puts on cat-eye sunglasses, makes her way towards the end.

"Oh, my god! It's Sexy Kim!"

Monica, Brandi, and Robyn are wedged between a group of college kids and a dreadlocked couple. The bitches all wear baby tees with miniskirts, Air Walks without socks.

"Nice dress, Sexy Kim!" Monica giggles. "All the retards will love you!"

"Yeah, Sexy Kim!" Robyn adds. "We just saw this retarded kid in a wheelchair. He'd be totally perfect for you!"

"It would be hard for him to run away from you, Sexy Kim!" Brandi laughs.

They look at each other. Laugh harder. Right when Kim walks past them, she gathers all the saliva in her mouth. *Pfffft!* It lands on Monica's right shoe. She sashays away in her black lace sundress, admiring the curves of her shadow. If they come after her, they'll lose their place in line.

"You stupid fucking whore!"

"No matter how much weight you lose, you're always gonna be a fat, retard-fucking wannabe!"

"You're so ugly a blind guy wouldn't want you!"

In line, Kim can't stop smoking. Tar and poison scrapes at her throat and lungs. Walter's running the cash register and answering phones at Brendan's shop. She wonders what he looks like now, with sideburns and a weightlifting routine.

Neil doesn't know he's coming back. They're afraid he might rat her out to her dad. Deborah's in on the secret. But Kim can't see herself throwing her arms around Walter tomorrow. There's no envy when she sees other couples together. People say absence makes the heart grow fonder. She's not so sure if she agrees.

The skater boys and Kurt doppelgangers still ignore her, every last one of their dates cute and small-boned. But there are guys who do hold her gaze, nod at her, give her a hint of a smile. They're her age, or a little order. Decent. Or awkwardly attractive, like the guy with the sideburns and Fugazi shirt, who stops and says, "Hey, how's it going?"

"Okay." She glances at him. A nervous smile stretches across her face. A gap between his front teeth. Protruding Adam's Apple. Gray eyes. Her fingertips touch her cheek. "I'm totally looking forward to seeing Sonic Youth."

He nods. "Me too. Did you see them at Castaic Lake a few years ago?"

Of course her mom didn't let her go. "I wish. Did you?"

"Yeah, it was great! They played 'Burning Spear!'"

"Holy shit!"

She lowers her chin. Their eyes meet. The area between her navel and crotch tingles. There's a disconnect between the soles of her Docs and the cement.

"Dude!" One of the guys he's with punches his arm. "We need to get in line!"

He sighs. "Yeah. We do." Waves at her. "See you inside."

They look back at each other before he and his friends disappear into the crowd. She knows she looks like she munched on a canary, has an ecstatic cigarette. Hopes they'll run into each other later. They'll get each other's numbers, make plans for a date. A long conversation over Mexican food. Wandering around with no destination and not giving a fuck. His kiss goodnight filled with possibility. There will be artsy films and rock shows. Abandoned movie theatres and amusement parks. Gray days at the ocean. When they do it, she won't be afraid to show and tell him what she likes. What feels good.

"I don't know, d-do you know what you don't like, then? That would really help," Walter says.

She tosses her spent cigarette into the dirt, stomps it out. Right. Her boyfriend is coming back tomorrow. She groans, digs her fingernails into her palms. How could she forget so easily? Why does he still have to be her boyfriend? She tries to take back that thought. She's looking forward to their reunion. Honest.

It'll be so nice to see him again. But even nicer if she sees Fugazi Guy later. No. She loves Walter. She's going to be Mrs. Riordan someday. What's Fugazi Guy's real name, anyway? Walter could've been busted for aggravated assault, but he still loves her. She still loves him. She needs to be a better girlfriend.

She wanders up and down the midway during the Mighty Mighty Bosstones. Casually observes the tables of

politically correct organizations. Feminism and
Vegetarianism? Good. War and pornography? Bad. Hippie
clothes and jewelry? Very bad. A sunburn so early in the
day? Fuckin' A.

When Possum Dixon plays the second stage, she stands
still and smokes. Their male model of a front man assaults
his upright bass, howls into the microphone. Their presence
and music much darker than she remembered. She and
Walter saw them when they opened for X back in
December. He had hugged her from behind as they swayed
together. They did it for the first time that day. She felt
truly close to him.

When the band plays a manic rendition of *In Buildings*,
she remembers when Walter said that song reminded him
of her. A lost moment in a crowded concert hall eight
months ago. Part of her wishes Walter would stay up north.
Her other part, the sentimental one that's prone to guilt,
wins.

After she emerges from a green porta-potty, she's
heading back to the main stage when a hand closes around
her wrist.

"Lose fifteen more pounds and maybe you'll be hot,
Kimmy." A low, taunting voice. Weasel laugh.

Kim gasps when she sees Kevin. A smirk peeks from
gray stubble. Skin dangles beneath his chin. The lines
under and around his eyes are even more pronounced. His
white hairs even more obvious. He could never pass for
twenty-seven. But he could easily beat the shit out of
Walter through sheer, stupid strength.

His friends are two equally creepy guys in faded T-
shirts and ripped jeans. They all have beer guts. Three

pairs of eyes give her goose bumps. Try to see through her dress, through her skin. Three pairs of yellow teeth grin back at her.

The one with blond hair nudges Kevin. "Hey, is that the underage slut you fucked in the ass?"

"Yup, right up her virgin poopie. It was so nice and tight."

Kim's mouth opens, but her scream remains lodged inside her throat. She just stands there. Unmoving. Her sunglasses rest on her head when they should be obscuring her eyes. Why didn't she pull them back down? Maybe Kevin wouldn't have recognized her if she did.

The last guy, a Latino with black curls, laughs. "She's definitely a two." He winks, steps closer. Kim's blood boils so hard it's about to rupture her veins.

Kevin's free hand caresses her right side. "She love us long time!"

"Let's stuff her like a turkey!"

"I bet she'd love to have all three holes filled at once!"

Her asshole puckers. The knots in her chest and shoulders pull tight. Tears trickle down her cheeks. Kevin and his creepy friends laugh, high-five each other as she trembles. The more she tries to get away, the more he holds on. Her skin burns skin from the sun. The trapped scream threatens to burst inside her. She tries again. Nothing comes out. They nudge each other and laugh harder. Kevin leans closer, eyes slipping down the front of her dress. The familiar stink of his sweat. She wrinkles her nose, breathes through her mouth.

Someone's watching. She turns towards a group of older teenage boys sitting in the grass. They wear baggy shorts, flannels tied around their waists. The curves of steel pronounced beneath the leather toes of their Docs. All six of them are silently observing. Kim makes eye contact with the largest one. Shaved head, tattoos covering his muscular arms. His bare torso hard and defined. Between two pierced nipples, a black tattoo of the latter K in a shield over his heart. The same tattoo Kurt had. Even though she can't stop shaking, she pulls her navel to her spine. He looks back at her. Her lashes flicker. He nudges one of his friends.

"Check out those dick-sucking lips." A wheezing sound flies from her throat as a paw squeezes her left tit. It slips down the front of her dress, twists her nipple. Her teeth clatter together. More laughter. "Her pussy stinks," Kevin takes his hand from her dress, pinches her ass. "but her poopie's the best hole I've ever fucked."

She tries to wrench away. He still doesn't let go. If her scream stays captive any longer, she's gonna pass out. She stares at Kevin incredulously. The places he pinched continue to sting. If they hadn't met on a party line, she never would've let him into her house, let alone inside her.

Back then, all she wanted was a band. That way, she could get away from her parents. Be beautiful and loved. Especially loved. She was never as fat and ugly as certain people claimed. She could've done better than a thirty-four-year-old loser who lives with his mom. After all he's done, this is the last fucking straw.

She hears herself hyperventilating. Three living, overgrown versions of Beavis and Butthead cackle. Her scream comes out as a quiet mewl. One of the assholes goes, "awww. " She's still shaking, but rage has pushed fear aside. Seriously, how dare he?! She just wanted him to love her. To save her. But this is her one chance to save herself. If she plays her cards right, he's a dead man.

One. Two. Three.

"My name's not Kimmy, you old pervert! So let go!" She tries to pull away again, but Kevin still won't let go.

"Whatever! Your name is too Kimmy!"

"What is it, then? Skanky?" One of his friends ask.

Kim takes a deep breath. "Ow! Ow!" She yanks her wrist back. Kevin holds even tighter. She looks over at the large, tattooed guy with helpless eyes. One of his friends looks at him. He nods. Good thing she didn't put her sunglasses back on. She can feel the liquid eyeliner and mascara running down her cheeks. "You're hurting me!"

The six guys get up. Their leader a foot taller than Kim. Wider, taller, and in better shape than Kevin and his friends. He inches into the peripheral next to Kim and Kevin. "Let go of her, Old Man."

Kevin lets go of Kim's wrist, throws his hands into the air. "Come on, she and I are friends!"

"Why would she be friends with you, Grandpa?"

Her lips curl downwards in distress. She rubs at her wrist. Widens her eyes at the large, tattooed guy. "Thank you."

He leans closer. "My pleasure."

A small crowd has gathered, watching with quiet intent.

Kim smiles at Kevin, waving her sore wrist back and forth. "You're stupid for admitting you fuck underage girls in the ass. Like, how old are you? Forty?"

"What are you talking about? I'm twenty-seven!" He's followed by a black cloud of jeers and snickers.

"Yeah, right. Take out your ID and prove it!"

"Fuck that!"

The large, tattooed guy laughs. "You're one unlucky bastard if you have that many white hairs and wrinkles at twenty-seven."

"Hey!" One of his friends yells at the people walking by, pointing at Kevin. "This guy's forty, but he buttfucks underage girls!"

More whispers and murmurs erupt. More people gather around.

"Hey, hey, that's not cool!" Kevin squares his shoulders, puffs out his chest. The large, tattooed guy scoffs. Gives him a derisive glance.

"Well, it's not cool to be a pedophile!" Another one of his friends says.

"Who rapes underage girls?" A girl asks.

"He does!" The large, tattooed guy points at Kevin. Kim catches his class ring on the middle finger of his right hand.

Heavy carved brass with a stone the color of fire. "He and his friends gang rape underage girls after shows!"

"Oh my god! I can't believe they let those perverts in here!"

"Yeah! He deserves to die!"

Kevin gives Kim a stupid grin. "Come on, Kimmy! I taught you how to play guitar and got you into all these cool bands! You can't do this to me! Fucking tell them we're friends!"

"Why the fuck would I be your friend, you old pig?" Kim asks. "And quit calling me Kimmy!"

"Why would a pretty girl like her want to be friends with an old loser like you?" The large, tattooed guy asks. He fixes his warm brown eyes on her. She tugs at a strand of her hair, smiles coyly.

"But Kimmy, you loved it when I fucked you up your..."

"Die!" She cups her right hand. Makes a hard, fast arc towards Kevin's face. A loud crack of clarity and power. Her palm hums happily. The heart charm from the wristband Walter gave her sways in approval. People laugh and cheer. Kevin's friends slink away, but they're blocked by the crowd.

The large, tattooed guy nods at Kim. "Good hit, Babe."

She winks. "Thanks, Darlin'."

A stream of Kevin's saliva lands onto her cheek. "You little bitch!"

One of the guys grabs Kevin, holds his arms behind his back. Their leader takes a swing. His cinder block fist, his class ring, collides into Kevin's face. A moist crunch. It's such a lurid sound that everyone gasps. Kevin responds with a pained "uhhh!" Blood trickles onto his upper lip. The next blow lands in his gut.

Kim politely excuses herself. The crowd parts for her. Better those guys than Walter. She slips her sunglasses over her eyes, saunters away from the melee. Wipes Kevin's filthy saliva off her cheek with the back of her hand. Taints her hand. She digs around her purse for a napkin. Spit keeps eating at her skin. It doesn't matter how much she tries to rub it off. If she had a bottle of Everclear, she'd bathe in it. She chucks the dirty napkin onto the ground. Splashes lukewarm water from the three-dollar bottle she bought onto her cheek, pours the last of it onto her hand. Behind her, people are chanting "Pedophile! Pedophile!"

Security pushes past her, sweaty and heaving as they rush in the opposite direction. Kim takes a deep breath, and strolls towards the exit.

40

Stuck in afternoon traffic. Not even close to rush hour. Rolled-up windows block the heat. Cold air blows onto Kim's face. Nothing louder than Mazzy Star on the stereo, or she'll flip out. Step too hard onto the accelerator and start a chain reaction on the 405. The police had to have been called by now. She imagines the Irvine PD swarming into the crowd, hitting concert-goers with batons, slapping handcuffs around belligerent wrists. They're probably looking for her, but she's long gone. She sighs and does the unthinkable. Lights a cigarette in her mom's car. The first rush of nicotine burns away her sadness.

Less than an hour ago, she got the most justice she'll ever get. The most she needs, anyway. Walter will be leaving in a couple hours. She needs to be a good girlfriend and call him before he does. She keeps checking the rearview mirror. No colored lights on top of black and white cars. No one following too closely. Hopefully Kevin's been beaten unconscious. The bastard better not rat her out, on top of everything else. The cars trap her. No escape from this free-floating steel prison.

She heads towards Via Verde Avenue, the exit closest to home. There's no way she's getting off there. Multiple levels of freeway in the distance. Every time she passes that structure, she can't help but visualize a 7.3 earthquake destroying it. The sky will rain dust, chunks of concrete. Broken glass and crushed steel everywhere. Palm trees will snap in half. She used to like palm trees when she was little. They're beginning to annoy her.

At the last second, she merges onto the 210. Turns off the stereo. The foothills are covered with smog, and waiting for a lit cigarette. Kim needs to lie down. Needs to use a phone. The exit to Downtown San Dimas is coming up. Should she? It's an outlandish idea. She can't believe she's thinking it. Getting closer. Her hands barely able to hold the steering wheel. She can't feel her foot on the gas, but she's being pulled in that direction.

Kim doesn't get out of the car. The engine runs as she stares at the beige stucco building. The lights are off in room 216. She's ten minutes away from home. Her parents will want to know why she's back from Lollapalooza so soon. That, and a bunch of other questions.

She tilts her head back. Sighs. Her body can move just fine. Hand on the door. Feet landing onto the blacktop. Thick, heavy air bleeds into her lungs. She still can't believe she's doing it, but she is. What if she can't check in because she's not eighteen yet? The guy at the front desk barely looks at her ID before running her dad's credit card. One adult. Smoking. He walks towards the back wall, where the room keys hang. She hears herself request room 216.

It's available.

She takes labored steps up the metal stairs. A man and woman are having loud sex in 115, open windows airing out the sordid details. A TV is turned all the way up. Her palm lingers on the handrail. She forces herself to go up the last three steps. Stops in front of the green door of 216. Faded brass numbers. Brass knocker. The shades are drawn. Her hand in mid-air, key hanging in limbo. It's hard to even stick it into the lock and turn it.

The door clicks shut behind Kim. That musty smell suffocates her. She runs to open the shades and windows. The sunlight and outside world reassuring. The couple in 115 are still going at it. Traffic on Arrow Highway a perpetual hum. She switches on all the lights. Everything is the way she remembers. Forest green carpet. Blue and white striped walls. Old wooden furniture.

She sits down on the bed, moves her arms, looks over at the wall. She's not nailed to the wall, watching Kevin fuck the dead girl. She lies on her side, punches in her calling card number before calling Walter. The knots return to her chest and shoulders. She lifts up her legs, swings her free arm. *Come on, please be there.*

"Hello?"

"Walter! I'm so glad you picked up!"

"Are you okay? Why aren't you at Lollapalooza?"

She cries as she tells him what happened in a hushed voice, but neglects to mention that she caught herself straying. He takes long drags from his cigarette. Huffs as he exhales. The curtains flap uncertainly in the hot summer breeze. The sound of him breathing is no longer her sanctuary. Not when she's stumbling over her words. When she's done, she sits up. Leans forward.

"I-I told you not to go alone!"

She holds the phone a few inches away. "I felt like I had to, no matter what!"

"I knew something like this would happen!" She hears a banging noise. "I'm your boyfriend a-and I'm not done with him yet!"

"Walter!" She wedges the phone between her ear and shoulder, rubs at her forehead. "I say when it's over between him and I, not you!"

"Not when I should've been there a-and y-you fucking flirt with strangers to get them to kick his ass!"

"I did what I had to do! He wouldn't let go of me, and it was my one chance to get back at him!"

"Wh-When I come back, he's dead!"

"No!" Her palm slams onto the mattress. "You promised you wouldn't mention this anymore, Walter!"

"But I love you, Doll! I can't help it!"

She tilts her head back, closes her eyes. Blows through pursed lips. "If you can't help it, then don't come back tomorrow! Or ever!"

"Y-You don't have to yell at me! But like I said, i-it's not hard to feel that way when you love someone so much!"

The ceiling's whiter than she remembered. Falsely pure. "I'm sorry, Walter. I shouldn't have yelled at you. It's been a long day, you know?"

"I know. Th-That's why I'm coming back to take care of you."

Walter talks her ear off as she looks out the window, foothills disappearing into the dusty sky. She hears herself lying through her clenched smile. She can't wait to pick him up at the bus station tomorrow morning. Or for him to take her to breakfast at IHOP and fuck her all day. Oh, yeah, it's been four months since they last fucked. She misses him so much. She can't wait to feel him inside her again, especially since she's on the Pill now.

And really? He's got a present for her? No, it wouldn't be a surprise if he told her what it was. Of course her parents don't know she's there. But why is she back in the same motel room she was raped in a year and a half ago? Jesus Christ, why?

She starts crying again, repeatedly slapping the mattress. She felt like going back, okay? She just felt like it. She doesn't need to fucking justify herself. No, stupid, unless someone breaks in, she won't get raped a second time. She's sorry she called him "stupid." She didn't mean it that way.

Kim's relieved when her calling card runs out and they're disconnected.

At Denny's, she has a Grand Slam breakfast for dinner. The steady supply of coffee and cigarettes ensures she won't be getting much sleep tonight. It's the first time she's been there without Walter. She eats slowly, stares off into space. It's nice not having him playfully step on her feet or feel her up under the table. It's nice not having to talk to him, or anyone else besides the waiter. Once again, the guilt returns. She tries to talk herself into believing that she's looking forward to seeing him tomorrow morning. That she still loves him. She swears she does.

The lights will stay on all night in room 216. She runs back and forth across the carpet, howling. Stands against the striped wall with her arms above her head before diving face-first onto the mattress. Screams into it until her throat's raw. Her knuckles numb from punching it so much. She stands, jumping up and down and shouting obscenities until she collapses.

Kim's sedate enough to watch the ten o'clock news. She sits at the edge of the bed, her mouth wide open as she keeps shaking her head. Apparently, an underage girl was sexually harassed at Lollapalooza. Other guys stepped in and a mini-riot broke out. Kevin is in critical condition at the UC Irvine Medical Center. His two creepy friends are luckier.

Eleven people have been arrested, including the ringleader. Former high-school football star, Zack Hilter. Security and police can't locate the underage girl, who's wanted for questioning.

She collapses backwards onto the bed, as if Kevin's vengeful ghost shoved her, his invisible palms burning her skin. Her chest tightening as she hyperventilates, arms trembling at her sides. Legs twitching. Like she's about to drown and the last thing she's gonna see is his smug baby face, so she squeezes her eyes shut. Wills her world black and the dead girl returns.

She doesn't know how much time has passed when she comes back to life. The light from the ceiling, from the nightstand, is the blinding truth.

Kim is still breathing, still mobile, still alive. But it doesn't stop her from reaching down and making sure she hasn't been visited by the ghost of a creepy loser who's in critical condition. After she makes sure she's as untouched as she can be, she exhales through clenched teeth.

"Come on, you disgusting son of a bitch," she breathes, grinding her knuckles into her heart to squeeze out the dirty air, "stay alive for me."

At the same time, she knows she's safe. For now. Chances are, Kevin won't be able to talk because his jaw's wired shut. Because he's sleeping beneath a warm blanket of painkillers. Even if he could talk, he's not going to rat her out. If he does, he's going to incriminate himself. The police will want to know how they met, the nature of their relationship. Her word against his. Not that she wants to get involved, but having that power makes her sing all the Hole and Nirvana songs she still knows by heart, including "Rape Me." Tears stream down her cheeks as she imagines a million dead girls rising, taking themselves back.

So why does it feel like part of her's missing?

"What am I gonna do now?" She asks the ceiling. "Huh?"

It doesn't give her any answers. All she can do is keep singing. Keep waiting for the pounding at the door that hasn't arrived.

At one in the morning, her voice deflates to a rough whisper. She's silent as she soaks in the tub, then lies down on the bed. The musty sheets are a shroud, but she can come back to life whenever she wants. Seven more hours until Walter arrives. Every time she looks at the window, she thinks she sees a swirl of red and blue lights waiting for her. Every time she looks at the clock, the green digital numbers keep pushing forward.

She'd rather stay in bed than meet Walter at the bus station.

One last cigarette before she closes her eyes. Constantly opening them to check the time that refuses to stop. Barely breathing as she listens and makes sure the random footsteps and voices outside aren't looking for her. But wouldn't the pigs have already found her if they wanted her that badly? She sighs, shakes her head, then laughs at herself. Three and a half hours to go. She officially turns eighteen nine minutes after six. Manages to croak out "Happy Birthday."

One more hour is left.

ABOUT THE AUTHOR

Randi Black is an aging rocker chick with an MFA in Writing from the School of the Art Institute of Chicago. For more information, please visit her website at http://www.randiblack.com or come say hi at ms.randi.black@gmail.com